MIDNIGHT FIRE

A JAGIELLON MYSTERY 2

P.K. ADAMS

IRON KNIGHT PRESS

Midnight Fire

Copyright © 2020 by Patrycja Podrazik

All rights reserved. This book or any portion thereof may not be reproduced or used in any manner whatsoever without the express written permission of the author except for the use of brief quotations in a book review.

ISBN 978-1-7323611-7-1 (paperback)

ISBN 978-1-7323611-6-4 (ebook)

Cover designed by Jennifer Quinlan

Map by Deborah Bluestein

All characters, other than those clearly in the public domain, and place names, other than those well established such as towns and cities, are fictitious and any resemblance is purely coincidental.

Published by Iron Knight Press

www.pkadams-author.com

Twitter @pk_adams

Facebook P.K. Adams Author

CONTENTS

Poland/Lithuania under the Jagiellon Dynasty c.1550

MOSCOW
RIGA
Baltic Sea
Tsardom of Russia
VILNIUS
NERIS
GDAŃSK (DANZIG)
Ducal Prussia
MINSK
WISŁA (VISTULA)
Grand Duchy of Lithuania
GORNITSA
Kingdom of Poland
WARSZAWA (WARSAW)
PRAGUE
KIEV
Kingdom of Bohemia
KRAKÓW (CRACOW)
LWÓW (LVIV)
DNIEPER
VINNYTSIA
BAR
N
W
E
S
Kingdom of Hungary
Ottoman Empire

Cast of Characters

The Royals

Bona Sforza	Queen Consort of Poland and Grand Duchess Consort of Lithuania
Zygmunt August	Queen Bona's son. King of Poland and Grand Duke of Lithuania (titles he shares with his father, Zygmunt Stary)

Poles

Sebastian Konarski	Caterina's husband
Emilia Grabowska	Sebastian's sister and Caterina's sister-in-law
Leon Grabowski	Emilia's husband and Caterina's brother-in-law
Beata Kościelecka	Queen Bona's lady-in-waiting
Marcin Kromer	King Zygmunt Stary's secretary
Jakub Zaremba	Knight escorting Caterina to Vilnius
Piotr Opaliński	Duke Zygmunt's chamberlain
Piotr Frikacz	Duke Zygmunt's courtier
Florian Zebrzydowski	Duke Zygmunt's courtier
Augustyn "Rotundus" Mieleski	Duke Zygmunt's private secretary

Lithuanians

Barbara Radziwiłł	Duke Zygmunt's mistress
Mikołaj "Rudy" Radziwiłł	Barbara's brother

Barbara Kolanka	Barbara Radziwiłł and Mikołaj Radziwiłł's mother
Rasa	Caterina's chambermaid
Milda	Barbara's kitchen maid
Oksana	Milda's chambermate
Cook	Worker with Milda in Barbara's kitchen
Jurgis	Milda's cousin
Jovita	Barbara Kolanska's parlor maid
Dimitr Siemaszko	Steward of the Radziwiłł estate
Ostafi and his wife	Owners of the Under the White Swan Inn
Captain of the Palace Guard	

Italians

Caterina Konarska	Queen Bona's former Lady of the Chamber
Giulio Konarski	Caterina and Sebastian's son
Cecilia	Giulio's nurse
Lucrezia d'Alifio	Queen Bona's lady-in-waiting
Maria d'Aragona	Marchesa del Vasto, distantly related to Queen Bona
Alessandro Perenti	Court musician to Queen Bona
Gian Lorenzo Pappacoda	Queen Bona's courtier and favorite
Giovanni Francesco Nascimbene	Duke Zygmunt's physician

Germans

Karl von Tilburg	Habsburg ambassador to Vilnius (visiting)

Rules of Pronunciation Relevant to This Story

Letter group "dzi" is pronounced like j in *John* (thus the name Radziwiłł is pronounced Raj-viw)

Letter w is pronounced like v in *vat* (thus the river Wisła is pronounced "Viswa," and Wawel Castle is pronounced "Vavel")

Letter ł is pronounced like w in *water* (thus the name Radziwiłł is pronounced Raj-viw)

Letter j is pronounced like y in *young* (thus the name Jakub is pronounced "Yah-khub")

Letter g is pronounced like gh in *ghost* (thus Jagiellon is pronounced "Ya-ghye-lohn")

Letter e is pronounced like eh in *egg* (thus the name of the village of Niepołomice is pronounced "Nye-poh-woh-mitseh")

Common diphthongs
Sz is pronounced like sh in *shop* (thus the name Dantyszek is pronounced "Dan-tysh-ekh")

Cz is pronounced like ch in *check*

Ch is pronounced like h in *hang*

Rz is pronounced zhe

"-cki": a common ending of Polish last names is pronounced "tsky", unlike in English the c is not silent.

Glossary of Terms

Bibones et comedones (tipplers and devourers)—a sixteenth-century semi-clandestine society of courtiers who devoted to their spare time to eating, drinking, and lovemaking. In addition to these activities, they produced poems and pamphlets that satirized life at the Jagiellon court. Their members play a prominent role in the first book of this series, *Silent Water.*

Hetman—supreme commander of the army.

Starosta—senior administrative official of crown territory or district, similar to county sheriff.

Szlachta (pronounced shlah-ta)—lower nobility, equivalent of England's landed gentry.

Wojewoda (pronounced voy-e-voda)—chief administrative officer of a province, a territorial governor.

Złoty (pronounced zwoti)—Polish currency unit dating back to the fourteenth century. The name translates as "golden."

Note on forms of address

Pan—Sir. Equivalent of Italian "Signore." *Note*: like all Polish nouns, it is subject to several conjugations, hence the form "Panie" that appears occasionally in the text. That happens when someone is addressed directly (vocative case) as opposed to being referred to in the third person (nominative case).

Pani—Lady, if the woman is married or widowed. Equivalent of Italian "Signora."

Panna—Lady, if the woman is unmarried. Equivalent of Italian "Signorina."

1

On the Road to Kraków
Early June 1545

We set out from Bari on a journey that we hoped would save our son's life toward the end of May in the year 1545.

It was altogether different from the grand progress I had made twenty-seven years earlier as a lady-in-waiting to the young Bona Sforza, heiress to the Duchies of Bari and Milan. She was on her way to Kraków to meet her new husband, Zygmunt, King of Poland and Grand Duke of Lithuania. We stopped in Venice to watch carnival festivities, stayed in Graz long enough for a hunt, and sojourned at the court in Vienna, where Emperor Maximilian treated us to a feast in a manner that befitted a future queen. At our final destination we were greeted by cannons booming from the city walls, cheering crowds, and the entire Polish court awaiting us outside of Wawel Cathedral.

This time, we rode in a simple carriage as part of a train of merchants, stopping overnight at travelers' inns, eating the watery stews they all seemed to offer or our own provisions or whatever unspoilt food we managed to buy in villages along the way. But I was glad of the swift pace, for each day brought us closer to the renowned physicians in Kraków who might be able to help our ailing boy.

Glancing at Giulio as we rattled over yet another rutted road, I shuddered to see how frail he appeared. The recurring fevers that afflicted him, starting when he turned four, had stunted his growth and weakened his limbs. He did not look like a boy of nine. How could he? He spent more time in bed than playing outdoors with other children. As a result, his skin had a pale, almost translucent quality, an effect only enhanced by his dark brown eyes with flecks of amber. Those eyes, so like his father's, glowed unnaturally large and bright in his thin face. My old friend Lucrezia Alifio, who still served as a lady-in-waiting to Queen Bona, insisted that the royal physicians in Poland could lessen his suffering, perhaps even cure him. Watching Giulio now, I hoped that this journey would prove her right, for none of the Italian doctors we consulted had succeeded in helping him. I also hoped that Lucrezia told the truth when she wrote that Her Majesty would be glad to see me and happy to help my family in our predicament.

"Do you know what I'd love to see when we get to Konary, Caterina?" Sebastian Konarski, my husband of twenty-five years, said from his seat across the rocking carriage. "I'd love to see the woods still as thick as they were when I was growing up. We'll need a lot of timber for the repairs," he added, appraising the large pines, ashes, and beeches rolling past our carriage windows.

It is not a thing one would normally admit, but the inheritance of Sebastian's family estate after the death of his elder brother Feliks was a godsend to us under current circumstances. Just five miles outside of Kraków, it gave us a place to live and an income to enable us to stay in Poland for as long as necessary to see Giulio restored to health. Sebastian's hopes for abundant wood had a high chance of coming true. Northern Europe was, after all, the land of endless forests. The woods we were traveling through had started in the Austrian territories and continued through Bohemia, which, according to the calculations of the leader of our caravan, should be coming to an end soon. Any moment now, we would cross the borders of the Kingdom of Poland, with less than a hundred miles separating us from Kraków.

The day was hot, but the broad canopy of leaves kept our path in a pleasant shade. After a while, the buzzing of insects and the twittering of birds soothed Giulio and his nurse Cecilia into asleep. Giulio curled up on the same seat Sebastian occupied, and Cecilia's head lolled on her ample chest next to me. After ten days on the road, with fitful nights tossing and turning on uncomfortable pallets and long hours of riding in a carriage with little to relieve the tedium of the journey, I rejoiced to see them able to sleep at last.

"It surprised me to hear that Feliks let the estate decline so much," I said, referring to the letter we had received from Konary's caretaker two weeks before our departure from Bari. We wasted no time in making our decision, putting our affairs in order, and setting out for the north. "But after the death of his son and then his wife," I added on reflection, "perhaps it's no wonder he lost interest in managing his affairs." I winced, realizing that, wrapped up in my own family's troubles, I had not stopped to consider the blows life had delivered to my late brother-in-law. His only son, Adam, thirsting after a soldierly adventure, had joined the army of Jan Tarnowski and headed east to the Grand Duchy to fight alongside the Lithuanians against Moscow. During the battle of Homel in 1535, the boy, only eighteen years old, was struck by an arrow and killed.

"Feliks never recovered from Adam's death." Sebastian's eyes strayed to Giulio with a concern I often saw in them but which he almost never expressed aloud, for fear of adding to my own worries. I had once appreciated his restraint, but these days it seemed like a way to avoid talking as we had in the early years of our marriage—about everything, happy and sad, honestly and openly. I missed those days.

The carriage rocked and shuddered as the wheels hit a rut, and the jolt awoke Cecilia with a start. She opened her eyes, blinked, saw that her charge was still asleep, and promptly nodded off again. I turned to the window, where the forest appeared to be thinning. More sunlight streamed through the tops of the trees, most of which looked like pines. I could not mistake those tall, narrow silhouettes. A sudden breeze hit my nostrils with the pungent odor of sap, which trickled in long rivulets down the ancient trunks.

As the air filled with that sharp, invigorating scent, I recalled with astonishing clarity the March morning when one of Queen Bona's maids of honor, who had been in my charge, was executed outside the royal jail for murdering two men of the court. In the moments before the executioner raised the axe, just such a breeze swooped across the river. Cooler than today's, it too smelled of pine and spring and life. In all the years I lived in the south of Italy, I had seldom encountered that aroma. I did not realize, until now, how its absence had helped me bury the past for so long. But inhaling that fragrance brought back the memories of the injustice Helena Lipińska had suffered and the revenge she took, for which she paid with her life. I knew even before leaving Bari that my return to Poland would force me to revisit that dreadful winter of 1519, but I had not expected it to be so soon or so sudden. The weight that settled on my chest told me that I had overcome my guilt and grief, but not completely. They lurked deep inside me and would last the rest of my life.

We sat for a long time in silence as I contemplated my son's sleeping face and the sheen of sweat on his forehead. I hoped he was simply exhausted, but I feared another bout of fever. After so many days on the road, we were all ready to stretch our limbs and sleep in a comfortable bed, without having to rise at dawn to spend hours jolted about in a carriage.

At length we entered a sizable village, with solid, limewashed cottages, busy animal pens, and sounds of clanging metal coming from a smithy somewhere out of sight. After the tiny hamlets of Bohemia, where ramshackle huts were shared with skinny pigs and scrawny chickens, and where people barely eked out a living farming small plots of land, this was the surest sign that we were now in Poland.

"One thing is certain," I said, feeling a new surge of hope. "The countryside has never been so prosperous as it is now due to the queen's reforms." When we left a quarter of a century earlier, Bona had just set out to overhaul the outdated farming practices, to build roads and bridges, all of which would in due course bring a significant increase in revenue for the Crown and make the Jagiellons' fortune one of the largest in Europe. In Bari, which she continued to rule through her representatives, we had only ever *heard* of her successes. Now we could see them with our own eyes. Perhaps we might even benefit from them.

"It will be good for us, too, once we're settled in Konary." Sebastian's words echoed my own thoughts.

But I could not help sounding a cautionary note. "After we complete the repairs."

Sebastian leaned forward and took my hand in his, squeezing it briefly. "Don't worry about that. Whatever the state of the buildings, I'll do everything in my power to restore the estate to what it once was." The fine lines around his eyes softened as he rubbed Giulio's foot. It was a measure of the boy's fatigue that he did not even stir.

With a sting of longing for happier days, I wondered when Giulio had become the main recipient of my husband's affection and caresses. I did not blame Sebastian. Our son's poor health had long been our main preoccupation, leaving little time for ourselves and for each other. And in all fairness, whatever tenderness I missed from Sebastian, he probably missed it from me in equal measure. I sighed, setting the concerns about the state of our marriage aside for later, because whatever he said, I did worry about the renovations, especially their cost.

To save money, Sebastian would supervise the repairs and even spoke of doing some of the work himself. But he was a gentleman by birth who had spent his youth as a royal secretary at the court in Kraków. True, in Italy we had farmed almonds, but Sebastian only managed the estate and kept its books, so the prospect of him doing manual labor made me uneasy. Still, I drew comfort from the calm assurance with which he seemed to approach this new challenge. Having no other choice, I decided to trust in Providence.

We found Konary's buildings in better shape than I feared. On examining its books, however, it became clear that for years the farm had generated barely enough income to cover basic upkeep. We would have to spend much of the money we had brought with us to fix leaky roofs and broken shutters, replace rusty hinges on the doors of the grain storehouse, and clean out the barn occupied by a handful of animals, although large enough to accommodate a hundred head of cattle.

A few days after our arrival, we took the estate's only carriage—its chipped paint and worn wheels suggesting that it, too, would require replacement soon—and drove to Kraków. We wanted to visit Sebastian's sister Emilia, who lived with her prosperous merchant husband on a street not far from Wawel Hill.

As we emerged from the wooded tract, I gasped at the familiar panorama of the city with its slanted red roofs. Kraków had spread out in every direction since the last time I saw it. But the proud bulk of the castle above the silver ribbon of the Wisła still dominated the capital, timeless as the river itself.

Its shape had changed somewhat due to the demolition of the east wing in the 1520s and subsequent new construction; yet it was still the Wawel I remembered, encircled by a stone wall that looked gray in the rain and almost white in the sun, with the copper-domed bell towers of the cathedral watching over the royal residence.

The castle held a special and conflicted place in my heart. Within its walls, terrible crimes had been committed on my watch, lives and futures destroyed. But I had also met Sebastian there and begun a new, unhoped-for, and happy chapter in my life. I looked at him, and only then did I realize tears were rolling down my cheeks. He smiled, but I saw a shadow of emotion pass over his face. For him, too, this journey brought a mixture of joy and grief.

As we approached, the bells of the city's churches rang out, but within the gates the subdued atmosphere in the streets struck me. As a crossroads of major trading routes and the kingdom's capital, Kraków was normally loud and bustling, but on that beautiful early summer day a strange hush hung over it. People seemed to move slowly and talk in soft voices. When they turned their faces in our direction, I saw worry lines or tears swiftly dabbed away.

Sebastian and I exchanged a puzzled look. The bells rang more loudly now, as they once had for Bona's arrival. But this time I heard something somber in their sound; their rhythm lacked the energy and joy I remembered. The slow and mournful cadence sent a shiver through me. Could it be for the king? Zygmunt—now nicknamed Stary, the Old, to distinguish him from his namesake and heir—was approaching his eightieth year and fast declining, according to Lucrezia.

"I hope it's not for His Majesty's soul," I said to Sebastian, who had served in Zygmunt's household during those dark events of 1519 and 1520.

"Me too," he replied, but I could see that he was worried. He liked and respected the old king, and I knew that Zygmunt's demise would cause him a great deal of sadness.

"Lucrezia wrote that his body is stronger than his mind," I added by way of reassuring him and myself. "There didn't seem to be any signs of impending death."

Before Sebastian looked away, I read in his eyes the same concern I had: the king's death might indefinitely delay our petition.

We continued the rest of the way in silence until we at last pulled up in front of Emilia's sizable stone-and-timber house, red-roofed like most of its neighbors. On this elegant street and in front of its polished exterior, our carriage looked even shabbier than it had in Konary. A maid in an immaculately starched white apron promptly appeared in answer to our knock. Her eyes, too, were red-rimmed and blurry from crying.

My stomach flipped. "What has happened?" I asked, steeling myself to hear my fears confirmed.

"A great tragedy, mistress." The maid struck a lamenting tone as she wiped her eyes with the cuff of her dress. "Our gracious queen has died."

2

Kraków
June 15th, 1545

I swayed on my feet. The emotion of returning to Kraków after so many years, the desperation with which I had awaited Bona's help, and now this terrible news threatened to overwhelm me. The queen was the healthiest person I knew; I saw her as indestructible. Were we too late? Had the hardship of the journey been in vain? What would happen to Giulio now?

"Is it true?" I asked Emilia, who came out swiftly on the maid's heels to welcome us. "Is Her Majesty dead? I always thought she would outlive the rest of us!"

My sister-in-law, who did not appear nearly as grief-stricken as the maid, frowned at my shocked reaction. Then her brow smoothed as she looked from me to Sebastian, who stood equally dispirited next to me. "Ah! There seems to be a misunderstanding," she exclaimed, pecking her brother on the cheek and drawing me into an embrace. "Caterina! You haven't changed one bit. I can't believe you just turned fifty-three!"

"What do you mean by 'a misunderstanding'?" I asked when I finally managed to extricate myself. When I had last seen Emilia—in 1520, the year of my marriage and departure from Kraków—she was a slender girl of sixteen with a fresh and bright complexion, like a ripening apple. Now she was overweight, with a double chin under a pasty white—though heavily rouged—face, which testified both to the prosperity of the house and an indoor way of living. I cast around for a way to return the compliment, but nothing came to mind.

She mistook that for another sign of distress. "Let's sit down." She took me by the arm and led us to her well-appointed dining hall. "There is a lot you probably don't understand about the present state of our kingdom. It was the young king's wife, Elizabeth of Austria, who passed away this morning, God rest her soul. The poor thing was only eighteen."

When Emilia's husband, Leon Grabowski, similarly portly though slightly shorter, joined us, the two of them set out to explain the complicated situation of the royal family.

"Fifteen years ago, Queen Bona decided to secure young Prince Zygmunt's future by having him declared king during his father's lifetime," Leon began as we settled at the long table in the oak-paneled hall that ran the length of the house. In front of us stood full goblets of wine as we waited for servants to bring the first course of our supper. "She was aware of her unpopularity," he continued, "due in large part to her interference in state affairs and the agriculture reforms that infuriated the landowners, the same ones who elect a new king after his predecessor's demise." As one of the leading city merchants, Leon had broad contacts at the court and was well-versed in its politics as well as, I suspected, its intrigues.

Sebastian and I nodded. We knew of Zygmunt August's elevation in 1530; but as the years went on, and his father continued in good health, the practical aspects of this peculiar co-kingship had lost their meaning, at least to us in faraway Bari. So much so that we had ceased to think of Poland as having two living kings—and, in due course, two queens.

"How was it received?" Sebastian asked.

"Not very well. In fact, the magnates' hostility toward the queen only increased, as they claimed she had preempted their privilege. But they had no choice but to accept it." Leon spread his arms. "I questioned the wisdom of that move as well, since the succession was all but guaranteed, and the election a mere formality."

"Her Majesty did no more than any mother would have to secure her only son's future," Emilia interjected with a firm toss of her gem-encrusted headdress, yet more evidence of the family's good fortune. A mother of eight, she had become so round that I wondered if offspring number nine was on the way. If so, she might be forgiven for ascribing such tender motivations to the queen. But I knew Bona better than anyone in that chamber. While I had no doubt that she was a devoted mother—I had seen that side of her often enough in my time—the move could only have been inspired by her desire to continue to wield power as her elderly husband declined.

Leon waved his hand dismissively at his wife's comment just as the doors opened and servants brought in a platter of roasted venison in a spicy sauce, bowls of stew, and loaves of white bread. It was surprisingly rustic fare, and it delighted me. Across the table, Sebastian's face showed me that he felt the same way.

When the servants retreated, Leon said, dropping his voice, "If you ask *me*, the queen cossetted the heir too much. Fulfilled his every wish, kept him from practical military training for fear that he would hurt himself, and when he was old enough provided women for his entertainment." Seeing my surprise, he nodded, while his wife tutted in disapproval of his mentioning such a thing at the table. "They say he prefers feasting and hunting to governing, and would sooner collect armor and weapons for display than wear them to lead men in battle."

I cut a juicy piece of the venison, and it tasted as good as it smelled. I chewed slowly, thinking about what I had just heard. "What did the old king have to say to that?" I asked.

"He did try to toughen the boy up," Leon replied. "When he turned eighteen, the king sent him to inspect the troops bound for Wallachia, but the youngster soon complained through messengers of hardships and poor health, and the queen implored her husband to bring him home. Now Zygmunt Stary's mind is feeble and his body frail, and he spends his days in bed, while his son stays in Vilnius most of the time, where he is grand duke. From what I hear"—Leon lowered his voice again, although the four of us were alone—"he's mainly enjoying himself with his friends—and women." He raised his bushy salt-and-pepper eyebrows meaningfully.

Emilia sent him another reproachful look. "You shouldn't say such things, my dear. The young king is—was—a married man."

I, who had served at courts in Italy and Poland, smiled inwardly at her naïveté.

I understood immediately why Bona had raised her son that way. It was a logical consequence of her ambition and her forceful personality. "The queen wanted to make young Zygmunt dependent on her," I said, "so she would become his confidant and chief advisor, perhaps even rule through him one day." *As she did through her husband.*

"That's exactly right, sister. Nobody would say it aloud anywhere near her, but that's what many at the court believed." I had never met Leon before today—Emilia married after we left for Bari—but my brother-in-law appeared to delight in gossip as much as any goodwife. I did not judge him for it. After years in the Italian provinces, I was starved for news of the goings-on at court. "It can't have been easy for a boy growing up like that," he opined. "Nor is it proper for a man to rely on a woman's counsel." He shook his head disapprovingly.

I took a draught of the excellent French wine as I mulled over what I had heard. So things had not changed much—first through her husband and now through her son, Bona tried to hold the kingdom's reigns tightly in her hands. It was the outcome of years of patient, determined, and at times ruthless maneuvering. And yet . . .

"Why did Zygmunt August marry a Habsburg?" I asked, thinking of the recently deceased Elizabeth. "It can't have been to Her Majesty's liking."

"Aye. The old queen adamantly opposed it. She wanted Anna Maria, daughter of Albrecht of Prussia, to strengthen the loosening bonds with that principality, or, barring that, a French princess. It was a big win for the Habsburg-friendly forces and a bitter pill for Bona to swallow when that marriage contract was agreed upon. But she seemed to have made her peace with it. They say she took good care of her daughter-in-law during her illness. And now, of course, Elizabeth's death opens the door to a second dynastic marriage."

"Rulers from all over Europe will be offering their daughters' hands to the newly widowed king as soon as Elizabeth is buried," Emilia said, excited.

"I can't wait to see who the queen will back." I had no doubt she would do everything in her power to stop another marriage to one of the many Habsburg princesses from the lands stretching from Hungary to Spain.

Emilia shifted in her seat, her eyes sparkling. "Oh, there are rumors flying up and down the kingdom!" Her plump hand fluttered to her chest, where her breasts threatened to spill out of the confines of her low neckline. "The daughter of the Duke of Ferrara has been mentioned, as well as Princess Marguerite of France, and even Mary of England! Imagine all the betting in the taverns," she added with a half-hearted note of disapproval.

If she were a man, something told me, she would be among the first to place *her* bet.

But neither she nor anyone else at the table that night had any idea of how vicious the ensuing contest would become.

3

July 10th, 1545

The young king was not in Kraków when his wife died. By then, he resided mainly in Vilnius, where he administered Lithuania in preparation for assuming the sole responsibility for ruling the two nations. I found it odd that he had remained away even as Elizabeth's health deteriorated, although it appeared that her death was unexpected. Messengers were dispatched with all haste to the ducal court that same day to inform Zygmunt August of her passing. After that, Kraków assumed the mantle of mourning as it awaited the widower's arrival and prepared for the young queen's funeral.

He did not enter the capital until the end of the first week of July, and the date of the burial was fixed for the tenth day of that month. Sebastian and I went to stay with Emilia and Leon again, and on the sweltering morning of the somber ceremony we made our way to Wawel. Leon, through his connections at the court, had secured for the four of us a place in the stands erected in the castle's forecourt, outside the cathedral.

Unlike the crowds that clogged the streets around the castle hill, we enjoyed shelter from the relentless sun, provided by blue- and yellow-striped awnings. Despite the occasion, I could not help but admire the new royal chapel. I had seen its foundations laid shortly before I left Poland, and in subsequent years Master Bartolomeo Berrecci had overseen its completion. Built in the Italian style on a square base, it had round windows surrounded by intricately carved decorations and a dome topped with a spire supporting an angel holding a crown and a cross. According to Emilia, the inside was full of sculptures and paintings commissioned from the most renowned European artists. The old king, nearing the end of his life, would have a splendid place to rest, as would future generations of Jagiellon rulers.

For now, though, we awaited another, far more premature funeral to begin. Pennants and banners surrounded us, snapping in gusts of hot wind from across the river. Alongside the black banners of mourning flew others bearing the double cross of the Jagiellons, the serpents and eagles of the Sforzas, and the red lions of the Habsburgs. I watched the embroidered animals, fluttering and undulating side-by-side in a semblance of coordinated movement that mocked the hostility between the royal houses they represented.

The irony was not lost on me nor, I felt certain, on those around me. Somehow, despite her maneuverings, Bona had been forced to accept this marriage, and although Leon insisted she had surrounded Elizabeth with the best care, I could not help thinking that the young queen's demise must have suited her. Indeed, rumors were already circulating—spread, Leon told me, by Habsburg agents in the city—that the young queen had not died of natural causes, and that her mother-in-law had something to do with it.

"The latest," Emilia whispered in my ear even as we sat waiting for the funeral procession to begin, "is that one of Elizabeth's maids died suddenly just days before the young queen after drinking a poison intended for her mistress."

I struggled to conceal my dismay. Mention poison, and fingers immediately pointed to the first Italian that came to mind. And there was no more prominent Italian in Kraków than Bona Sforza.

"But others say the girl died of a bad lung," Emilia went on without waiting for me to respond. "It's impossible to know the truth, and, in any case, I don't see how that has anything to do with Elizabeth, who was known to have seizures. It was those seizures that eventually claimed her life."

I took heart from Emilia's certainty, for I did not believe those rumors either. For one thing, the Habsburgs were prone to the same falling sickness that afflicted Elizabeth and had killed quite a few of them over the years. As for Bona, she may have been ambitious, stubborn, at times even ruthless, but the continuation of the dynasty meant everything to her. Once she accepted she could no longer prevent the marriage, she would have focused her energies on helping her daughter-in-law produce an heir as soon as possible, rather than get rid of her. I knew the old queen to be capable of many things, but not of murder.

All the same, I could well imagine her sighing a quiet breath of relief as morning dawned on the fifteenth day of June.

The sudden cascade of clangs bursting from the bell tower put an end to my musings. Next to me, Sebastian too heaved a sigh of relief. He reached for a handkerchief to wipe his forehead—where his hair had receded greatly since we met and was now more gray than brown—for the third time in the last half-hour. As he did so, the ornate iron gate connecting the castle to the forecourt opened with a metallic groan, and the cortege emerged on its short, somber procession toward the cathedral.

Piotr Gamrat led the way. I recognized him even from a distance: Bona's former advisor who now served as the Bishop of Kraków and Gniezno, the latter see making him Primate of Poland *ex officio*. During my brief service at the court years earlier, he had been a portly middle-aged man with a balding pate. Now stooped with age and completely hairless under his miter, he leaned heavily on his crozier, confirming the rumors about his failing health. Behind him, reining in their horses to match the bishop's doddering pace, were a dozen knights on fine chestnuts—half wearing the colors of the Jagiellons, the other half those of the Habsburgs. Immediately behind them four splendid white horses caparisoned in black velvet pulled a flat, open carriage bearing a casket draped in the same cloth. An enormous wreath of white roses lay on the casket beside a crown studded with jewels that sparkled in the midday sun. A flash of sorrow touched my heart at the thought of the young queen, one-third my own age, gone so soon from this earth.

The raised dais of the stands allowed me to peer over the heads of the people in front of me. From a distance I saw Queen Bona, clad in black from head to toe, stepping solemnly behind the casket next to her son, followed by bishops and deacons from around the realm. The clergy chanted a hymn; behind them walked row upon row of nobility and courtiers. I could not take my eyes off the queen until she disappeared inside the great church.

Always plump, Bona had expanded in every dimension except height over the years, an effect only enhanced by her mourning attire. The folds of her gown started at her bosom, then billowed out before falling to the ground in a straight line, making it impossible to discern her waist. Her face, as far as I could make out, was stern, even dour, yet one could not mistake the regal dignity that her straight posture and deliberate movements still conveyed. She was shorter than most people around her, but her majesty towered above them.

A sudden, unexpected emotion seized me. Almost thirty years earlier, I had watched her in that same spot as she stepped down from the carriage that had brought her from Bari to meet her new husband. She had been young and beautiful and smiling that day. A lifetime of struggle to acquire, maintain, and expand her power had stripped that beauty from her and left marks many would consider unflattering. But I knew that, were she able to go back, she would have changed nothing.

Queen Bona was where she wanted to be, and something told me that she was not done yet.

I caught only glimpses of the young king during the procession. He walked on his mother's far side, and her bulk hid his slim figure from my view. But after the funeral came a reception, where I had the chance to observe him for the first time.

Most of those attending belonged to the family and the highest ranks of the realm: officials, nobles, senators, and bishops. Of the small number of seats set aside for other guests, Lucrezia had secured two for us. Walking to the new banqueting hall, I marveled at the extent of the renovations that had taken place since my departure from Bona's court. As with the new burial chapel, the influence of the Italian style of building and decoration was evident inside the castle. I saw new coffered ceilings; larger and airier rooms, with windows and doors that opened from the arched arcades; and many sumptuous tapestries that enhanced the residence's air of grandeur despite the black ribbons draped on the gilded candelabras and wall-mounted sconces.

The tables had already been set when we arrived, and it did not take me long to realize another difference: the food was Neapolitan. Seeing my surprise, Lucrezia explained that Bona had long since made good on her threat to bring Italian cooks to Kraków. Nicolo Maria de Charis, a native of Naples, served as their chief at present. I took in the platters heaped with chunks of octopus and cod fried in olive oil, pork rolls stuffed with raisins and pine nuts, flattened wheat cakes garnished with herbs and cheese, bowls of pickled vegetables, and trays of oranges and grapes. As I did so, I thought of old Michałowa, who ruled the castle's kitchen when Bona and I first arrived in Kraków, and how the poor woman must be turning in her grave.

As the reception began, I studied Zygmunt August discreetly. Dressed in a black doublet under a short cape edged in gray sable, a gray feather in his cap, and no jewelry, the king cut an appropriately somber figure. He sat between his mother and an officious-looking man of middle age who wore clerical garb but also the insignia of Grand Chancellor, who therefore must have been Samuel Maciejowski. Zygmunt frequently leaned toward one or the other of them to converse.

Yet I detected no signs of mourning in his face, whose swarthy complexion betrayed his Italian heritage. He had delicate, almost feminine features that I recognized from the medallion Bona had commissioned from the Italian artist Gian Maria Padovano, a copy of which I had seen in Bari some years earlier. It showed Zygmunt as a boy of twelve. That childish face had displayed affability and charm, with big dark eyes, well-defined eyebrows that resembled his mother's, and a pensive expression. Now it seemed that only the pensiveness remained. He had a serious, even brooding air, but somehow it failed to convey grief. It was more like boredom. He looked as if he wished he were somewhere else.

"You're very curious about the young king, Caterina." Lucrezia's voice reached me.

So much for discretion.

"I am," I admitted. "Since I came back to Kraków, I have heard"—I hesitated—"quite a lot about him."

Lucrezia laughed. It was a brief and joyless laugh, and it pained me. In her youth, she had been a cheerful, even frivolous girl, in love with gowns and pearls, whom I'd had a hard time keeping away from male courtiers and servants alike.

But after she accidentally discovered Helena's second murder victim, the queen's secretary Ludovico Mantovano, she underwent a deep transformation. She refused all offers of marriage and had remained with the queen to this day. Like every other woman in the hall, she wore black, but something told me that for her it was not just temporary mourning attire. The lobes of her ears, once pierced, showed two barely visible indents, which suggested that she had not worn jewelry for years. Her only adornment was a silver chain necklace with a cross pendant. Although in her early forties, she looked a decade older—the once-luscious olive skin of her face thin and lackluster, pulled at the edges by graying hair gathered severely under her black headdress.

"Most of it is probably true," she said. She tried to sound neutral, but a note of disapproval crept into her voice nonetheless.

I did not know how to respond. I raised my goblet and sipped wine—still Lombard, Bona's favorite—savoring its forgotten flavor, rich and slightly tart, with a taste that lingered. The act of drinking helped me stifle the questions forming on my tongue. A funeral reception was not the right place to indulge in gossip.

"How sad that Queen Elizabeth died when he was away," I said instead.

The scoffing sound Lucrezia made was barely audible, but it reached me all the same. "I doubt he sees it that way," she said.

"What do you mean?"

She took her time answering. I knew she needed to use the right words. And the right tone of voice. When she spoke, I needed to lean sideways to hear her above the murmur of the surrounding conversations, subdued though they were. "The young king has a mistress in Vilnius, a woman named Barbara Radziwiłł," she said.

This was hardly shocking news. Zygmunt's father had supported many mistresses in his day, and from families far less distinguished than the Radziwiłłs, who were counted among the leading Lithuanian nobility.

But Lucrezia had not finished. "Those who travel between the two courts say he is very much in love and has foresworn all other women for her, including his wife."

My eyes rounded. *That* was unusual. Royal marriages were arranged, and nobody expected the king to be lovingly devoted to his queen. Still, he had a duty to produce an heir at least.

Lucrezia smiled sadly when she saw my surprise. "Poor young queen, she returned from Vilnius alone in the spring. So abandoned did she feel there that the company of her mother-in-law—who, as you know, has little warmth to spare for any Habsburg—appealed more to her than her husband's indifference."

I shook my head as pity for Elizabeth filled me. Married off at such a young age, burdened with expectations she could not fulfill through no fault of her own, she must have experienced nothing but disappointment and humiliation in her short-lived role. I remembered seeing a portrait of her when the news of the royal marriage reached us in Bari. It showed a pretty young girl wearing a Spanish dress and a melancholy smile. I glanced at the king as he moodily beckoned an attendant for more wine and felt concern as I realized that the future of the monarchy rested on his shoulders.

After the reception, we lined up to pay our respects to Zygmunt and his mother. In the throne chamber, there were three thrones now: two for the elder royals and one for their co-ruling son. One of them was empty, the old king being too frail to attend any of the day's events. I wondered if Elizabeth had had one, too, and it had already been removed. I turned to ask Lucrezia, but she had disappeared.

From up close, the impression I'd had of Zygmunt August only intensified. The last time I had seen the heir to the throne of Poland-Lithuania was in the summer of 1520, when he was a red-faced, howling infant, already at the center of everyone's attention. This intense interest in the kingdom's only male heir continued, from what I'd heard, into his childhood and adolescence. The result was a young man of good looks but capricious temperament. A man raised by women and indulged by them, despite the fact that one of these women was as strong and forceful as any man. Or perhaps because of that.

I approached the thrones and dropped into a curtsy. "My deepest condolences to Your Majesties."

Zygmunt nodded with perfunctory courtesy. My face held no familiarity for him. But not so for his mother. At first, the queen bestowed her customary icy blue gaze on me, full of studied graciousness and regal detachment. Then I saw a spark of new alertness in them as her mind began working through its store of information. Within seconds, it found what it was looking for.

"Contessa Sanseverino—Signora Konarska." Bona was as sharp as ever. "We have been told of your return to Kraków." She gave me a small smile, the first I had seen on her face all night and a sign of high favor.

"Indeed," I replied. "My husband and I brought our son to Poland in search of a cure for his fevers." I felt nervous as soon as I said it, for I had not intended to bring up the reason for our visit just then. Lucrezia had already promised to arrange an audience to present my request, although things had understandably gotten delayed due to Elizabeth's death. In mentioning my concern, I might have gone against protocol. But Giulio's health was never far from my mind.

The queen's stern face softened momentarily with a look I also remembered—one of motherly empathy—before she recomposed her features. In that, too, she had not changed: she was still loath to show the world what she perceived to be the weakness of emotions. "Yes. Lucrezia mentioned it to us. What ails your son?"

"He is prone to bouts of the fever that affects some people so severely in the southern regions of Italy," I replied, aware that Zygmunt was already talking to the next courtier in line. "He's still weak from the journey, but we thank God he hasn't suffered another attack yet."

"We are glad to hear that." She continued to look at me, but I could see that she was thinking of something else; I could almost hear the wheels spinning. "When this is over"—she made a small gesture to encompass the gathering, although I suspected she meant the mourning period—"we will arrange for one of our doctors to examine your boy."

The finality of her tone suggested dismissal, and I curtsied again, gratefully. "Thank you, Your Majesty."

As I moved away from the throne, I felt exhausted after the long, busy day, hot and emotional. It must have been close to nine o'clock in the evening, the summer night had just fallen, and I wanted to go back to my sister-in-law's house and rest. I also had another reason to withdraw. Jan Dantyszek was among the guests at the reception and not far away, having paid his respects to the king and queen before me. Now the Bishop of Warmia, he had been the third of Helena's victims in the winter of 1519, and the only one who survived.

He must have been approaching sixty, but he was still a handsome man, though stout. The golden-brown wavy hair he once liked to show off now fell gray and limp from under his cap. He had exchanged his courtier's doublet for ecclesiastical robes, but he looked as confident and at ease in the presence of power as ever. He did not recognize me, it seemed, but his face was burned indelibly into my memory. A quarter of a century earlier, we had spent a terrifying several hours in the cellars under the castle kitchens as Helena's captives, and only the timely arrival of Sebastian saved us from death that night.

I was glad Dantyszek had gone on to rebuild his life, to use his considerable talents to serve the kingdom and the Church. But I had no wish to speak to him. Anything we said to each other would force me to revisit that terrible time, and although I could never forget what had happened, I wanted to keep the memory as far from me as possible. Neither Lucrezia nor Bona had brought it up, although for different reasons. I doubted the queen had given it much thought during the intervening years, while Lucrezia's feelings were probably even more complicated than mine. Whatever the case, I welcomed their discretion and preferred not to dwell on the past.

Trying to stay as far away from Dantyszek as I could, I went in search of Lucrezia. I finally found her talking to the queen's musician Alessandro Perenti, a young Veronese, who was taking a break from playing a mournful tune on his cithara. I bid her goodnight and left the banqueting hall with as much haste as propriety permitted.

Minutes later, I was descending the gentle slope of Wawel Hill toward the city under a starry summer sky, its cloudlessness promising another clear day tomorrow. Above me, in the royal chapel, the young queen was spending the first night of her eternal repose under the layers of marble, gold, and already wilting flowers.

4

August 5th, 1545

After two months in Kraków, I had a better understanding of the factions and power plays at the court and of Bona's own situation. She stood on shakier ground than I had thought. Elizabeth's death may have cleared the path for a marriage more to her liking, but powerful forces opposed her. And those forces had a great deal of influence over her son, based on the gossip that went around.

At their head was Grand Chancellor Samuel Maciejowski, who sat on the king's left side during the funeral reception. Similar in build and military-like bearing to his predecessor Stempowski, he, too, wanted closer relations with the Habsburgs. Jan Tarnowski, the army's hetman—its supreme commander—and one of the leading nobles of the realm, was Maciejowski's most important ally. For reasons I could not fully understand, King Zygmunt appeared to be sympathetic to that political line and took advice from both of them. This meant that the queen's influence waned steadily as the old king handed more and more power over to his son, in direct contradiction to her expectations and hopes at this point in her life.

I crossed the colonnaded inner courtyard of the castle, its flagstones still wet after the overnight rain that had pleasantly cooled the air after weeks of incessant heat. This same courtyard had once been the scene of my desperate trek in knee-deep snow to the castle kitchen in search of the missing Jan Dantyszek, followed by the longest and most terrifying night of my life. I tried to keep that memory at bay as I approached Lucrezia, who was waiting for me at the bottom of the steps that lead to Wawel's elaborate arched entrance.

She greeted me warmly and inquired about Sebastian and our children—Aurora, recently married, lived with her husband in Rome—and I thanked her for her note confirming the audience for today. But when we entered the cool interior of the residence and retraced the familiar path to the queen's gallery, we did so in silence. I had already noticed during our first meeting that the sight of me, while bringing a fond smile to Lucrezia's face, also revived painful memories. I had seen it in the haunted look in her eyes before she averted them. We had not spoken of it then, and we remained silent now, but Helena's ghost was with us, like a heaviness in the air.

The presence chamber of the queen's apartment was crowded, but the composition of the attendants differed greatly from what it had been in my day. For one thing, there were no maids of honor; young women served Zygmunt August's wife, not Bona—and when his wife died, her household was dissolved. The new queen, when Zygmunt August remarried, would have to form her own.

Three female attendants accompanied the queen. Beata Kościelecka, whom I had last seen as a spunky five-year-old, was a lady-in-waiting and the old king's illegitimate daughter. She would be in her late twenties now. There was also Elisabetta Colonna, a few years older than Beata and a descendant of the dukes of Urbino. As such, she was Bona's cousin and currently served as the Lady of the Queen's Chamber, my old post. The third woman looked vaguely familiar, but I could not place her until Lucrezia introduced her as Maria d'Aragona, Marchesa del Vasto. Then I knew: tall and thin, with dark eyes shining with avid curiosity and a shock of unruly black hair barely contained by her headdress, she had to have been related to Giovanna d'Aragona, the Princess of

Montefusco, who had stayed at the court in the early 1520s. As it turned out, Maria was her niece.

There were also three men in the chamber, not counting Perenti, who sat in a window alcove softly tuning his instrument, ready to play whenever the queen desired. Bishop Gamrat huddled in a chair, looking even more frail than he had a few weeks earlier at the funeral. His right hand shook even though he pressed it to his stomach to try to still it. His presence suggested that despite being responsible for the two most important dioceses in the kingdom, he was still Bona's advisor. Behind a small desk perched a young man—he could not have been more than twenty—who served as her secretary. I remembered him from the funeral, when he walked behind the queen, his beardless face streaked with tears.

Finally—bent close to the queen and whispering in her ear when I entered—was Gian Lorenzo Pappacoda. He wore silver-striped puffy breeches that reached to his mid-thighs, shapely in tight white hose. A small ruff of nearly translucent lace, starched stiff, encircled his neck. That, together with his slithering proximity to the queen's chair and his fawning demeanor, made him the purest example of a courtier, a man with no job other than to flatter and entertain, and thereby make his fortune. He reminded me of a young Dantyszek, but more shameless and less charming. In fact, his face—though it could have been considered handsome, with its olive skin and carefully tended black beard—had something cunning and shifty about it. And nowhere was the impression more powerful than when one met his eyes: small and so dark they were almost black, their look calculating and greedy. I took an immediate dislike to him, not suspecting that my repulsion would one day come to haunt me.

The queen smiled as she responded to Pappacoda, although I did not catch her words. The smile revealed a row of browned teeth, the result of her lifelong enjoyment of sweet confections—which, judging by her girth, had not abated. As I waited for her to address me, I took stock of the other changes that had taken place in her, seeing her as I did up close and in the full light of day for the first time in a quarter of a century. The rumors were true: she had aged badly. I was a year older than the queen, and although I was not so vain as to believe everything my sister-in-law said about my looks, I had a slimmer waist, a smoother face, and—based on the little that was left uncovered by Bona's austere white cap—less gray hair. The loose robes of shiny, dark-colored velvet in which she was draped only heightened the impression that her shape resembled a tree trunk more than an hourglass. Once again, I recalled the alluring young woman who swept into Kraków with trunks full of fashionable gowns in bright yellows, icy blues, and passionate crimsons. Noblewomen across the kingdom once imitated her style. I doubted they did anymore.

Despite the smiles she had for Pappacoda, I saw signs that Bona's temper had gotten worse over the years. Her once full and voluptuous lips were now pale and pinched, to the point where she resembled Suor Modesta, the strict disciplinarian at the convent I had attended in my youth. The permanent lines running down both sides of her prominent nose gave her a stern look even when she was benevolently disposed. When angry, she must terrify her subordinates. Much of it probably grew out of her long and bruising tenure as Poland's queen, for she had never been an obedient and submissive wife in a country whose customs demanded nothing else. She exceeded her husband in political astuteness, determination, and the ability to take advantage of opportunities. She had made a fortune—and lots of enemies—by investing in land and reforming agriculture. She had fought many battles, triumphed and failed, and she had the scars to prove it.

"How has young Giulio been?" the queen asked after the introductions were completed. "We trust there has been no return of the fever?"

"There has not, and we are grateful to God. But he's still very weak," I replied. That was not strictly true: Giulio, while still spending most of his time indoors, had in fact been able to get out of bed and move around the house more than when we had first arrived in Kraków. There was even a little more color in his cheeks, and his appetite had improved. But none of it meant that he would not suffer another attack—in the past, there had been times when he felt stronger before inevitably relapsing. I withheld that information from the queen for fear that she would decide he did not need to see a royal physician. "Sometimes the period between relapses lasts for months," I said instead.

The queen nodded vigorously, as if she had extensive experience of the way fevers worked. I remembered her distraction during our brief conversation at the funeral reception. She was certainly more attentive now, and I saw deep concern in her eyes. For my son's health? I found that hard to believe.

I was wondering if I should ask her for help directly when she spoke again. "We believe it would benefit your Giulio to be seen by a competent doctor, of whom there aren't many." I inclined my head, my heart leaping with hope, even as I registered the sarcasm of her last words. Bona still despised physicians, it seemed.

"Fortunately, we have a few in our employ with deep and extensive learning in the medical arts," she went on, and I listened to this praise, half-surprised and half-amused. Perhaps she had softened toward medics as she got older and needed them more, although she looked healthy enough to me. "Here's what we think." She raised a forefinger. "It would be best for the boy to be seen by an Italian physician, given that his affliction is common in our native land. Unfortunately, the two

Italians who serve us are currently away from Kraków—de Valentinis is back home tending to his ailing mother, and Nascimbene is with the young king in Vilnius."

My heart sank. "When do you expect them to return, Your Majesty?"

"It's hard to say. Nascimbene will be with my son until the end of the year at least, and de Valentinis—that depends on how his mother fares."

"What about the Polish doctors?"

The queen shrugged. "They are both good surgeons, but they know little about herbs and potions. They don't have the experience to deal with your son's condition," she stated authoritatively.

I knew better than to argue with her. I would not have had the chance, either, for she was speaking again, smoothly and firmly, which told me she had already thought this through. "There is a weekly convoy to Vilnius, carrying dispatches and consignments from the court. You and your son could go with it to see Nascimbene. It's the safest way to travel."

The suggestion amazed me. I took a deep breath and tried to gather my thoughts. I was supposed to leave for Lithuania so soon after making the arduous journey from Bari? And with Giulio? He was better, but I feared that more travel would weaken him, perhaps even sicken him again. Was it worth the risk? And what would Sebastian say?

When I looked at Bona, she was studying me calmly, but there was a tense and calculating look in her eyes. I had no doubt she knew exactly what was going through my mind.

Behind me, I heard the door of the chamber open, and the queen's eyes turned in that direction. With an air suggesting expectations fulfilled, she flipped her left palm up and beckoned to the newcomer with a practiced movement of her fingers, swift and commanding. I looked over my shoulder to find a man of spare build, with a narrow, intelligent face framed by thick gray hair spilling from under his cap. He wore a tight black doublet, a chain of office rested on his chest, and he carried a sheaf of papers under one arm. Clearly a secretary, but a high-ranking one because I had seen him during the funeral reception seated at the same table as the queen and her son.

"Leave us," the queen commanded, and we women dropped into a curtsy. The men bowed. "You stay, Caterina," she added as the others made their way out of the chamber, with the notable exception of Pappacoda. He remained motionless by the queen's chair, his eyes trailing the others as they left. Bona had always had favorites whom she would take into her deepest confidence, and Pappacoda was obviously the latest of them.

The commotion gave me more time to consider the offer. Admittedly, it was generous. As much as I did not look forward to another journey, I knew that a convoy could cover the distance between Kraków and Vilnius in a little more than a week in good weather. Moreover, she would pay our expenses, and it would be a chance for Giulio to be seen by one of the best physicians in Europe. What kind of mother would refuse such an opportunity?

When the doors closed behind the last of the retreating courtiers, the queen gestured toward the newcomer. "Pan Marcin Kromer, His Majesty's chief secretary. My husband's," she clarified. "Signora Caterina Konarska, my former Lady of the Chamber."

We nodded at each other. I tried to hide my puzzlement under a polite smile. What did the old king's secretary have to do with my son's health or my journey to Vilnius?

"So what do you think of my offer, Caterina?" the queen asked in her usual direct manner. She was never one to leave too much silence hanging over a gathering. I also noticed that she switched away from the royal "we." Now she was speaking to me as she had in the old days—more intimately. Suddenly, I felt more at ease, despite Pappacoda's unsettling presence.

"It is a kind and magnanimous offer, Your Majesty, and I thank you for it." Bona acknowledged my words with a curt but gracious incline of her head. "However, I have to consult my husband before I accept."

"Of course."

In the brief silence that followed, as I awaited a dismissal that was not coming, my eyes strayed to Kromer before I could help myself.

"I wish to be honest with you, Caterina." The queen spoke again. The worry I had seen in her eyes at the beginning of our meeting intensified. There was a new sadness in them, too. Something was clearly eating away at her. "There is a reason why your journey to Vilnius would also be very helpful to *me*."

"In what way, Your Majesty?"

Bona inhaled, her ample chest swelling. Somewhere under the loose robes the seams of her bodice must have come close to snapping. The opaque lace with which she now covered the bosom she had once loved to display expanded with her breath, making her look more than ever like a puffed-up owl.

"You may be aware that my son has had the care of the Grand Duchy since His Majesty my husband ceded the position to him last year," she said. Then, with a note of bitterness, she added, "He's back in Vilnius now."

I thought it odd that young Zygmunt had left less than a month after his wife's burial, but something told me that Bona's bitterness had more than one cause.

I was correct.

"I have been hearing some very troubling news from the ducal court," the queen continued, growing more dispirited as she went on. Whatever was coming next, it was clearly difficult for her to talk about. "News of an affair my son has been conducting with a certain woman of a rather disreputable character."

I did not know what to say to that. Barbara was a noblewoman from a prominent family. I knew nothing else about her, and therefore thought it best to hold my peace.

Bona continued with barely a pause. "I'm told the young king is very smitten with her"—her mouth twisted in a grimace of distaste—"and that her family is plotting to convince him to marry her."

Disbelief must have been painted all over my face, because Bona nodded vigorously in emphasis. Although she remained outwardly calm, I sensed fury building up inside her. Her fingers squeezed the arms of her chair until her knuckles showed white. I understood why: a marriage of her only son and heir to the throne that brought nothing in terms of alliances or territorial possessions would be a disaster.

"Surely His Majesty wouldn't—"

"Oh yes, he would!" Bona exclaimed. "My son does what he wants, and if it hurts me, so much the better!" Her voice rang with bitterness again, and her eyes glistened with tears—a weakness she abhorred—before she determinedly blinked them back.

I stared at her. In truth, what could I say? That she had raised him that way—to put his own interests and pleasures above everything else? I could not utter such words to the queen, yet I felt pity for her, and her brief moment of vulnerability touched me.

"I am very sorry to hear that, but what does it have to do with my journey to see Doctor Nascimbene?" I asked cautiously.

The reply was swift. "I want *you*, Caterina, to speak to my son while in Vilnius and dissuade him from taking this step, which would be a catastrophe for the monarchy."

Speechless, I struggled to rein in my thoughts as they scattered in a thousand directions. From a corner of my eye, I registered Pappacoda's darkening face. It seemed that the queen's favorite disliked me as much as I did him. Or perhaps he resented the familiarity with which she treated me.

Bona gazed at me unwaveringly, still as a statue, until I gathered my wits and asked, feebly, "I, Your Majesty?"

She nodded gravely.

"But why would King Zygmunt listen to *me*, a person he doesn't know, a woman? Surely, such a mission would be better accomplished by an official envoy . . ."

She cut me off. "He won't speak to any of my men. He refuses to see them."

I raked my mind for an argument to refute *that*. "Even if that's the case," I said after failing to find one, "that doesn't mean that he will listen to me. After all, I would be acting as Your Majesty's emissary, too."

"Not officially. You would be traveling at my recommendation to see Nascimbene, who serves as my son's personal physician. My son loves children; he will sympathize."

So that was the plan. Now that I understood, the silent presence of Kromer spoke volumes. It told me that the old royals presented a united front in their opposition to the marriage, and that I would undertake the mission on behalf of both of them. It made sense, I realized.

"He will agree to see you," the queen added, "if you ask for an audience as an Italian married to a Polish nobleman and seeking help for your son. Only when you stand before him will you unveil your other mission—my sincere supplication for him to abandon the idea of marriage to this woman for the good of the state. He will hear you out. You are my last hope, Caterina." She strove to keep her tone level, but I could see how humiliated she was both by her son's indifference and the necessity of asking others for help.

I felt sorry for her. Watching her power wane must be one of the hardest experiences of her life. Only at the breaking point would she beg her son like that. But I knew her well enough to understand that she would do what she had to, not just because of her sense of dynastic pride but also out of a genuine concern for the future of Poland-Lithuania, surrounded by enemies wolfishly eyeing her throne. She cared about that, and I respected her for it. But could I help?

Then I thought of my son again. The queen's mission and the future of the state aside, this was my best chance yet to help Giulio overcome his illness and have a healthy childhood. If Sebastian let me travel to Lithuania, I would. I would travel to the ends of the earth to save my child.

"I will talk to my husband, and if it is within my power, I will go to Vilnius," I said.

Bona acknowledged this with a nod, and I thought I saw her tense frame relax slightly. Next to her, one corner of Pappacoda's full lips lifted in a smirk in which I saw a fleeting annoyance. But I had too much on my mind to give it another thought.

Lucrezia escorted me to the castle courtyard. In the early afternoon, it was drenched in sunlight reflecting so brightly off the white stone of the colonnade that I had to squint. Heat dried the flagstones under our feet and sizzled in the air again. The courtyard was deserted, except for the guards standing sentinel by the gate leading to the forecourt. Everyone else, it seemed, had sought refuge in the cool interior of the castle.

"The queen says her son refuses to receive any of her men," I remarked as we descended the steps from the main entrance. Whether or not Lucrezia knew about Bona's offer, like anyone else who spent more than a day at court, she must have been aware of their feuding. "I had no idea the break between them was so deep."

"It's even worse than you think," she said quietly. "He believes that Her Majesty wants to have Barbara Radziwiłł assassinated. That's why he won't see anybody who comes from her, and why he won't let them anywhere near his mistress."

I gasped, incredulous. "That's not true, is it?" The Bona I had known in my youth would not have considered anything so heinous, but the woman I had just left was hurt, humiliated, and desperate. And she still held sufficient power to issue such a command and expect results.

Lucrezia scoffed. "Of course not."

"Then why would he think that?"

"Some of his advisors, including Chancellor Maciejowski"—Lucrezia's voice was barely above a whisper—"have been turning King Zygmunt against his mother for a long time. It doesn't help that she's Italian."

Being Italians ourselves, we both knew how deeply rooted our reputation was in that regard, and not entirely without justification. Some prominent nobles in our lands—including women—had indeed dispatched their political or personal enemies using secretive methods. But to paint everyone of us with the same brush? If the highest officials in the realm perpetuated such slanders, and the young king lent them credence, any one of us stood in danger of a grave accusation for the slightest of reasons—or no reason at all.

We reached the middle of the courtyard and stopped to bid each other good-bye.

"Thank you for arranging this audience," I said. Lucrezia had no chance to answer before an oddly high-pitched sound, something between the yelping of a dog and the braying of a donkey, cut her off. I looked around for the source of the noise but could not find it. The guards remained unmoved, clearly not perceiving any danger.

Lucrezia gave a small laugh when she saw my bewilderment. "Come with me," she said with an air of mystery.

She led us toward the gate that connected the courtyard with the queen's private garden. She pushed the gate open, and we entered a large space enclosed by the castle wall. It looked much as it had when Bona first set it up: the flower beds arranged in the form of a chessboard, delineated by neat paths, and a large trellised loggia covered in creeping vines and rosebushes in the far corner. But there was one difference. The section of the garden to the right of the gate had been cordoned off from the rest by a stockade of sorts, taller than a person's height and made of vertical iron bars.

Behind those bars were three of the strangest animals I had ever seen: sandy colored, with thin legs and curving necks topped with narrow heads that ended in large, fleshy lips, curved into a perpetual roguish smile. But the oddest feature was their backs—not flat like a horse's but raised in a hump.

As I stared at them, I heard Lucrezia's voice next to me, amused. "They are called camels."

"Camels," I repeated. "I have heard of them."

"They come from the warm regions of the world, where they are used much like pack horses by caravans crossing the great desert." Then she added, "The queen received them as a gift from Roxelana, the wife of the Turkish sultan, Suleiman, whom they call the Magnificent, as a gesture of gratitude for her efforts to promote peace between them."

"I see." I continued to gaze at the animals. Despite the semblance of perpetual smiles, they seemed restless as they stepped around their enclosure aimlessly. I had the impression—perhaps enhanced by the shape of their heads, elongated and tilted up at a slight angle—that they sought to escape. Their tawny fur had dry and gray patches like those one might find on mangy dogs, adding to their forlorn air.

Scattered piles of apples, pears, and carrots gave off a ripe scent, but the camels did not nibble at them. Every now and then, one of them made that whining-braying sound, which seemed to make the others even more restless.

"And she sent three of them?" I asked, puzzled. What use could Bona have for these exotic pack animals in the heart of Kraków?

"She sent five," Lucrezia said. "But two of them died."

I regarded the beasts again. They had come from a different world, where hot winds blew every day and winter did not exist. No wonder their companions had not survived for long. Even in the height of a Polish summer, when they should have been comfortable, the remaining three were anxious. They would probably meet a similar fate soon.

Royalty always wants to bend everything to its will, I reflected. To make things work according to decree. But some things cannot be controlled. There is no cheating nature, no taming its laws. In the end, nature always prevails.

I returned to Konary the next day.

Sebastian was out on the estate supervising the repairs. We had seen little of each other since the day we attended Queen Elizabeth's funeral. I knew he would not return before supper. Too impatient to wait, I went through the apple orchard and down the sloping hill toward the farm buildings. He was there, among the laborers hired to replace the roof over the large barn that overlooked several acres of pasture and a pond. He was wearing a shirt and breeches, but no doublet in the heat. I wished I had the same freedom to shed my constraining bodice and voluminous skirts and walk around in a cotton shift. Fortunately, the countryside was breezier than the city.

He saw me, and I waited for him in the shade of a large tree at the edge of the orchard, its long branches dotted with the small, rounded shapes of new fruit. A week earlier, they had been green, but now the globes had acquired a faint pink blush. In a month or so, the branches would sag low and heavy under the weight of ripe red apples, and I wondered with renewed apprehension if I would be here to enjoy them.

I considered my husband as he walked up the path. Despite his fifty-five years, he was mostly lean, although the trace of a belly could be seen under his shirt, open at the collar to reveal chest hair as much gray as black. Gray threaded his beard, too. Although he still walked with the grace of his youth, I noticed with a pang of sadness that his movements were slower now. I wished he did not have to do this work himself, but I was also aware that he saw it as a respite from the tension of our son's illness. He had not told me that—it had been a long time since we talked about such things honestly—but I knew that a part of him looked forward to the work, which took him away from the infirmary-like atmosphere of the house.

Up there on the hill, Giulio still spent most of his time in bed under Cecilia's watchful eye. He took an interest in his late uncle's library of some one hundred volumes and was working his way through the treatises on agriculture, art, and politics, including an early copy of Machiavelli's popular work on the most desirable qualities in a ruler. I had also seen him read Castiglione's *Il Cortegiano*, which, to my knowledge, had not yet been translated into Polish. Giulio did not understand much, if any, of it, but he enjoyed putting the words and sentences together, and it warmed my heart to see him so happily engaged. If only his physical strength returned enough to allow him to run through the woods and swim in the pond, like other boys his age did during the long summer days.

"I didn't expect you back so soon." Sebastian kissed me lightly on the cheek. It had also been a while since we embraced with ardor.

When I left for the audience with Bona, I told him I might stay in Kraków for a few days to visit Beatrice Roselli. A former maid of honor to the queen, Beatrice had married Gabriel Morawiec, a northern magnate who had a palace on the outskirts of the city, and I looked forward to spending time with an old friend living in such luxurious circumstances. But the queen's unexpected offer had caused me to return home immediately.

"There is something I must tell you," I said, getting straight to the point. The sooner the decision was made, the better.

We took a path away from the orchard and the barn and walked toward the pond. The road skirted the pasture under the shade of a row of old planted oaks whose leaves rustled in the breeze. Long reeds grew over the far side of the pond and gave shelter to hundreds of frogs. Their loud, rhythmic, strangely soothing croaking could be heard as far as the house after dusk. We had almost reached it by the time I finished recounting my conversation with Bona.

"She wants you to go to Vilnius to talk her son out of a marriage?" Incredulity colored Sebastian's voice.

"Yes. I would do that at the same time as I would consult his Italian physician regarding Giulio's fevers," I reminded him quickly.

He shielded his eyes as he gazed over the pasture where a dozen cows, far fewer than the farm could accommodate, grazed lazily, their tails intermittently whipping one or the other side of their hind parts to swat flies. He mulled over the news for a long while, then said, "She's using you. Do you realize that?"

I straightened my spine, vaguely piqued that he did not trust me to see that for myself. "Of course. That's what she does. Nevertheless," I added, equally pointedly, "it is an opportunity for our son to be seen by a competent doctor. You cannot deny that."

His eyes shifted toward the house. "So you think it's worth it?" he asked, his voice softer.

I took a deep breath. "Yes." I had been thinking about nothing else since the previous day and decided that it was best to accept the offer. I would do it first and foremost for Giulio, and if in the process I could prevent Bona's son from making a terrible mistake, so much the better. Although I had no idea how to accomplish the latter. "I'll take Giulio to Lithuania, if you give me your leave to do so."

"I'll go with you."

We were silent for a while as I considered his words and he waited for my reply. I surveyed the estate around us. We had brought it to a semblance of life again after several masterless months. But the fields that had not been plowed and sown in the spring, and the decrepit state of some of the outlying buildings, spoke of much work that remained to be done. I turned to Sebastian and saw, in his face, a yearning to see it through.

"There is no need, my love." On the spur of the moment, I used the term of endearment we spoke to each other so often early in our marriage. Instead of comforting me, it reminded me again of the intimacy we had once shared and seemed to have lost. "We will go as part of a train of merchants and courtiers who travel regularly between the two courts. We'll be safe."

He frowned. "I don't like the idea of you both on the road for so many days." The conflict was plain in his face.

"We will be fine," I repeated.

His gaze traveled beyond the orchard and up the hill again. "I'm worried about how Giulio will handle it. He's still recovering from the journey from Bari. Perhaps we should wait until Doctor Nascimbene returns to Kraków in December. Isn't that what the queen said?"

I strove to hide my impatience. "She said he *should* be back, but she cannot be certain. What if the roads become impassable for months? Have you forgotten what winters here are like?" My mind was made up, and I would do what I could to stop Sebastian from revoking his permission. "Then we'll have to wait until next spring, by which time Giulio might have a relapse."

Sebastian studied me with sudden concern. "You miss the excitement of court life, don't you, Caterina," he said with a trace of reproach. "You gave it up all those years ago, but you haven't forgotten it."

I opened my mouth to protest but could not find the right words. For, in truth, he was right. The circumstances of my quitting royal service were still a thinly healed wound, prone to reopening if I were not careful. But time had blunted the pain and cast the other aspects of my life at Wawel—the banquets, the hunts, the sleigh rides, and, yes, even the fashions—into a softer light, tinged with nostalgia.

"You know exactly why I left the court," I said sharply. "It was the right decision, and I have *never* regretted it. But I won't lie to you"—the words came out before I realized I was saying them—"the prospect of spending a few weeks in Vilnius intrigues me. It will be good to reexperience court life again for a short time."

I felt color rising in my face as my pulse raced. A strange elation enveloped me as I tasted the forgotten feeling of being honest with my husband, the freedom that came from trusting that I could tell him anything and he would understand.

We held each other's gaze, and Sebastian's eyes remained inscrutable. "I will go with you then," he repeated.

I shook my head. Then I pointed toward the pasture and the farm beyond. "We both need to escape from the things that have preoccupied us for such a long time. You have the renovations, and I have this mission for the queen."

The anxious gaze he cast in the direction of the barn and the workers told me that I was right.

"We'll be safe," I assured him again. "We'll be under the queen's protection." Then I added, "If all goes well, we'll finally find a cure for Giulio." I inhaled deeply. "Just imagine—it will change our lives."

5

Late August 1545

The night before we set off for Vilnius, a powerful thunderstorm blew over Konary, cooling the air once again. It toppled one of the old oaks by the pond and tore some of the branches off the apple trees in the orchard. Miraculously, the repaired parts of the barn roof withstood damage, although a section inside was flooded.

Sebastian rode with us to the city, a trip that took almost five hours instead of the usual two because the driver had to stop occasionally to clear fallen branches and other debris off the road. I wondered if the departure would be postponed; in fact, a part of me hoped, for Giulio's sake, that we would spend a night at Emilia and Leon's house before setting out, but that was not to be. Evidently, Queen Bona still approached every project with the same determination, energy, and single-mindedness. No pesky storm would delay *her* plans. It was no wonder, I reflected, as I settled myself, Giulio, and Cecilia in a spacious carriage with gilded knobs and soft cushions, for the very future of the monarchy was at stake.

As the train of carriages left the castle's forecourt and descended the hill toward the city's eastern gate, dark clouds hung heavy and ominous in the western sky, a reminder of last night's storm. I tried to quash a superstitious worry that this did not bode well for the success of my dual mission. As it happened, I later learned that on that day, the twenty-seventh of August, Bishop Gamrat died—the only man, Bona later told me, who had never betrayed her trust.

Four people rode in my carriage. To my surprise, the queen appointed Maria d'Aragona, Marchesa del Vasto, as my companion on the journey. If she was anything like her aunt Giovanna—and from the little I knew of her, that appeared to be the case—she would not stop talking until we reached our destination. Just the thought of it caused a headache to form in my temples even before our driver whipped the horses into motion.

Sure enough, the marchesa's presence gave rise to a constant buzz of observations and commentary as we left the walls of the capital and made our way toward the bridge over the Wisła through suburbs of increasingly smaller and more rickety houses. And like her aunt—who, Maria informed me, was currently staying in Paris at the court of François I, to whom she was also distantly related—she seemed oblivious to the effect her talk had on those around her. Giulio fell asleep quickly, lulled by the swaying motion and Maria's incessant chatter, so there was at least a silver lining in that.

Besides ours, three more carriages composed the train, which was protected by men-at-arms in royal livery riding in front and bringing up the rear. I did not know who our travel companions were as they were never introduced to us, but from their dress and manners I surmised they were high-ranking courtiers. The eight of them avoided us throughout the journey, taking their meals together while discussing business in low voices. Like me, they were on a mission—or missions—for the old royals, and the well-guarded, bulky trunks tied to the roofs of their carriages testified to the importance of the goods they were conveying between the courts. Yet in the summer of 1545 Poland-Lithuania was relatively peaceful, and I wondered if their tasks could be as sensitive as mine.

The queen assigned a knight by the name of Jakub Zaremba to protect us. He arrived wearing armor over a padded tunic, and a pair of greaves and gauntlets. Taking off his helmet and revealing dark golden hair and a reddish-blond beard, both untouched by gray although he looked to be well into his thirties, he introduced himself as Her Majesty's trusted man, whose task it was to deliver us safely to Vilnius. Perhaps to stress his credentials, he added that he was a deputy to Bernard Pretwicz.

That impressed me: Pretwicz was a famous military leader, whose bravery and tactical skill in fighting Tatar invasions had earned him widespread admiration and respect, as well as the nickname *Terror Tartarorum*, Terror of the Tatars. Tatar mothers were said to invoke his name to rein in unruly children. Pretwicz was a Pole from Silesia and therefore had German ancestors; nonetheless, he enjoyed the queen's favor due to his success in containing the threat to the southern borders. For his service, she had named him the *starosta*, or administrator, of the town of Bar in the Podole region, part of her dower lands. Since then, the castle at Bar had become the base from which Pretwicz and his troops organized their expeditions against the Tatars. I had learned all this since my return to Poland, such was the fame of the man and his exploits.

Zaremba did not talk much, which was unsurprising in a soldier, but having him ride alongside us for days offered opportunities for chatter. Thanks to Maria's endless curiosity, I soon learned some interesting facts about him. At Bar, for example, Captain Pretwicz had chosen Zaremba to lead clandestine and reconnaissance work prior to launching expeditions into Tatar territories. His tasks involved secretly observing the enemy, tracking and capturing individual warriors for questioning, and—he even hinted—infiltrating encampments in the guise of a captive in order to gather information. It all sounded very dangerous and brave, and I listened rapt as a child caught up in a fairytale.

Having such an accomplished knight in charge of our escort gave me peace of mind. His military successes aside, Zaremba's air of quiet efficiency and self-assurance, seemingly without arrogance, reminded me of the young Sebastian, a fact I noted with some consternation. I should add that he looked nothing like my husband. In addition to his fair coloring, he had a faintly pink, healed battle scar running from his left temple, under his ear, and down his neck, disappearing into the collar of his gambeson, and his skin was more weathered due to his outdoor life.

I soon discovered another advantage of traveling under the queen's auspices. Instead of stopping overnight at drafty inns with bad food, unpleasant odors, and dirty blankets, we stayed at comfortable cottages on the rural estates that were part of Bona's ever-growing landholdings. Here, too, I was able to see the effects of her agricultural reforms, especially as we came closer to, then entered, the borders of the Grand Duchy.

Lithuania had always been poorer than the Crown, a reality manifested in smaller and more scattered villages where the peasants barely made ends meet at the best of times and went hungry when harvests were poor. The towns, too, were less populous and showed little of the prosperity of their Polish counterparts. Yet the lands administered by the queen were visibly more affluent, with larger fields worked by well-fed laborers. I remembered the queen's early ideas about merging fields, rotating crops, and installing capable administrators, and the results were on display throughout her lands. How sad and ironic, then, that all this power and wealth could not buy her son's affection.

By and by, I also discovered a benefit to Maria's presence. She was a veritable fount of information (again, like her aunt) about private details of the lives of everyone at court, both in Kraków and Vilnius. As we broke our fast in a large caretakers' kitchen early one morning—Cecilia was feeding Giulio upstairs in our room—I asked Maria whether the young king's love affair was indeed as serious as the queen feared.

Her eyes lit up with excitement, and even more color rose in her over-rouged cheeks—another family trait. "Zygmunt is very much taken with Barbara," she said, settling herself more comfortably across the table from me. A flagon of wine and a platter of fresh cheese and warm bread stood between us, making my mouth water. I ate as she talked with barely a pause for breath. "Before, his affairs were short-lived. No sooner would rumors start circulating about a new mistress than that woman would be replaced by another. After he married, Queen Bona tried to persuade him to be more discreet about his passions, and when his wife's health began to deteriorate, she even sent him women of pleasure, if you know what I mean." She winked. "A friend from Vilnius wrote me that he did indeed avail himself of their services in order to appear more restrained, but once he met Barbara he sent them all back to Kraków. As you can imagine, the old queen was furious." She chuckled. "That was more than a year ago, and there has been no talk linking him to anyone else since then."

So the affair had started quite a while back, even before Queen Elizabeth's final illness. Again I felt pity for the young woman, barely more than a child, thrust into the middle of so much licentiousness and deception. "How did he meet her?" I asked. "Was she Elizabeth's lady-in-waiting?" Royal mistresses often advanced along that particular pathway.

Maria shook her head and leaned forward, as if to ensure I did not miss a word. An unlikely possibility, even when she whispered. "They met when the king visited Gieranony, the seat of the magnate Gastold family, into which Barbara had married. She was a young widow by then; her husband died the year before. That's where she and the king fell in love." She pressed her hand to her bosom in that age-old gesture of women talking about fairytale romances.

I remembered Bona's words about Barbara's allegedly bad reputation and considered asking about that, but I did not want the servants coming in and out of the kitchen to overhear us. Besides, Maria was already continuing her story, her tone gossipy once again. "Soon after the king returned to Vilnius, Barbara followed him, staying with her mother at the Radziwiłł palace, which is next door to the ducal palace. How convenient! The king took to organizing masquerades and tournaments for her and had a passage built from his residence to the Radziwiłł gardens to be able to meet with her secretly."

I shook my head slowly, both because the story was unlike anything I had expected and because the extent of Maria's knowledge impressed me. Too bad women could not serve as court officials; her skills in information gathering would be truly invaluable in that role.

"A year is not a very long time," I said, "and he has never tried to marry a mistress before. Perhaps the danger isn't quite as serious as Her Majesty believes."

She shrugged. "Who can tell? He apparently confided in his most trusted courtiers that he wished to marry Barbara. But he *is* known to be fickle. He tires quickly of women and luxuries—always looking for the next plaything. He has recently taken an interest in tapestries and is expanding the collection his father started at Wawel. He's having the most expensive specimens sent to Vilnius from all over Europe . . ."

She went on, but I stopped paying attention. As I recalled everything I had heard and seen of Zygmunt August, a picture coalesced in my mind of a man who was spoiled and selfish.

In some ways Bona's indulgence of him was understandable: he was her only son. She probably experienced some guilt as well. In the fall of 1527, she was pregnant when she decided to join her husband on a hunt in Niepołomice. But a terrible accident took place: a bear charged toward the queen, and her horse, spooked, reared and threw her off its back. Miraculously, Bona survived, but that same night she gave birth to a boy who died within hours. After that, she could have no more children, and the future of the dynasty came to rest on the slender shoulders of young Zygmunt.

If that explained why his mother had done everything to protect him and cater to his every whim, though, the result was a man whose predominant concern was his own pleasure rather than the well-being of his subjects. I knew how seriously Bona took her own responsibilities as queen, and I could only imagine her disappointment as she watched Zygmunt grow into the role that destiny prepared for him.

"... her family is nothing if not greedy and ambitious," Maria's words reached me through my musings. I turned my attention back to her. "That brother of hers, Mikołaj—they call him Rudy, the Red, because of his auburn hair and beard—wants to elevate the Radziwiłł clan over all the others in Lithuania. And now that the king's path to marriage is open once again, he'll do everything in his power to put his sister on the throne." She nodded as if this were a foregone conclusion and took a rare sip from her cup. I had already noticed that her near-constant talk prevented her from eating much—perhaps that was what kept her so thin. "They say," she added the moment she swallowed the wine, "that Rudy wants to be elevated to a dukedom, a goal that would be greatly facilitated by having a royal connection."

There was a limit, however, to Maria's knowledge. When I asked her if Zygmunt's advisors were equally against the marriage, she shrugged. "Some are, and some aren't. It varies as he grants privileges or withholds favors to get this courtier or that on his side." But she was much less interested in high politics than in amorous intrigues. For insights on the former, I would have to talk either to the courtiers who traveled with us—an option that did not seem promising—or to Jakub Zaremba.

❧

The opportunity came at the end of the fifth day of our journey. We had just left Mazovia and entered Podlasie, where we stopped for the night at a manor house outside the village of Gornitsa. It was still light when I tucked Giulio into bed.

"Did you enjoy playing with your toy soldiers today?" I asked him as I felt his forehead. It seemed a little warm—or was it my imagination?

He nodded. "When the carriage wasn't too shaky."

I sighed. Polish roads were hardly comfortable to travel on, but those in Lithuania were worse. "We're halfway there, darling. When we get to Vilnius, you'll have a solid floor to play on."

His eyes lit up. "Then I can have a real battle!"

"Yes." I smiled. "And I'll buy you some more soldiers."

"Before Doctor Nascimbene examines me?" he asked eagerly.

"We'll see." My hands were still roaming over his forehead and cheeks, as I tried to gauge if he was warm from the road or from fever. His eyes did not have the unhealthy shine that came with a fever, and that was good news. Still, I was anxious. "Setting up an appointment with Doctor Nascimbene is our main goal. Once we've done that, we'll go toy shopping. How does that sound?"

"Sounds good, *mamma*," Giulio replied. "And when I'm healthy and strong, I'll join Hetman Tarnowski's army like Cousin Adam did."

I ruffled his hair. "I hope by the time you grow up those border wars will have come to an end. Going to war isn't something to aspire to, darling. Cousin Adam died at Homel, remember?"

"But he died a hero!"

"That's true." I sighed again. "But I want my son to live a long and healthy life. That's why we're going to Vilnius."

If only that were the sole reason!

Giulio nestled into his pillow and yawned. "I can't wait to get there," he mumbled, already falling asleep.

"Me neither," I said, watching him drift off. "You're very brave, and I'm so proud of you," I added in a whisper as his breath slowed and evened out.

A few moments later, I was descending the darkening staircase from the upper floor, a candle in hand, when I saw a faint orange glow through one of the windows.

I paused on the landing to see better—the glow came from the edge of the estate near a grove of trees—and discerned several figures clad in dark flowing robes, outlined against what appeared to be a bonfire. Around me, the house was quiet. Our fellow travelers must have already retired, and the count who held the estate from the queen was away. Overcome by a curiosity sharpened by days of tedium on the road, I decided to see what was going on.

I let myself out through the front door, walked around the house, then across the expansive lawn toward the light. The evening was cool and refreshing, perfect September weather with just a whiff of the earthy scent of autumn in the air, warm enough to be outside without the feeling of my chemise and petticoats sticking to my skin from perspiration.

As I came closer, the figures that had earlier seemed to be milling around aimlessly, now proved to be circling the orange-yellow flame, raising and dropping their arms in a coordinated, rhythmic fashion as they did so. I stopped about halfway between the house and the gathering, not wanting to encroach on this strange ceremony. It brought to my mind Midsummer Eve celebrations popular in Poland on the twenty-third of June. But this fire, although sizable, was not as large as the bonfires lit along the Wisła, nor did the participants carry flowers or lanterns to be floated on a stream or a river. Besides, we were closer to the autumnal equinox than to the summer solstice.

As I pondered this oddity, I felt more than heard a movement behind me. My stomach clenched. But for the figures around the fire I was alone, and the twilight was swiftly turning into night. I should have considered the risk before venturing outside, but it was too late now. I turned and lifted the small lantern I had taken from a table by the front door. I had kept it covered with my other hand so as not to alert the others to my presence. Now I held it out in front of me like a sword. Then I exhaled with relief when I saw the familiar figure of Jakub Zaremba, out of his armor and wearing a light belted tunic and a pair of tan hunting boots. His shoulders were covered by a cloak whose deep red color, like wine, acquired rusty highlights in the glow of the fire. He looked like any member of the gentry out on a walk to survey his land, except for a sword still buckled to his side. A soldier never parts with his weapon.

"It's you." I lowered the lamp, wondering why I had not heard his footsteps sooner. I must have been quite taken with the spectacle at the edge of the woods.

He inclined his head. "Forgive me. I didn't mean to startle you." His beard was neatly trimmed, which offered an interesting contrast with his rugged features, and I realized that I rarely saw him without his helmet. "I thought you might be the person walking away from the house."

I gave him a guilty smile. I should have expected that he would follow me. In the last few days, I had found that his protection extended not just to the road; he was also never far from us when we stopped overnight. Bona's concern about my safety was touching, even if her ulterior motive was clear. For his part, Zaremba was discreet, but I felt his presence even when I could not see him. Yet somehow, I had forgotten about him tonight. "I saw the light and came out to have a look," I explained, pointing toward the fire. "It's still early." I had always been a night owl, and it would be another two hours at least before I was ready to go to bed.

Zaremba's eyes followed the direction I indicated. "Ah." He squinted as he considered the scene. "This is common throughout Lithuania. You'll see it more often as we ride deeper into the duchy."

"What is it?" I asked. "What are they celebrating?"

"It's not so much a celebration as worship." He pointed to the right of the bonfire. "Do you see that large tree, a little apart from the grove behind it?" I nodded, peering at the outline of a thick trunk, the reflection of the flames licking its bark. "It's a sacred oak," he explained. "It's the object of their ritual; around the fire they pray to their gods and thank them for the gift of nature and its bounty as the harvest gets underway."

"Gods?"

He chuckled, a deep but surprisingly soft sound. I had not even seen him smile before tonight. "Grand Duke Jogaila may have converted to Christianity more than 150 years ago, but paganism is still strong in the countryside. The peasants here worship whatever they can—groves, brooks, even snakes."

I stared in wonder. In 1386, the pagan Jogaila, the ruler of Lithuania, had married Jadwiga of Poland, queen in her own right by the time she was eleven years old. The union gave rise to the Jagiellon dynasty. Nearly two centuries later, it was facing the challenge of Protestantism in the various lands it ruled, but here was proof that for the simple folk such conflicts meant little: they still happily adhered to the beliefs of their ancient forefathers.

"How do you know so much about it?" I asked.

There was a pause before he answered. "I was born in Poland," he said, "but grew up in southern Lithuania, where my father served as a soldier, protecting the border from Tatars." A tight note entered his voice as he continued to gaze at the bonfire. I wanted to know more, but the look in his eyes was faraway and withdrawn. I sensed an invisible barrier between us.

"It sounds like the young king tolerates these beliefs," I said instead.

Zaremba cleared his throat, his eyes focusing again. "He ignores them. He abhors confrontation, and that includes in the religious sphere. As a result, the court in Vilnius attracts many who flee persecution for not adhering to orthodoxy in places like Muscovy."

I cast my mind back to the multinational, multilingual court at Wawel in my youth. *Like father, like son.* Except in one thing: the young Zygmunt's decision to follow his heart rather than political calculation in the choice of a woman to share his life.

"Liberty of worship is a farsighted policy, for it protects the realm from being weakened by internal strife." He turned to me. "Though some believe that external threats to our security weigh much less on our grand duke," he added.

The glow of the fire sharpened the contours of his face and smoothed out the lines, showing how handsome Zaremba must have been when he was younger. Alone with me, he proved himself knowledgeable and well-spoken, different from the officious, at times gruff military man who rode by our carriage during the day. I was right in guessing that I could learn more from him.

"Are you referring to the rumors of his marriage plans to Barbara Radziwiłł?" I asked cautiously. I did not know how much he knew about my mission.

"I am. Some say it's love, others an act of rebellion against his mother. But whatever the case, it will bring no good. A marriage like that would divide us in a way the religious conflicts have failed to do, for it would force the nobility of both nations to take sides."

"So you think there *will* be a wedding?" I prodded, still trying to sound casual. The worshippers across the field had now moved away from the fire and encircled the oak, raising flat vessels similar to plates aloft in a gesture that appeared to mimic an offering.

"He has mentioned it to his advisors," Zaremba said. Then he added, with a slight shrug of his arms, "but I don't believe he has taken any steps yet."

His words confirmed what Maria had told me a few days earlier—that the king had been confiding in his trusted men and buying their support. But trust was a scarce commodity at court, so it was no wonder word had already reached Bona. I understood now that her fears were justified, and the weight of my mission felt heavier on me than ever.

"It's a shame the relations between the queen and her son are so strained on account of this affair," I said.

"They were already strained by the time she learned of it." He hesitated, and I wondered if he wished to abandon the subject. But before I could speak, he continued. "They began to deteriorate fast when the idea of handing over the administration of Lithuania to the young king was first raised. It was a move his father wanted, on account of his frail health, but his mother opposed." Zaremba lowered his voice, although the peasants were too far away to overhear us and were now chanting a tune, apparently oblivious to anything outside their own circle.

"She opposed it because it would have meant sharing power, even if it was with her own son," I said, grasping Bona's motivations immediately.

Out of the corner of my eye, I saw him studying me, and I knew that his curiosity was piqued. "That's correct. She was right about that, too. He won't allow her to interfere in the duchy's affairs any longer, even though she has extensive possessions here." He swept an arm out. "Ten years ago, she was the power in Lithuania, even more so than her husband. Now she has no say." He shook his head. "I don't think anybody expected that this is how he would throw off the yoke of maternal love."

The bonfire was dying, and the cloaked figures began to disperse. The rite was over. A chill crept into the air as the heat of the fire lessened and darkness enveloped us. We turned toward the house, where the only light came from the kitchen area. It was dim, suggesting that the servants had retired and left only one oven burning overnight.

"You said the nobility will be forced to take sides if an engagement is announced." I returned to the topic that was at the heart of my mission as we began crossing the darkened lawn.

"Some already have—the Radziwiłłs, of course, who also supported the investiture of young Zygmunt as grand duke against Her Majesty's wishes."

I fought a sudden urge to ask Zaremba to come to the kitchen with me and have a cup of wine or that delicious pear cider we had drunk at supper. But it would have been an unseemly invitation from a woman, especially a married one. I wondered if he was married, too.

"The key?" I was jolted out of my thoughts by Zaremba stretching out an open palm toward me.

My face crumpled. "I forgot." Mortified, I silently cursed myself: there were spare keys on a peg by the door. Now the servants had gone to bed, and we were locked out. What were we going to do?

Zaremba frowned, as if remembering something. His hand went to his pocket, patting it. "Oh, never mind." His face broke into a smile. "I have it. The steward gave me one when we arrived, just in case," he added sheepishly.

He stepped ahead of me, pulling the key out of his pocket, and I raised my lantern to shed more light on the doorway. He bent down for a brief moment, as if to adjust a buckle of his boots, then inserted the key in the lock. He tried a few times to turn it, then grunted. "It's stuck. The key must be new and untested." He looked over his broad shoulder at me, his face apologetic.

I moved closer with the lantern, but he held out his arm. "It's all right. I can see."

"Should we wake the servants?" I asked anxiously.

"No need," he said through clenched teeth as he wiggled the key again. "I can manage." He leaned forward and applied force, using both hands now.

After a minute, I grew worried again. "Perhaps it's the lock?"

He shook his head and gave it another twist. I heard an audible click. He exhaled. "There." His breath came faster now. "Done." He returned the key to his pocket and pushed the door open.

Inside the hall, he turned to me with an air of someone ready to take his leave, but I forestalled him. "Who else is likely to side with the king?"

Zaremba looked amused. "You ask a lot of questions, signora." Before I could find a suitable reply, he added, "Her Majesty instructed me to provide any information you need. Anything that helps you accomplish your mission." So he did know. "Unfortunately, nobody has the answer to *that*."

I felt a stab of disappointment. He must have noticed, for he said, "I shouldn't be surprised if Chancellor Maciejowski did, however."

I inhaled sharply. If Maciejowski backed the young king, then Hetman Tarnowski would almost certainly follow suit. The most powerful men in Poland after the two Zygmunts allied against Queen Bona.

She was indeed alone. And when her husband died, she would be powerless.

6

September 6th, 1545
Sunday

We arrived in Vilnius shortly before noon after eight days on the road. The city greeted us with an overcast sky hovering over a warm late summer day.

Entering through one of the southern gates, we proceeded directly toward the ducal palace. The capital of the Grand Duchy was smaller than Kraków, and more of its houses were built of wood, but many looked new. There was much construction going on, some of it in stone. It also had wider streets that were easier to negotiate, even though a recent rainstorm had left them as uneven and muddy as their Polish counterparts under similar conditions. Overall, Vilnius had the appearance of a city in transition, suspended between the old and the new, with a whiff of promise yet to be fully realized.

After about a mile, the main street curved, and we emerged onto an even wider road. Zaremba leaned toward my widow, a smile curving his lips as if to impart that I was in for a surprise. He pointed ahead, and I leaned out to look, gasping at the view. It was quite impressive, even though the palace, a half-mile or so ahead of us, was not nearly as large as Wawel. But it was less a jumble of styles than the royal castle in Kraków; in fact, the three-story structure had an elegant and harmonious look to it that Wawel lacked. That and the gray color of its stone, a deep steely hue that suggested less weathering, told me that it was built more recently. Beyond and to the right of the palace, an older-looking defensive complex, walled and surrounded by brick towers, stood on a small hill.

Zaremba must have followed my gaze, for I heard him explain, "The Upper Castle was built by Duke Gediminas some centuries past. The dukes of Lithuania resided there before the dynastic union with Poland."

Across from me, Maria d'Aragona chuckled. "Pan Jakub was a competent escort on the road, and he's an equally competent guide through Vilnius."

"We were lucky that the journey passed without incident," Zaremba said modestly.

"I have been to Vilnius before, too, you know." The marchesa pouted, but her eyes flickered with mirth and mischief. "Though I can see why Pani Caterina would rather be shown around by a seasoned courtier and soldier such as yourself."

My cheeks warming, I cast about for a riposte, while Zaremba laughed his soft, deep laugh that I had come to like. A droll note crept into his voice as he played along with Maria's joke. "And that there is the cathedral"—he pointed west with an exaggerated flourish—"and the statue of Vytautas the Great nearby."

I slid down the bench, a bit too hastily. Maria remained where she was, still grinning widely, but Giulio followed me, and we stuck our heads out the other side of the carriage. We were still playfully jostling for space when a sizable church came into view. Across from its entrance was a tall, narrow belfry whose bells were summoning the faithful to High Mass. The scaffolding wrapped around two sides of the cathedral proclaimed that it was under renovation.

"It suffered extensive fire damage a few years ago," Zaremba explained.

I could see that the work sought to imitate the classical style, with rows of marble columns supporting the entrance below a decorative triangular tympanum crowned with larger-than-life figures of saints and a round domed chapel.

"It's like the old buildings in Rome, *mamma*!" Giulio's dark eyes were wide and his voice reverently quiet, as if he were inside that church. I smiled as I ruffled his chestnut hair. Italy was still home for him.

We kept gazing at the cathedral until the carriage swerved, and we passed through the gate and entered the large four-sided courtyard of the ducal palace.

I had expected to visit the palace long enough to request an audience with the king, then be taken to some accommodations arranged by Bona in the city. But to my surprise, a set of rooms was ready for us. I doubted the queen had requested it directly, given her son's refusal to receive her envoys. Rather, someone from the old king's office must have arranged it.

The rooms, small but comfortable, consisted of a sitting chamber and two bedchambers. Their location in the northern wing on the third floor gave us a good view of the river Neris and the villages on the opposite bank, which I found charming. With our windows close to the corner of the building, I could also catch a glimpse of extensive gardens on the eastern side of the grounds. I wondered if they were the same gardens that the duke used to meet secretly with his mistress. As casually as I could, I asked the maid assigned to us, a girl named Rasa, if the gardens abutted the Radziwiłł estate. In response, she nodded with a knowing smile that all but confirmed my guess.

Rasa had just started to unpack our trunks when Maria arrived, bringing word of a banquet in honor of Barbara that night.

How she had learned about it so fast, I had no idea. It must have been the first thing she'd inquired about. Whatever the case—and despite my tiredness—the idea excited me. I was intrigued by the unlikely romance between Zygmunt and Barbara, but I also dreaded the mission entrusted to me. Given how moody and temperamental the young king was said to be, I feared he would be angered by my embassy, refuse to allow Doctor Nascimbene to see Giulio, and send us away. For that reason, I decided to present our case to him first and bring up the queen's plea only after the medical consultation was over. That gave me some assurance, although I had yet to decide how best to approach Zygmunt. For that, I needed to get a better understanding of him and his court before I spoke to him. I had to observe.

I tasked Rasa with pressing my best gown for the evening and waited impatiently until the sun went down.

Maria wanted to accompany me, of course, but I was deliberately vague on when I planned to leave and told her I would meet her there. I wanted my first impressions of the palace and the king to be my own, without the filter of her commentary.

I followed Rasa's directions to the banqueting hall on the second floor of the palace. I walked through a series of hallways and spacious chambers with whitewashed walls and wooden ceiling panels decorated with tiles, whose patterns I immediately identified as Eastern, even with my limited experience of such décor. Many were geometric, square or round, and some were painted in rosettas, like the stained glass in our cathedrals. The predominant hues were various shades of blue, with red, green, and yellow speckled among them.

In many chambers, there were shelves stacked with books and manuscripts. There must have been hundreds of them.

Besides that, exquisite tapestries depicting royalty and other great lords with their families hung on almost every available wall, as well as scenes of battles, hunting, mythical beasts, and biblical themes. A martyr clutching a cross to his chest and lifting his soulful face to the heavens hung next to a group of nymphs bathing naked in a garden pool. I admired the varied and impressive collection and understood the reason for its growing fame throughout Europe.

The corridors were filled with art. I passed pedestals with ceramic vases and ancient-looking amphorae. I stared at marble figures positioned in niches and alcoves, some of them barely clad and holding lyres or bunches of grapes in their hands. Many of these could have graced any Italian *palazzo.*

By the time I arrived at the banqueting hall, I believed the story I had heard before my departure from Kraków: that a papal ambassador had once asserted in a letter to Rome that the Vilnius palace held more treasures than the Vatican itself.

Despite the palace's smaller size, the hall was almost as large as its equivalent at Wawel. Here, too, richly colored and finely woven tapestries decorated the walls. A fire blazed in an iron hearth at one end of the room, and most of the windows were thrown open to mitigate the heat. The scents of late summer flowers drenched the air. From a far corner, strains of a soft melody of harp and lute floated above the buzz of conversation. The windows, I could not help noticing, gave onto the ducal gardens. And tonight, Barbara would be the guest of honor. How appropriate.

I saw right away that the ducal court was younger—as well as louder, more garish, and more casual. Clearly, Zygmunt did not cultivate the stately solemnity that accompanied many gatherings in Kraków. Watching him on the raised dais surrounded by young men of the highest rank—talking, laughing, slapping each other's shoulders, and winking at women who pretended bashfulness while basking in their attentions—it seemed as if the court had been taken over by the members of the *bibones et comedones* society of my youth. I recalled Zygmunt's demeanor only a few weeks earlier in Poland, seated at his mother's table during the funeral reception, looking restless and bored.

He could not have appeared more different now. His beaming face, the color in his cheeks above his trimmed beard and moustache, and his easy movements all attested to his being where he belonged, at home. He was dressed splendidly in a black velvet doublet, its sleeves slashed with white satin. A small ruff of snow-white lace framed his neck, and similar lace embellished the cuffs at his wrists. An enormous swan feather rose from his cap, rimmed with diamonds the size of beans, and a large gold ducal ring glistened on his left hand. The amount of jewelry on the duke and the lords and ladies around him would put Wawel to shame. In addition to the earrings and necklaces, their clothes were sewn with precious stones in such abundance one had to squint when they moved, for the gems caught the light from the hearth and the dozens of candles blazing in the candelabras all around.

I checked to left and right, before and behind me, without discovering a woman who might be Barbara. Curious. A chair on Zygmunt's right stood empty—was it reserved for her? On his left lounged a stout man of about thirty with a curly copper beard and equally copper hair, barely tamed by his cap. That beard was spread on a large ruff, like a platter, conveying the owner's pride in its size and thickness. He could only be Mikołaj "Rudy" Radziwiłł. The Red.

Less boisterous than the other men at the top table, he surveyed the chamber with a gaze that appeared leisurely, a small smile playing on his lips, but I could see that he in fact missed nothing. His entire posture radiated confidence and satisfaction. His seating assignment indicated that he was

Zygmunt's closest advisor. Did he already see himself as the duke's brother-in-law as well? From Zaremba, I knew that he had the ambition to follow his father to the post of hetman, the supreme commander, of the army. And as Zaremba had noted, becoming royal kin would greatly facilitate that.

I spotted Maria at a table in the middle of the hall and made my way there. I took the empty seat next to her, which I assumed she had saved for me. She did not notice my arrival, for she was busy talking to a lady wearing a traditional Lithuanian cloth headgear that covered her hair and looped under her chin like a wimple, intricately embroidered and sewn with seed pearls. Maria's distraction suited me well as it allowed me to continue observing the assembly while we awaited Barbara's arrival.

Or rather, I awaited her, because the other diners had long since begun their meal. Perhaps I had misunderstood, and she was *not* the guest of honor. All around me, I saw chunks cut from the stuffed swans that graced the center of each table and trays of roasted chickens containing nothing but bones. Platters of oranges were heaped with peels, and servants were already refilling bowls of olives, chestnuts, raisins, and almonds. I helped myself to a seasoned mix of figs and beans and a wing of roasted turkey sprinkled with rosemary. Somewhat to my surprise, I found the drink in my cup to be Malvazia, a sweet Greek wine, rather than Italian. Was that a subtle statement on the duke's part, I wondered?

The volume of conversations fueled by the servants' diligent refilling of the cups was rising when I spotted Jakub Zaremba at a table ahead of us. He sat with his back to me, his attention focused on the main table. Only once in a while did he turn his head slightly toward the man seated next to him to exchange some words. I smiled, thinking how this reserve matched his soldierly persona, even if his outfit for the evening did not. He wore a red doublet, a frilly-collared shirt, and a velvet cap decorated with a gray feather. But for his sun-browned skin and the faint scar, a stranger would never guess he was a military man.

Wondering if he had his sword on him, I became aware that the voices floating from Zaremba's table spoke German, although I could not be sure if he and his interlocutor did. I looked more closely and realized that the other men at the table had the look of the Habsburg envoys I had seen in Kraków. The chief difference between them and the Polish and Lithuanian courtiers was their austere dress: their caps remained undecorated, their doublets buttoned up to the necks with only a trace of lace visible, and they wore no jewelry. The elegant cut and the quality of the cloth, however, testified to good taste and wealth.

Their presence surprised me at first. I had already heard Russian spoken around the palace, which matched the court's reputation for offering a refuge to boyars who ran afoul of Prince Ivan in Moscow. But I had not expected to find a tableful of Germans here. Then again, the Jagiellons had been related to the Habsburgs by blood and marriage for several generations; in fact, that most likely explained their diplomats' presence in Vilnius. With Queen Elizabeth barely cold in her grave, they must have been trying to forge another marriage alliance already. If so, then, in a way, they were my allies.

The servants brought in desserts, large silver trays filled with sugared confections in the shape of winged eagles, lions, large-petaled flowers, and unicorns. For a lack of anything better to do—Maria was still talking to her neighbor, who, as far as I could tell, had not yet uttered a word—I strained my ear to catch the German conversations. In my youth, I had a passable knowledge of the language, although I always understood more than I could speak. Now I realized how much I had forgotten. Despite picking out a few words, including *König* and *Fahrt*, I was unable to make anything of it.

Increasingly bored, I was about to turn to Maria when the volume of conversation suddenly abated and heads turned toward one corner of the hall. A sense of anticipation filled the air, as if the gathering awaited the beginning of a performance by a troupe of players, lowering their voices but not stilling them, whispering to their neighbors, and pointing their chins toward the stage.

Except there was no stage. Instead, as I followed their gaze, I noticed an iron-bound door I had not seen before, tucked next to the hearth. It opened from the inside, and a woman—alone—stepped across the threshold and into the hall. Dressed in a gown of cream and rose silk, with wide sleeves edged in delicate white fur and a pearl-sewn bodice cinched around an impossibly small waist, she paused in the glow of the fire. The flames caught the brilliant shine of her dark hair, loose under a wine-colored velvet cap decorated with the same pearls as her belt. She stopped just long enough to focus the eyes of the assembly on herself before proceeding, in a movement that was both fluidly graceful and demure, toward the main table.

It was Barbara Radziwiłł.

And she knew how to make an entrance.

I could not tear my eyes away, wondering what was so mesmerizing about this woman. Her outfit, although rich, was modest in comparison to some of the other ladies in attendance. Nor was she the most beautiful. With a complexion that was almost white, like the surface of an alabaster vase, a melancholy look in her large dark eyes, small, bud-like lips, and a willowy frame, she could not have been more different from the ruddy, robust, wide-hipped ideal of femininity so popular in these parts. What was it in her that appealed to a man who had been surrounded by the most voluptuous women all his life? Then I realized it must have been that freshness, a certain exoticism, and a hint of fragility that attracted him.

"Isn't she enchanting?" Maria's voice in my ear jolted me back to the moment. When I turned to her, I saw an expression of naked admiration on her face. I would come to learn that Barbara had that effect on people: even if they believed the stories about her—and Maria certainly did—they could not help but be captivated by her.

And those stories were not at all flattering. During our last overnight stop before Vilnius, Maria told me everything she had heard about Barbara's past. We were staying at a cottage in a village on the river Merkys, and I suggested a walk along its picturesque bank to stretch our legs and admire the leaves that were beginning to turn. By the time we returned, refreshed and invigorated, I knew about the rumors that had been swirling around Barbara for years, even before she met Zygmunt. According to them, she was unfaithful to her late husband, who—to be fair, Maria emphasized with a great deal of sympathy—was old, short, and limping, for all his prominent positions as a *wojewoda* and a member of the Gastold family. Barbara's alleged lovers represented most of the magnate families in the duchy, including Pac, Sakowicz, and Astikai. Her dissolute lifestyle was said to be the cause of her barrenness, for she'd had no children with Gastold, nor any of the others.

But now I found myself wondering how much of it was true. The image was utterly at odds with the understated elegance and refinement of the woman before me.

"She is indeed very charming," I said as I watched Barbara reach the empty seat next to Zygmunt. He rose, took her delicate, long-fingered hand in his and bestowed a kiss on it, his eyes never leaving her face. In them, I saw a devotion and a deference I would never have expected from a man I had come to think of as proud and capricious. Barbara's face softened in a sweet smile, and for a brief moment, which nevertheless seemed to stretch, they were alone in the hall, perhaps—as far as they were concerned—in the entire world. The gathering had fallen silent.

Finally, Zygmunt's gaze turned, almost reluctantly, from his mistress, and with a gesture of his palm he motioned the assembly to continue their feast. Then, still holding Barbara's hand, he helped her to her seat as the chatter resumed. Within moments, they were deep in private conversation, their attention solely on each other. I took a few bites from my plate, still studying Barbara, who did not touch her food; instead, she fastened her eyes adoringly on the king's face as she smiled or offered replies to his words. Bona, I realized suddenly, had never looked that way at her husband. Only once or twice did Barbara's eyes stray, briefly, to the room. But when they did, it was with a hint of challenge, her chin rising ever so slightly, and I sensed that the doll-like fragility was misleading.

It was impossible that she was unaware of the rumors surrounding her. Yet she embraced the role of the royal mistress without apology. I sensed a fierce ambition lurking underneath that pleasing surface. She wanted to be queen, perhaps in her mind she already was, and she wanted the men and women gathered around her—many of them higher-born than herself—to become used to the idea.

Each time Barbara's eyes returned to Zygmunt's face with a look that offered both promise and submission, she seduced him again. Now I could see that indefinable quality that went beyond the simple allure of an attractive woman. For burning inside her was a passionate, perhaps even reckless nature. And Zygmunt was completely in thrall to it.

At length, I forced myself to turn back to my table. Ahead of me, I could see the back of Zaremba's head; he sat, still as a statue. I would have given a lot to know what was going through his mind. Did he still think Barbara an opportunist at the service of her and her family's ambitions, or was he convinced by the display of affection between her and the duke?

Then it occurred to me that both could be true at the same time. Barbara could have fallen in love with Zygmunt despite his status, and his status might appeal to her as much as it would to any other woman in her place. In a world in which royal affection offered riches and prestige beyond one's wildest imaginings, and in which there were many who would snatch that affection for themselves if they could, perhaps she was simply protecting what destiny offered her along with love. If so, who could blame her?

My mind reeled back twenty-five years to that winter when I had fallen in love with Sebastian Konarski. Ours was a different story, without political stakes, but we did face obstacles of our own. I was a widow in diminished circumstances, and my failure as the Lady of the Queen's Chamber had left me with few options but to return home. We could easily have missed our chance at happiness. We might no longer gaze into each other's eyes the way the duke and Barbara did, but I still appreciated what we had once shared.

And so, having to plead with Zygmunt to heed his mother's advice became more distasteful to me than ever. It also seemed futile, for one thing was certain: Barbara made an impression. Whether it was admiration or criticism—and I saw a fair amount of the latter on the faces around the hall—few people remained indifferent in her presence.

It was an enormous power, and Queen Bona was right to fear it.

It was past midnight when the banquet came to an end. Tired, I rose from the table to find Zaremba staring at me, before his features melted into a polite smile of acknowledgment. For an awkward moment, neither of us moved, not sure what to do. Then he walked up to me.

"I didn't expect to see you here tonight," he said with mild reproach.

I was puzzled. Surely, Bona's protection did not extend to regulating my activities in Vilnius? "I thought it would be good to see His Majesty before I spoke to him in person on such a delicate business," I said coolly.

"Of course." He hastened to agree as if he realized he had spoken out of turn. With a gallant gesture, he extended his arm toward the great door, but we were forced to hang back until the press of people dissipated.

"Where are your rooms?" I asked once we exited the hall, and immediately regretted it.

"The same floor as yours, opposite wing," he replied casually.

"Oh." I did not know what else to say and glanced around for Maria, but she had disappeared.

"So what did you think?" Zaremba asked.

"About what? Oh, the duke." I hesitated. I was not sure how much I should say before I had a chance to think more on it. "He appears taken with Barbara," I replied vaguely, repeating what I had heard from so many people in the last few weeks.

"What about the rest of them?" he asked again as we passed through the chamber where the bathing nymphs hung next to the martyr saint. I averted my gaze, abashed in his presence, but Zaremba did not seem to notice it.

"The rest? Do you mean the courtiers at his table?"

He nodded.

"Well, they seem young and fond of entertainment ..."

Zaremba gave a short bark of laughter. "They do, don't they? Zygmunt doesn't surround himself with experienced and strong advisors, people who have their own views, only with opportunists, idlers, and sycophants."

Those were harsh words, but I could not deny their plausibility. Again I saw this behavior as a consequence of Bona imposing her will on both her husband and her son until the latter flew the coop for the freedom of Lithuania.

"Barbara's brother, Mikołaj Rudy," I said, "is he one of them?" I thought back on the imposing red-haired figure, with a gravitas the others did not possess, and the shrewd eyes with which he took in everything that went on in the hall, especially after his sister arrived.

Zaremba rubbed his beard. "An opportunist? Yes. A sycophant? Probably. But definitely not an idler. He wants to be a *wojewoda*, perhaps even a hetman one day. That's more than can be said about the rest of that lot. If you ask me, he wants to rule Lithuania."

"Rule? How?"

"Not directly, of course." We started climbing the staircase to the third floor, our steps echoing off the stone. "But *de facto*."

"Surely, the king's favor—even if it's a brotherly kind of favor—isn't enough to amass such power? Does Rudy have a support base?"

Zaremba looked at me with something akin to admiration. "That's a shrewd observation, signora. The queen knew what she was doing when she selected you as her envoy." The compliment gave me unexpected pleasure, and I felt the heat of a blush rising to my face. At the age of fifty-three I had not thought that possible anymore. "But to answer your question," he went on, "the basis of power is land, and the Radziwiłłs have plenty of it. They used to have even more. Like many magnate families, they were forced to mortgage their holdings to help pay for the army to defend us against Muscovy. But when the time came to reclaim their estates, Queen Bona demanded they provide proper documentation of ownership. Those who couldn't produce all of the required papers lost their possessions, which she then bought up. Now she's the largest landowner in the duchy and makes a fortune off her properties, which they resent."

"And they still want their land back?"

"Of course. All of those families—the Gastolds, the Kiszkas, the Wolans, and many others. But it's the Radziwiłłs who have maneuvered themselves into the best position to press their claims. That's why they supported Zygmunt's ascension to the duchy even before he'd met Barbara. In fact, I wouldn't be surprised if they arranged that meeting to further strengthen their hand."

I pondered this. If Zaremba was correct, then—regardless of her own feelings—Barbara was a pawn of her family, a means of regaining wealth and strengthening power. What a sad position to be in! With a sense of dismay, I realized that I wanted it all to have a bigger meaning than petty family politics. "Perhaps their marriage would aid the cause of Polish-Lithuanian union," I said. It was not a far-fetched idea: while co-existing in a commonwealth under one dynasty, the two nations remained administratively separate. For years there had been calls for a formal political union, which—its proponents believed—would bring great benefits to both parties.

Zaremba glanced at me with a bemused expression. "You think that because Polish magnates support the union, the Lithuanians do, too, but that is not so. Magnates like Rudy Radziwiłł are jealous of the power they have accumulated in the duchy and fear, perhaps justifiably, that it would be diluted. Captain Pretwicz"—he added, referring to his famous commander—"was in a council meeting with the king a few months ago and told me that Radziwiłł and others of his ilk had pressured Zygmunt to oppose a formal union."

So Barbara's family's position was entirely self-serving. The enormity of the threat to Bona's interests became even more clear to me. Quite apart from the dynastic implications, the Radziwiłłs' rise would be her fall. Her power in Lithuania—and in due course in Poland—would all but vanish. But what if the king and Barbara really loved each other? Was the attainment of one goal worth sacrificing the other?

I blinked, as if that could relieve the headache building up somewhere behind my eyes. I had been right in hesitating to accept this mission. There would be no winners here. Whatever happened, someone would pay with heartbreak or humiliation.

We stopped at the door to my chambers. "I hope you succeed where others have failed," Zaremba said. His wish sounded heartfelt, but I heard little optimism in his voice.

I struggled for a response; nothing seemed adequate. "I'll do my best," I said. It was the only truth by which I could swear. My headache intensified, and I wanted to retire.

"Perhaps this is a task that requires a woman's touch," he added unexpectedly, in a tone that caused something to lurch in my stomach, an anxious but not entirely unpleasant feeling. Why did he care so much? What was he trying to say?

The sudden silence between us offered no answers. The corridor was dimly lit by oil lamps set in holders wide apart, and I could not see the expression in Zaremba's eyes, which, although blue, were now dark and shadowed under his brows.

"We shall see, and hopefully soon." The sooner the better, for I did not know how much more of this tension I could sustain. "God give you good night."

I closed the door behind me, then paused, listening. It was some moments before I heard his footsteps as he moved away down the corridor.

In the sitting chamber all was quiet, and the fire was dying in the grate. The maid had already left, and the others were sleeping. Then I saw a white rectangle on the table. I picked up the paper, luxuriously thick and edged in gold leaf, broke the seal that held the two ends together, and read:

His Grace Duke Zygmunt August
requests your presence at a private audience
tomorrow afternoon, at three o'clock.

I folded the invitation, surprised. I had not expected this kind of efficiency from such an informal court. In Kraków, far more stately and better organized, it could take weeks to be admitted. I took a deep breath, my chest swelling with anticipation and anxiety in equal measure.

For better or for worse, my mission was about to begin.

7

September 7th, 1545
Monday

Despite the tapestries, the artwork, and the goblets of wine instead of mugs of ale, the atmosphere in the antechamber had something of the tavern about it. Young courtiers lounged around on cushion-strewn benches in poses of casual ease or played chess at tables inlaid with mother-of-pearl. I recognized two from the court in Kraków. Piotr Frikacz and Florian Zebrzydowski had accompanied the young king to Queen Elizabeth's funeral, and I remembered Lucrezia rolling her eyes. "Libertines and good-for-nothings," she had commented. "The queen believes they are a bad influence on her son." Looking at Frikacz now, with his pouchy stomach and florid complexion, as he regaled a group of courtiers with a story amid loud outbursts of laughter, I could see her point.

Chamberlain Piotr Opaliński bade me wait until the preceding audience ended. A mild man in his early fifties, he wore a dark blue velvet robe and a simple black cap without any adornments. His demeanor, polite and serious, stood in stark contrast to the others. He did not express his opinion in any obvious way, but I sensed that he did not care much for the youths who idled around the antechamber. The queen had spoken fondly of Opaliński, so either he had received his appointment at her recommendation or, more likely, acted informally as her eyes and ears around the Lithuanian court.

My wait lasted a quarter of an hour, during which Opaliński offered me a goblet of tokay. Clearly the duke had a predilection toward sweet wines. I took only two sips, finding the Hungarian less to my liking than the Greek from the banqueting hall. But such was not the case with the courtiers: before I was ushered into Zygmunt's presence, a servant had to bring up two more flagons to replenish their cups.

The audience chamber was one of the most luxurious I had ever seen. Gilded wallpaper lined its walls, and tapestries hung everywhere. Gold tassels tied back window curtains of the finest moss-green velvet. The windows, like those in the banqueting hall, gave onto the gardens. Spots of red and yellow already touched the tops of the trees along the far wall, which once separated the lovers—a breathtakingly beautiful view when framed by the curtains. Beyond the trees were the gray stone walls of the Radziwiłł residence. I wondered if Barbara still lived there or whether she had moved into the ducal palace.

Zygmunt August was alone save for his secretary, Augustyn Mieleski, an obese man of around thirty appropriately nicknamed Rotundus. Mieleski's head was almost completely bald, except for a spare, tawny ring from one ear to the other around the back, and his cheeks had a rosy glow that gave him a benevolent look. Zygmunt sat on a raised chair near the windows under a tapestried baldachin bearing the coats of arms of the Jagiellons and the Sforzas as well as the emblems of Poland and Lithuania. It was a movable canopy of state, for I had caught a glimpse of it the day before, while passing by the formal reception chamber on the floor below.

In response to the warmth of the afternoon, the duke wore a sleeveless jerkin of black and red leather cut in the Neapolitan style with a row of silver buttons on the right side of his chest. His white silk shirt had wide sleeves that gathered at the wrists, finely embroidered there and around the collar. A silver clasp secured his short black velvet cape at the neck. With black hose and breeches, the latter striped with the same velvet as the cape, the ensemble was elegantly understated and flattered his frame, slim but strong, a testament to his love of hunting and the outdoors. A feathered cap rested on his slightly curling brown hair. From up close, his skin looked even more swarthy, a clear Aragonese trait.

A gilded Italian sword was strapped to Zygmunt's belt, and he cut a soldierly figure, even if he did prefer to collect armor rather than wear it into battle. As I had two months earlier, I found only a passing similarity between the young man before me and the serious, wide-eyed boy in the Padovano medallion. His eyes were still large and dark, and there was a melancholy look in them when he was not speaking, but something in the set of his full lips was both sensual and cynical and must have resulted from his overindulged, undisciplined youth.

When the door closed behind me, he beckoned me with a hand adorned with the ducal ring.

I approached his chair and curtsied. "Your Grace," I addressed him with the title Opaliński had advised me he preferred. Did he deem himself unworthy of "Your Majesty" while his father still lived? Or was the demand intended to irritate his mother, who had single-handedly caused him to be elevated to the title of "king" when he was all of nine years old, the mother who had later so vocally opposed his assumption of the ducal role? I suspected the latter.

"Signora Konarska." He motioned me to rise, which I did gratefully. "You have come to Vilnius all the way from Bari, by way of Kraków, to seek a cure for your son?" He spoke in fluent and elegant Italian, only slightly accented. Despite his feud with his mother, his speech, attire, and taste in art showed that he was deeply attached to his Sforza heritage. It made me feel more warmly toward him.

"I have," I replied, pleased to see that he had taken the trouble to prepare, and that he was proceeding straight to the point. In that, he reminded me strongly of Bona. "Giulio has suffered from recurring fevers for some years now, and none of the physicians we consulted could help him. My husband comes from Kraków, where we were advised to seek help from Doctor Nascimbene, whose expertise is widely praised."

The duke's eyes narrowed, as if he were trying to recall something. "Did your husband once serve at the court of my father?"

Despite his courteous tone, my breath froze. Why was he asking this? Was his next question going to be about my service to Bona? If so, he might throw me out without giving me a chance to see Nascimbene.

"Yes, Your Grace," I said, striving to keep my voice even. A film of perspiration broke out on my upper lip.

"I thought your name was familiar."

"My husband remembers His Majesty King Zygmunt as a kind and generous lord," I said quickly, and truthfully enough. "That's why we have decided to petition Your Grace for this favor." I did not know how much longer I could keep up this vagueness.

"Yes," he said slowly, his mind still searching for something that seemed to elude him. "How old is your son?"

"He has just turned ten, but he looks no more than seven, because of the frequent illness that has kept him in indoors and in bed for such a long time."

Zygmunt's eyes softened, momentarily erasing the polite reservation with which he had treated me so far. Lucrezia, Maria, and Zaremba had all spoken of his secretive and distrustful nature, but when I described the effects of Giulio's condition, he seemed genuinely affected. "Then we will do all we can to help him have a healthy and carefree childhood." For a few heartbeats his eyes seemed to glaze over with emotion, but he recovered quickly, and the mask of regal detachment returned to his face.

Like mother, like son.

"Thank you," I replied.

The duke gestured toward his secretary. "Pan Mieleski will arrange a consultation with Doctor Nascimbene as soon as possible."

"Yes, Your Grace." Rotundus bowed and scribbled something on a parchment that rested on a portable desk supported by straps slung around his bull neck.

"Is there anything else, signora?" Zygmunt asked, his tone still benevolent.

If there was any time that I had his goodwill, it was now. But how could I use it to ask him not to marry a woman he loved for the sake of the national interest? And how could I reveal *now* that I was acting as his mother's messenger? The impossibility of the task rendered me mute. I was afraid for Giulio. I wanted to believe that the caring and compassionate Zygmunt I had glimpsed would not take back the promise made to a desperate, pleading mother, but was not his own mother equally desperate and pleading, and yet he remained unmoved? The words I had been sent to speak would not form on my tongue; it was as if they turned to ash in my mouth.

"Well?" The duke tilted his head, and in that moment the door from the antechamber opened.

Zygmunt's eyes traveled over my shoulder, and a warm smile broke on his lips. "My dear Mikołaj! Come in."

I held my breath. Mikołaj Rudy passed me and took the chair closest to the baldachin on the duke's right side. He did not wait to be invited, and he sat casually, thighs spread, one silk hose-clad leg folded under the chair, the other out and at an angle, the tip of his pointy shoe swaying idly. His whole demeanor exuded an air of familiarity so great that it bordered on proprietorship.

Dismay and relief fought inside me. Dismay because the Radziwiłłs' presence in the palace and the duke's favor they so obviously enjoyed meant that Bona had already lost, and in due course the country might lose, too. But also relief that fate had intervened by sending Rudy into the audience chamber in that precise moment and prevented me from having to complete my task for the queen. I did not want to succeed, if it meant standing in the way of two lovers who seemed so devoted to each other. And if I failed to persuade Zygmunt, which was far more likely, I would only incur the displeasure, perhaps even hostility, of the man who would soon be the sole king of Poland.

I left the audience in a kind of fog, struggling to reconcile the mixed outcome of my efforts. My son would finally see a competent physician, yet I had let Queen Bona down. When I first reached Vilnius, I had planned to ask for another audience, after Doctor Nascimbene examined Giulio, to thank the duke for his help and present the queen's case, come what may. But after today, I understood, deep inside, that I would not take that step. In the end, I would use the Radziwiłłs' power as my shield.

In my sitting chamber, I found Giulio on the floor, playing with painted wooden blocks. With intense concentration, he stacked them into a structure resembling a fortress. In a chair by the hearth, Maria greeted me with a cheery smile. She held a porcelain bowl of sugared almonds in her lap. It was all I could do not to grimace, because she was the last person I wanted to see. I needed time alone to sort out my thoughts.

"*Guarda, mamma!* Look!" Giulio called. "Maria brought me a present." He pointed to the blocks with a delighted expression.

"Marchesa del Vasto," I corrected him, sending Maria an apologetic look. I felt a stab of guilt for my ungenerous thoughts, for as exhausting as the woman could be, she was also kind-hearted.

She waved her hand. "I asked him to call me Maria. I don't like formality."

I walked to the sideboard, poured a cup of wine, and held it out to her.

She shook her head. "I've been invited to a party tonight, so I'll stick to these for now." She picked up a couple of white-coated oblong shapes from the bowl and popped them into her mouth. "They're my favorite snack."

I sat in the chair opposite hers with a sigh.

"How was the audience?" she asked.

"The duke has agreed to arrange a consultation for Giulio with Doctor Nascimbene."

"I'm happy to hear that!"

I smiled. I wanted to be polite, but I also really wanted her gone so I could rest. I said nothing, hoping she would take the hint.

She scrutinized my face. "You look tired, Caterina."

"I am. I might lie down for a bit."

"What you need is a distraction and some relaxation," Maria stated, as if I had not spoken at all. "I have an idea. Come with me to the baths."

"What?"

"I was planning to go to the baths before the party. You should come with me."

I frowned. "But they are for men!"

She chuckled. "Here in Vilnius, both men and women go. It's very"—she searched for the right word as her eyes twinkled—"interesting." She settled on that when she saw the alarmed glance I sent in Giulio's direction. But he was too intent on planting miniature blue-and-yellow flags on top of one of the battlements to pay our conversation any heed. "I visit every time I'm here. What do you say?"

I must admit I was a bit shocked, although I tried not to show it. After all, it was none of my business how Maria spent her time. She was not married, and, as a distant cousin to Queen Bona, she was highborn, so she could get away with what might be scandalous for a woman like me. If the *bibones et comedones* were still active in Kraków, she *had* to be a member. Briefly, I considered asking her, before remembering that Giulio was with us.

"Thank you, but no. I've never been to one, and I don't think I should start at my age."

Maria's eyes rounded in mock stupefaction. "What?! You don't look a day over thirty-five!"

"That's not true." I pushed a stray lock of hair that had fallen on my forehead back under my headdress. I cannot deny that I was flattered. "But it's nice of you to say that."

"I mean it. We'll have a grand time." Then she added, as if she only just realized a possible reason for my reluctance. "Nothing unseemly happens there, at least not in the baths I go to, but you can bump into courtiers from the palace and foreign visitors. Who knows, maybe Zaremba will be there?" She winked.

I ignored the innuendo. "No, really. I must prepare Giulio for the doctor's visit, and when that's over, we'll return to Kraków as soon as possible."

Maria looked momentarily disappointed. "I'll go to my chambers and get ready. Send me word if you change your mind." Then she added, for she was not one to be put off easily, "If not today, maybe some other time."

When she was gone, I returned to the chair and took a few almonds from the bowl. Through the windows, I watched the pearly clouds float majestically across the pale blue sky. Despite the lingering warmth, the days were getting shorter.

Outside I saw the first signs of approaching dusk; it would be dark in less than an hour.

"I'll go lie down, *mamma*," Giulio said, rising from the completed structure. He was smiling, but he looked tired, and a sheen of sweat covered his face. My heart constricted. *A few more days, my dove, a few more days.*

He came to me, and I kissed his forehead. "You built a beautiful fortress. Now go rest. We'll see a doctor soon, and he'll make you better."

Cecilia came out of their chamber to take Giulio just as a knock on the door rang out. I expected Rasa, come to light the candles and make up the fire for the evening, but instead Zaremba appeared when Cecilia opened the door.

"Jakub!" I tried to sound welcoming, but I doubt I succeeded. His presence again robbed me of the chance to rest. Still, I invited him in, and he took the chair Maria had vacated. He looked tense, and it occurred to me that perhaps he, too, could do with a visit to the baths.

I offered him the almonds, but he refused with a distracted air. "How did your audience go?" he asked instead.

"Giulio will see the doctor, but I'm afraid I failed in my other mission. What the queen asked me to do is impossible." The words came out of my mouth bluntly, but I was glad of it. Denying the truth would have been worse.

A shadow of dismay crossed his features. But perhaps that was a trick of the fading light, for when I glanced at him again, his face was composed and difficult to read. Silence enveloped us as I focused on my restless hands in my lap. Another person disappointed in me. A sense of inadequacy crashed over me with a force I had not felt since my time as the overseer of the queen's maids of honor.

Across from me, Zaremba exhaled as if he had been holding his breath this whole time. "I'm sorry to hear that," he said, his voice almost resigned. Then he added, perhaps reading my dismal thoughts from my expression, "Don't blame yourself, Caterina. It was always going to be a difficult task, with the odds stacked against you. You're not the first to have failed in this."

I lowered my eyes, embarrassed. I did not tell him that I had not even tried to state my case before the duke. I accepted that I was a failure, but I did not want him to think of me as a coward too.

"I hope to leave Vilnius with the next convoy heading for Kraków," I said, eager to change the subject. "You'll be returning to Bar to rejoin Captain Pretwicz and his troops, I assume?"

"My orders are to see you to Kraków safely first."

"Oh." I was baffled by how glad this made me feel. "I see."

Zaremba's eyes remained on me for a few moments longer. Then he rose, and I followed him to the door. Before he opened it, he turned to me. Darkness deepened in the corners of the chamber, rendering the features of his face less distinct. I wondered why Rasa had not arrived.

I opened my mouth to say something—although I was not sure what—and felt his hand on my waist, light but firm. I knew I should resist, but I did not take a step back or move to push his hand away. I just stood there, my breath coming faster and shallower, loud in my ears, where his familiar address—Caterina—was still ringing.

Zaremba moved closer. The solidity of his thighs pressed against my skirts. His musky scent sent a tingling wave I had not felt in years through my limbs. A warm and pleasant languor spread through my body. He lowered his face, his lips hovering inches from mine.

What was he doing? What was *I* doing? Fog filled my mind again, as it had a few hours earlier, although for an entirely different reason. Then my husband's image emerged from the fog. Sebastian appeared before me the way he had looked that winter night long ago at Wawel: dark-haired, dark-eyed, with a small smile and an air of mystery about him. We stood in the chamber he occupied as a royal secretary, hard snow peppering the windows, and he was about to kiss me just as the cathedral bell struck the hour and broke the spell.

The clarity of the vision made me gasp, and I took a step back. "What are you doing?" I asked, looking away, although by now it was almost completely dark. Where *was* Rasa?

"I'm sorry," he said. His voice was calm, not apologetic. "I got … carried away. You have a way about you, Caterina …" He made a move as if to step closer again.

I held out my hand. "Please don't."

A knock on the door startled me. Zaremba stepped nimbly aside, and I hastened to open it.

"It's you!" I wanted to greet the maid in a stern tone, but it came out almost cheerful. In truth, I was weak with relief. "I was wondering when you'd come!"

She picked up the basket of firewood next to her feet. In the crook of the other arm she held several wax candles. "I'm sorry, my lady. The cellars were low on candles, but there was a delivery in process. I had to wait until the crates were opened."

I waved her in, and she bobbed two small curtsies to me and Zaremba before heading for the hearth.

With a swift step, Zaremba was over the threshold. "God give you good night, signora."

"And you, my lord."

I closed the door and almost ran to the sideboard. Maria's winking face floated before my eyes, and I shut them forcefully. I poured and drained a good measure of wine as Rasa struck the flint repeatedly until she was able to coax enough sparks to light the kindling.

A few more days, and we will be on our way back home. A few more days.

8

September 9th, 1545
Wednesday

The summons came two days later, in the morning. After breaking our fast in our chambers, Giulio and I were accompanied by one of the duke's junior secretaries to the southern wing of the palace, where Doctor Nascimbene's exam room was located on the ground floor next to a small infirmary. I thought the escort a thoughtful gesture.

Doctor Nascimbene was ancient: a man of seventy, small, spare, and slightly stooped. With a long, pointy beard and a cap too large for his head, with a top that tilted sideways, he looked like a wizard from one of the tales Giulio and I read together. My son stared at him with wide eyes, timid and curious in equal measure, and the corners of his lips trembled with what could have been either suppressed laughter or the possibility of tears.

I put my arm around his shoulders, then addressed the physician. "We are very grateful to His Grace and to you for agreeing to see us, *dottore*."

The old man nodded benevolently. His pale blue eyes turned to Giulio and glinted with a spark of mischief. "And how old might you be?"

"Ten," Giulio answered, barely audibly. I squeezed his shoulder for courage. "I'll be eleven come next spring," he added, a bit more loudly.

"That's a serious age, indeed." Nascimbene's voice was mildly high-pitched. It too would not be out of place in a tale of wizardry. I wondered if it was his real voice as he turned his back on us, revealing a small hunchback. When he turned back again, he held out his palm. A dark, square shape rested in the middle of it. It was a piece of marzipan, a great rarity. "But I hope not so serious as to prevent you from enjoying a little treat." He lifted his hand a little higher in an encouraging gesture as he brought his wrinkled face closer. Round spectacles perched at the end of his nose.

Giulio looked at me with hopeful eyes, and when I nodded, he took a timid step forward and snatched the confection from the doctor's hand. "*Grazie*," he said as the marzipan vanished into his mouth, and a smile of delight brightened his face. The treat, and the fact that the conversation was unfolding in Italian, were quickly putting him at ease.

Nascimbene turned to me with a smile that revealed a surprising number of teeth for one his age. Clearly, he himself did not indulge in sweets too much. "I am told that your son suffers from recurring fevers?" he said, his voice lower now and unexpectedly strong.

I silently chastised myself for my doubts when I first saw him. Despite the outward signs of frailty, Nascimbene's mind was still sharp. "Yes," I replied. "Since he was four. We lived outside of Bari until last spring, when we brought him to Kraków to seek help at Her Majesty's court."

The doctor motioned Giulio to sit on a raised bench by the window. The view showed the main city street leading up to the palace gate. We had ridden down that street only three days earlier, although it seemed longer than that. I had expected to wait a week or two before being seen, but we might accomplish our goal much sooner. Suppose we were back on the road to Kraków with the convoy leaving Vilnius on Saturday? At least this part of my mission was going well.

As Giulio was stripping off his little doublet and shirt, Nascimbene asked me to describe his symptoms in detail. I recounted the fevers and chills, the headaches, nauseas, muscle aches, tiredness, and pallor. A few of the more severe attacks had also included convulsions, followed by a state of semi-consciousness that was neither sleep nor full delirium.

"And how are you feeling today, young man?" Nascimbene asked as he began his examination.

"Not bad," my son replied. "Just a bit weak."

The physician pulled down each of Giulio's lower lids, looked into his eyes while holding up a candle to the side of his head, and examined the inside of his mouth. He also checked his pulse, palpated his ribcage, and measured the length of his arms and legs.

"Would you say that you have felt generally better since your arrival in Poland?" he asked.

Giulio tilted his head back, thinking. Bored with the lengthy exam, he had been fidgeting and shuffling his legs in the air under the bench, but now he stopped, as if struck by a thought. "Yes," he said wonderingly. "I have. I've had fewer headaches, and my arms and legs haven't hurt as much."

My heart leaped. While I had, of course, noticed him faring better in the past few weeks, I had not allowed myself to hope too much. I had been waiting for a relapse, expecting and dreading it every day from the moment I opened my eyes. And there were still days when he had sweats and was too tired to get out of bed. This illness, I had to admit, had my mind in as powerful a grip as it did his body.

Nascimbene handed him a bell-shaped vessel and pointed to a cloth partition. "Go behind this and provide a sample of your water."

As Giulio was attending to the request, the doctor said to me, "There is a slight yellowish tinge to his eyeballs, and he's not growing as fast as he should." I nodded, unable to speak for the constriction in my throat. "He's afflicted by a type of swamp fever. I say a type because cases have also been found in susceptible individuals in drier areas where swamps don't occur. But that only shows that bad air—*mala aria*—can travel far, although fortunately not so far as to make it impossible to outrun it."

"Outrun it?"

"Yes. The best thing you could have done for the boy was removing him from southern Italy. There are far fewer swamps in cooler climates, and their miasmas are less noxious."

Giulio returned with the vessel that was less than half-full. "I could only manage this little," he said guiltily.

"Not to worry, young man. This will be enough, although scant urination"—he spoke to me again—"is one of the symptoms." He swirled the contents before examining them against the light, his short-sighted eyes squinting behind his spectacles. "The color is paler than normal, which confirms my diagnosis. The fever stems from an imbalance between wet and dry humors."

"Does that mean he's no longer at risk of a relapse in Poland?" I asked, barely daring to hope.

He spread his arms in a gesture of uncertainty. "Not necessarily. It can take up to a year to fully recover once the patient has left the region whose air sickens him." Then, seeing my face fall, he added, "But your son is still young and his growth will have time to catch up. If nothing else gets in the way, there should be no difference between him and other boys his age by the time he's fourteen."

"So all we can do is wait?" I was both relieved and disappointed. My son would recover, it seemed, but it would take a long time, and we had traveled so far to hear such mixed news.

"Ah." The doctor raised a forefinger. "There is an infusion I can prescribe for him which, God willing, will help his humors return to the original balance faster. But with this malady, there are no guarantees," he cautioned. "Time is still our best ally."

He ambled to the counter, covered with an array of vials, bowls, jars, and various sizes of spoons, knives, and pestles. Atop the counter, a hatch of shelves and drawers held a variety of labeled boxes and bottles. He pulled two of the boxes out and lifted their lids. He took a wooden spoon and stirred their contents, making a soft rustling sound. He measured out a quantity of dried brown leaves and a similar amount of dried white flowers and placed them in a linen sack he produced from one of the drawers. Then he tied the strings of the bag.

"Sweet wormwood and yarrow," he said, handing it to me. "Brew one cup at bedtime every day for at least six months. This bag will last you for four weeks. You should be able to procure more from any apothecary in Kraków. If for some reason you can't, write to me, and I'll send another packet with a convoy from the court."

"I'm deeply indebted to you, *dottore*." I reached for a purse hidden in the folds of my gown and pulled out a gold sovereign.

He raised a thin leathery hand, dotted with liver spots, in a gesture of rejection. "No need, signora." He shook his head. "The grand duke pays for all treatments in the infirmary."

I waited for Jakub Zaremba until ten o'clock that night. I had not seen him since he came to my lodgings two nights earlier and we almost kissed. My cheeks burned each time I thought about how close I had come to betraying my husband, and I wished I did not have to see Zaremba again. But the queen had charged him with escorting us back to Kraków, and I wanted to go with the convoy that was due to leave in three days.

He had stayed away from the banqueting hall earlier that evening. Given what had passed between us, it would have been even more unseemly than usual for me to go knocking on his door, so I paced the sitting room as the tower clock chimed hour after hour and the darkness thickened outside. I grew more and more anxious until I realized I had no choice: I had to speak with Zaremba, or there might not be room for us in the convoy. I did not want to have to wait another week.

I went down the corridor, turned the corner, and knocked on the second door on the right, hoping nobody would see me. A long moment elapsed, and my stomach lurched. He might be out, and if so, I had no way of knowing when he would be back. What if he did not return before Saturday? Suppose he had gone to the baths or—the thought filled me with dismay—to one of the pleasure houses, which I'd heard were even more numerous here than in Kraków? Dismissing my fears, I raised my hand to knock once more and watched it trace an arc in the empty air as the door swung open.

Zaremba stood in front of me holding a goblet of wine in his hand. Clad only in his breeches and a shirt, open at the collar to reveal dark blond chest hair, he appeared to be getting ready for bed. I lowered my gaze and willed my legs to remain in place, for a part of me wanted to turn and run back to my chambers.

When he saw me, his face—which he had shaved, I noticed—registered a surprise that swiftly gave way to unease. "Signora Konarska." A moment passed. "What an unexpected pleasure." This time he forced a note of artificial cheer into his voice. He must have been drinking for a while, for he spoke rather too loud, his face had acquired a flush, and his eyes, despite the pouches of tiredness beneath them, had the glimmer that comes with too much wine. He must have had a rough day.

He swung the hand that held the goblet in a parody of welcome. "Do come in."

I hesitated. As much as I did not want to be alone with him, I was even more worried that someone might see us together. I took a reluctant step inside. "You've shaved," I said to cover up the awkwardness.

He ran his fingers along both sides of his jaw. "I'm going to try the goatee style, it's becoming very popular in Spain."

He closed the door and took a swig of his wine, and suddenly I felt thirsty. It had been a long day for me, too. My eyes lingered on his cup, and another awkward pause ensued, during which I wondered if he wished me gone. Finally, Zaremba cleared his throat and walked over to the sideboard.

I could not help glancing around his chamber. It was in a state of disarray, not unusual in the lodgings of a man who occupied them alone, although there were maids available to clean. For a moment, I considered suggesting that he avail himself of their services, but I stopped myself in time. It was not my place to give him that sort of advice.

Besides, my interest was caught by a round box resting on a divan that stood against the wall between two windows. It was powder pink and looked out of place among the masculine items strewn around the room—the dark red cloak he had worn at Gornitsa, thrown across the back of a chair; pieces of armor discarded on the floor; platters with crumbs on them; some papers on the table; and a pair of tan leather boots.

And then that pink box from a milliner's shop.

When I turned to him, he was watching me, his face tense.

"Have you been shopping?" I heard myself asking. It occurred to me that perhaps he was awaiting female company. That would explain his surprise when he opened the door.

Zaremba's gaze flicked to the hat box, and there was that discomfort again. "Yes. Uh … no. I brought it with me from Kraków."

I attempted a bit of humor. "It's not for you, is it?"

He laughed, but the sound had a forced quality to it. I was certain that he wished I had not seen the box. "It's a gift."

"For whom?" I asked, before I could stop myself. I have always been too curious for my own good.

He looked away. "For my wife."

"I see." In the silence that followed, I looked intently into the cup he had handed me. It was less than half-full. It seemed like he really wanted me gone. The thought, along with this new revelation, made me vaguely disappointed where I should have been relieved. After all, he was deceiving Pani Zaremba, not me. "Where is she?"

He looked embarrassed. "She stayed behind in Bar."

Finally, the truth was out. He was married, and he was a liar. Why should I be surprised? At least this would halt our strange dance. A fleeting fancy, nothing more, ended before we did something that we—or at least I—regretted. The thought made me feel better, and I took a draught from my cup. The wine was different from the Italian I was used to or the Malvazia served in the banqueting hall. It was not as sweet, with notes of cherry and plum but also a spicy aftertaste that was familiar, although I could not place it.

"Interesting." I lifted the cup for a closer inspection.

"Do you like it, signora?" Zaremba asked with a smirk. He was in full control of himself again, and the inebriation had given his demeanor a subtly insolent edge. Still, he avoided using my Christian name, and I was glad. It put us back on a more formal footing.

I ignored his tone. "I do. What is it?"

"Spanish, from Castille. It's one of the best to be found in the Habsburg domains. There are imperial envoys currently at court, and they travel with their own wine. I sat at their table last Sunday. Ambassador von Tilburg said they had gifted a barrel to the grand duke and have been sharing the rest with the courtiers. They are justifiably proud of it."

"That taste …" I took another sip and let the liquid roll over my tongue.

"It's black pepper."

I nodded, remembering. Pepper was a great rarity, brought by the Spaniards from overseas. It was so expensive I had only tasted it a few times in my life. "It hasn't been served in the banqueting hall."

He shrugged. "Perhaps the duke doesn't like it, or he likes it so much he drinks it only in private so it lasts longer." He laughed and raised his cup, as if offering a toast. "Whatever the case may be, Castilian happens to be my favorite, and the ambassador sent me a flagon as a goodwill gesture. My maid delivered it yesterday."

My eyes strayed toward the chamber, which had not been subject to any maid's attention in days.

"She's yet to clean," he explained, as if guessing my thoughts.

I finished the cup. The wine was indeed excellent. Who knew such a delicacy could come from a Habsburg land? I handed the vessel back to Zaremba. "We saw Doctor Nascimbene today, so we are free to go home," I said. "I came to ask you to secure a spot for us in the convoy that leaves on Saturday."

"Saturday? We could leave earlier than that." He seemed strangely eager. "There's a merchant caravan departing on Friday morning."

"Even better."

Zaremba swayed slightly on his feet, his eyes narrowing, and, for the first time, I realized just how drunk he was. I decided it was best to leave, but before I could move he turned away, bent over the chair and, gripping its back for support, rummaged under his cloak, the color of an autumn leaf. When he straightened again, he held a leather-bound book in his hand, a fine edition with pages edged in gold leaf.

"This is for your son." He offered me the book. "It's based on the legend of King Arthur and his Knights."

"Oh." I hesitated. "That's very thoughtful of you. But why?"

"A long journey away from home must be tiring, and he's probably bored. I thought he might find this entertaining."

I opened the book and read the title page: *La morte di Arturo*, the Italian translation of *The Death of Arthur* by Sir Thomas Malory. It must have been expensive. And hard to come by in Vilnius, or even in Kraków.

"Thank you." I felt warmly toward him again and chastised myself for it. If I had not just found out that he was married *and* likely had a mistress, I would have thought he was again looking for a way to seduce me. "I'll start packing first thing in the morning," I added by way of taking a leave.

I left his chamber with the book and a lighter heart than I'd had in weeks. I looked forward to a good night's sleep and to leaving in less than two days.

But, as it turned out, neither of those things happened.

9

September 10th, 1545
Thursday

I donned my nightdress, but as I bent to blow out the candle, a loud, urgent knock broke the silence of the midnight hour. I froze. What if Zaremba's lady companion had not shown up, so he got even drunker and decided to come to my chamber? I hastily wrapped a dressing gown around me and rushed to the door before Cecilia could open it; Rasa had already retired to the servants' quarters. The last thing I needed was for anyone to see Zaremba visiting me so late at night.

In the sitting room, I nearly collided with Cecilia. I hoped the low light from the embers of the dying hearth fire prevented her from seeing how flustered I was. "Go back to your room," I said in a loud whisper. "I'm sure whoever it is has mistaken our door for someone else's. I'll take care of it."

I waited until she disappeared before opening the door. The rebuke I planned for Zaremba died in my throat when I saw Chamberlain Opaliński outside.

"Signora Konarska." He made a small bow. He carried a candle in an iron holder, and in its flickering light his face looked anxious. "I apologize for disturbing you at this hour, but His Grace requests your presence. I'm afraid it's urgent."

It took a moment for me to grasp what he was saying, but when I did, my chest contracted painfully. "Of course, but … has something happened?"

"He'll explain everything. I'll wait for you out here," he said, politely but firmly.

I left him and set about getting dressed with the help of a perplexed Cecilia, whom I roused out of bed again. I had to be quick but also look presentable before Zygmunt August. I selected the same crescent headdress I wore for the first audience—my most expensive one, with a single ruby among the seed pearls that edged it. Fifteen minutes later, I was hurrying to keep up with the chamberlain as he walked briskly through the dim and eerily quiet palace corridors. I felt rattled, and however hard I tried to keep my mind blank, my thoughts kept going to the obvious place. Had the duke found out about my association with Bona? Had someone told him about my mission for her? To my knowledge, only Zaremba had that information, and he wanted me to succeed. Had he found a way to speak to the duke? Done what I should have? Yet in the last few days, he had seemed more interested in romance than in politics.

And what would Zygmunt *do*? Would he throw me out of the palace in the middle of the night and expel me from the capital? Would he have me reimburse him for Nascimbene's services? Fortunately, I had the money to pay him back. I could also find accommodations in a nearby village and wait until Friday for the merchant caravan to leave for Kraków. The worst he could do would be to confiscate my bag of herbs, although that, too, would be a temporary setback. Then, with a sinking feeling in my stomach, I realized that he could, in fact, do far worse: he could throw me in jail. He was, after all, the absolute ruler of this land.

After what felt like hours but could not have been more than ten minutes, we arrived at the duke's private apartments, where he had received me three days earlier. Neither courtiers nor servants filled the antechamber; there were only two stone-faced guards standing sentinel on either side of the inner door. My sense of foreboding increased. Surely, the duke would not take such precautions, act in such secrecy, solely to punish me for my inartful and unintentional deception?

Zygmunt August stood gazing pensively into the fire in his private sitting chamber. His doublet of black velvet and bronze-colored brocade and splendid coat trimmed with sable fur suggested he had not yet changed from his evening attire. At first I thought he was alone. Then I spotted Barbara Radziwiłł propped up on the silk-covered cushions of a chaise longue at the opposite end of the chamber. Her long, slender fingers stroked the head of a white cat, yet the tension with which her other hand gripped the fine woolen scarf wrapped around her shoulders revealed her disquiet. In the light of the candles burning in the sconces around the chamber, her dark eyes, wide and alert, shone with ill-disguised fear as she shifted them from Opaliński to me and the duke, then back.

In the corner closest to the fire two black hunting dogs lounged on a large pallet. I guessed they were Sybilla and Gryf, the duke's favorites, who always accompanied him to his hunting lodge at Knyszyn. They lifted their heads when we entered, their noses rising to sniff the air, but they laid them back down in response to a restraining gesture from Zygmunt. Despite the charged atmosphere, the whole tableau had a cozy air of intimacy and domesticity.

"Pani Konarska." The duke turned his head, although the rest of his body remained motionless. His expression was grave. "Rest assured that I didn't relish disturbing you at this hour, but the matter is of utmost importance." He spoke in Polish, no doubt for Barbara's benefit.

"I am at Your Grace's service."

He paced in front of the hearth, his steps heavy and his shoulders slumped. In fact, his entire body appeared weighed down by a great burden. "There is no easy way to say this," he spoke at length, "so I'll be direct. There has been a murder in the palace tonight."

My breath caught. "A murder?"

"I'm afraid so."

There was a moment of silence, during which I wondered why he would call me so late at night to tell me about it. Unless …

My stomach dropped painfully. Unless it was someone I knew. My mind flitted immediately to my son and his nurse, whom I had left in our lodgings. They were safe, so that left Zaremba, with whom I had spoken less than two hours earlier, and Maria …

"Is it the Marchesa del Vasto?" I asked, my mouth dry.

He shook his head. "A kitchen maid was found dead in my private kitchen around ten thirty tonight."

"Last night," he corrected himself, for it was almost one in the morning. "It seems she was poisoned."

I shivered, although I could never have met the maid in question. I wondered what her death had to do with me, but I saw no way to inquire directly. Instead, I asked, "In your private kitchen, Your Grace?"

"Pani Barbara and I"—Zygmunt paused his pacing, his open palm indicating his mistress—"keep a separate kitchen from the rest of the court. For safety reasons." A grimace twisted his lips.

I felt light-headed. I knew about the grand duke's suspicions of his mother's supposedly murderous intentions for Barbara. A surge of dread tightened my chest. If he blamed the queen for this murder, and he somehow found out I was in Vilnius on a mission for her—a mission to stop his marriage, no less—he would throw me in jail as a traitor and a murder suspect, and what would happen to Giulio?

A rivulet of sweat trickled down my spine, and my clenched palms were damp. My heart pounded against my ribs, pumping pure fear through my veins, and despite the chaos in my mind, one clear thought emerged: I had to run away. The moment this audience ended, if I still had my freedom, I would take Giulio and Cecilia and leave the palace at first light with just the clothes on our backs.

The duke continued, seemingly unaware of my turmoil. "Pani Barbara takes half a cup of wine at night to help her sleep." His eyes rested on her, full of tenderness and concern. "Normally the kitchenmaid brings it upstairs between ten and eleven o'clock, but last night she was late, so the chambermaid went to check on it and found the girl on the floor showing signs of a poisonous agent."

He began pacing again, and I waited for the ax to fall. But the silence stretched, and my anxiety subsided. If he believed me responsible, surely he would have ordered my arrest by now. But if he did not, why had he summoned me at all?

He stopped again and looked straight at me, his face strained. "We believe the poison was meant for Pani Barbara." He stated what I had already guessed. "She was the one who was supposed to die tonight."

Barbara brought her hand to her throat, and her eyes turned liquid with tears, although she held them back. From up close she looked more vulnerable than in the banqueting hall; fear replaced the air of confidence she'd had about her before. I now saw a woman who understood fully the precariousness of her position, the danger that threatened her. She also looked unhealthy: her face had a sallow tinge, and dark shadows under her eyes made her look older than her twenty-five years. Unbidden, Maria's words came back to me, repeating the rumor that Barbara suffered from the French disease. I pushed the thought back. Whatever the case, anyone who had narrowly escaped a terrible death could be forgiven for looking ill.

"Who would have done such a thing?" I asked, swallowing hard in expectation of a grave accusation. I steeled myself.

"Many people oppose our love," he said with raw honesty. Then his tone turned petulant. "They would see me marry some dull foreign princess with a limp or a jutting jaw and spend the rest of my life chafing at so unappealing a bond."

I had little doubt that by "they" he meant his mother and her faction. The passion with which he delivered that statement told me I had done the right thing in not mentioning her plea to him. I would have achieved nothing and damaged my own standing.

I tried to think of a response, but nothing seemed appropriate or safe. I wanted to avoid angering him further so that he would release me. I would leave Vilnius as soon as possible. If he did not intend to accuse me, I still had no idea what he wanted with me. To hasten my dismissal, I tried flattery. "I have no doubt Your Grace will find the culprit and punish him quickly."

"I will!" he said fiercely. "That's why I summoned you here."

So there it was. He would call his guards to haul me away to some dark, stinking cell where they would torture me to extract a false confession, then execute me. I saw it all so clearly that my hand flew to my mouth to stifle a sob rising in my chest.

I was on the brink of falling on my knees to plead innocence when the duke spoke again, sympathetic but determined. "I know it's been a long time since you were involved in something like this, but I believe your skills will be helpful. Solving this crime is a matter of utmost consequence for the state."

For a few heartbeats I had no idea what he was talking about. Then it became clear: he was referring to Helena's case. But how did he know of my involvement in it?

As if answering my unspoken question, he said, "After our audience on Monday, I directed Secretary Mieleski to find out more about you. Your name sounded familiar, you see. He informed me about your service to my mother"—that grimace again—"and how you tracked down the person who killed two courtiers at Wawel in the winter of 1519. That was before I was born, but I heard the story many times growing up, although it always referred to you by your maiden name—Sanseverino."

Sanseverino had been the name of my first husband, but the rest was true enough. I waited for him to bring up my current association with the queen, but he did not. Was it possible he did not know? Should I reveal it now? I probably should, I thought, but, once again, my tongue was tied.

"I also want it done discreetly," the duke went on, "and as a visitor from Kraków you will attract less attention than regular residents of the court. I will provide lodgings and food for you and your son at the palace until you discover the murderer." His tone made it an order, not an offer. Not for the first time, he reminded me of Bona. For all the discord between them, they were cut from the same cloth—determined, stubborn, and convinced they need only command to be obeyed. But they were royalty: they had the right.

"I am at Your Grace's disposal," I said. In truth, he left me no other option. At least he hadn't thrown me in jail. And who knew? If I could identify the culprit soon, I would still be able to depart this week. Perhaps not on Friday, but on Saturday . . .

"Thank you," the duke said simply. He rose from his chair, walked over to Barbara, sat at the edge of her chaise longue, and took her hand. He kissed it, then pressed it to his heart. "As long as I'm here, nobody will hurt you," he said, his voice soft and tender, as if they were alone. "I promise."

"I know, my love. I trust you completely," she replied. They were the first words I had heard from her. She spoke in Polish, with a melodic Eastern accent that enhanced the aura of fragility that hung about her.

She lifted her eyes, full of the trust she had just professed, to Zygmunt's face. An unspoken communication passed between them. The scene transported me back to the day when Sebastian walked me to my chamber after my meeting with Chancellor Stempowski about the note Helena had slid under my door. Before we parted, he looked into my eyes and said similar words: *You'll be fine. I'll make sure of that.* That was the moment I fell in love with him.

Watching them, my own memories fresh and true, I grasped that a genuine affection existed between Barbara and Zygmunt. The Radziwiłł family may have been playing a political game, but Barbara loved the duke, and he loved her. I glanced at Chamberlain Opaliński, whose face told me that, whether he liked it or not, he saw the same thing.

Zygmunt rose from the chaise longue. "The body is still in the kitchen, and Doctor Nascimbene is there. I didn't want anything disturbed until you had a chance to see it. Once you have, we will have the girl moved to the palace chapel so her family can claim her."

I understood. My work was to start immediately.

That was how I found myself, just before two o'clock in the morning, in a small kitchen which, judging by the number of flights of stairs we descended, and the narrow windows set just below the ceiling, was located below the ground level of the palace. On the way down, Opaliński explained that it had been carved out of the main kitchen the previous autumn and given a separate entrance from the corridor. A palace guard manned that corridor day and night. Only two people worked in the new kitchen: a cook and a scullery maid. The duke planned to build a staircase—he added—that would link the kitchen to Barbara's bedchamber directly, thus answering the question of whether she had moved into the palace.

The kitchen, although small, was fully equipped with a bread oven, a hearth with a spit, shelves and cupboards, a pantry, chopping counters, and a central table where the servants could roll dough and eat their meals. The larger kitchen next door kept it warm, even though the staff had long since extinguished its own cooking fire for the night. There were three people inside, but only two of them were alive.

I recognized Doctor Nascimbene and guessed the other—a middle-aged woman with swollen, red eyes and easily twice the size of the elderly physician—to be the cook. Like many of her profession, her face was permanently flushed from the heat of the ovens and hearths at which she spent her life. As we entered, she clambered laboriously to her feet.

Nascimbene acknowledged me with a nod and motioned me to follow him to the other side of the table, while Opaliński remained by the door. My pulse beat loudly in my ears as I made my way around the rough pine table until the corpse, whose legs I had already seen from the entrance, came into view.

I shuddered at the grim and pitiful sight. The unfortunate servant, identified by the doctor as Milda, was a slight girl with a shock of blond hair that had fallen out from under her cap and spread around her head like a halo. She lay on her side by the bench on which she must have been sitting when she was struck down. Her left arm was thrown out beneath her, but the right one lay close to her chest, its fingers still curled. Her shift was torn open at the neck, and together with the positioning of the fingers, it showed that she had clawed at her throat in her final moments. I understood why, too, for a grotesque grimace distorted her purple-blue face, and flecks of white foam had dried on her lips. Those lips framed a swollen tongue, pushed partly out of her mouth, indicating that she had indeed died of an ingested poison.

I said a silent prayer for this innocent soul. My pulse slowed, and my head cleared. A silver goblet stood on the table, half full of wine, undoubtedly the one she was supposed to carry up to Barbara's bedchamber. Already I could picture the death scene as it unfolded. Without the doctor telling me, I knew what had happened, and now I needed to find out by whose hand—and why.

I touched Milda's fingers and found them still warm.

"Dead less than four hours." Nascimbene sighed. "Such a shame. She was only sixteen."

A sudden fierce determination to avenge this wrong overcame me. The victim before me was poor, vulnerable, and younger than my daughter. I looked around. "Where is the parlor maid who found her?"

The cook remained on the other side of the table so as not to see the body. She pressed her hand to her bosom, which heaved as if she were about to start crying again. "Lina became so 'ysterical Doctor Nascimbene 'ad to give 'er a calming draft to put her to sleep," she said, her breath catching. "But between the screams she told us what she seen."

"And what was that?" I asked.

The woman's eyes filled, and she sent a pleading glance toward the doctor. He stepped in, perhaps worried that she, too, might need a calming draft. "Lina came to check on the wine for Pani Barbara as Milda was late with it. It was a few minutes past ten o'clock. She found her on the floor, still twitching, and ran out into the corridor crying for help, but most kitchen servants had already retired."

"She came banging on m'door, she did," the cook said, some newfound resolve surfacing. "I 'ave a room on this level, as I can't climb the stairs no more," she explained. "The guard in the corridor isn't allowed to leave 'is post, so Lina 'ad to run all the way up to 'is Grace's apartments 'erself. By the time I arrived, Milda was no longer moving. I waited wit' the guard outside as I was afraid to stay in 'ere alone."

"Who came back with Lina?"

"I did," Chamberlain Opaliński spoke for the first time. "Milda was already dead. Lina began to scream, and we couldn't stop her, so I had to release the guard to go fetch Doctor Nascimbene."

"The parlor maid was the only one I could help," the physician said sorrowfully.

"Was Milda alone when Lina found her?"

"Yes," Opaliński replied. "She said there was nobody else in the kitchen."

I looked around again, taking my time. The kitchen had two doors: one from the corridor, through which we had come in, and one in a side wall. An iron key hung on a peg next to the latter door. "Where does it lead?" I asked.

"Outside," said the cook, "It's our delivery door. Used to serve the whole of the old kitchen, but now they 'ave to bring everything in through the corridor from another part o' t'palace. The other cooks don't like it, they don't!"

Talking about something other than the murder, something as familiar and comforting as kitchen gossip and servants' grievances seemed to calm her.

"Is that how wine is brought in as well?"

She shook her head. "The wine comes from 'is Grace's own stores in the cellar."

"How often?"

"Every morning. The Master Cupbearer brings two flagons up." She pointed toward a cloth screen covering one of the shelves.

I pushed the linen fabric aside. On the shelf behind it stood two silver flagons with ornamental handles and curved beaks that tapered off gracefully. They looked similar to the ones from Bona's dowry, used to serve wine at Wawel in my youth. I wondered if they were the same flagons, and if so, did Zygmunt know? I inspected them to find one empty and the other only about one-third full.

"Do the duke and Pani Barbara usually drink all of the wine?"

"No. They rarely finish both flagons, and 'is Grace never drinks after seven o'clock," the cook replied.

I carried the flagon that still had some wine in it to the table. Instinctively, everyone leaned forward, but they maintained their distance and only craned their necks, as if afraid that something might jump out at them. Fighting a similar irrational fear, I lifted a candle and gazed into the flagon again. I could see now that the liquid inside was dark red, its surface glossy in the light. My stomach clenched at the thought of the deadly danger lurking underneath it.

Then I paused. "Do you know what kind of wine this is?"

The cook looked uncertain. "The duke usually asks for Malvazia. Sometimes tokay, but not very often."

I was puzzled. The wine in the goblet was neither. Tokay was the color of amber, and Malvazia was rose-colored.

"I'll question the Master Cupbearer," the chamberlain offered. "The duke has some Provençal wines in his personal store, but he drinks them only on rare occasions."

I moved the vessel around in a circle, thinking. Then, as a faint aroma reached me, I stopped, my heart skipping a beat.

I brought it closer to my nose and swirled the contents again, as the others looked on with growing perplexity. I inhaled and paused, the breath filling my chest. My mind worked quickly, and then I knew. I had smelled this only a few hours earlier, the distinct spicy odor of black pepper. I lifted the goblet that stood on the table, from which the unfortunate maid had taken her final drink. I held its filigree stem and repeated the process. It had the same deep and rich color and the same peppery scent.

"This isn't Malvazia *or* Provençal," I explained to my stunned audience. "It's Castilian."

"If you're correct, signora, this wine comes from the barrel gifted by the Habsburg ambassador," Opaliński said, his face blanching.

I extended the goblet toward him; after a brief hesitation, he leaned in and smelled it. "Yes. I recognize it too. And the color–" He turned and rushed out of the kitchen, and we heard him order the guard to take a message to those minding the duke's private cellars not to use that barrel's contents anymore.

I placed the goblet back on the table. "Pour this away when we're done here," I told the cook.

"Yes, m'lady," she whispered.

"When was the last time you saw Milda alive?" I asked her as the chamberlain returned.

The woman thought hard. "Just after eight last night, when we finished 'ere. When they dine privately, 'is Grace and Pani Barbara eat at six o'clock. They're done by seven, and we take an hour to clean up. Then Milda returns at ten to prepare the wine for Pani Barbara and carry it upstairs."

"And both of you followed that routine last night?"

"Far as I know, 'cept for the carrying upstairs, of course."

So there were approximately two hours, from eight to ten, during which the kitchen was empty of staff. It was the only time the Castilian could have been sneaked in. But how? There was always a guard outside, and this one had not reported seeing any strangers about.

"Why would Milda have taken a drink from the goblet prepared for Pani Barbara?"

The cook's eyes darted toward Opaliński, who gave a slight nod. "She wasn't just a kitchen maid but also … a taster." Seeing my puzzlement, she explained, "She 'ad to taste everything went on Pani Barbara's plate and in her cups, even water. Earned an extra silver talon for it every month." A sob rose in her throat. "That's 'ow much 'er life was worth!"

I frowned. "Shouldn't she have tasted the wine in Barbara's presence, not here, alone?"

The cook was silent.

"Anything else you should tell me?" I prodded, sensing that she was hiding something. "Every bit of information can help, no matter how trivial."

The woman burst into tears. "She was a good girl, she was! But she 'ad a tough life!" She put her palms on both sides of her pudgy face, like an old woman lamenting. "An orphan she was, never knew 'er mother nor 'er father, raised on strangers' charity, and out on the streets when she was no' yet fourteen." She produced a stained and crumpled handkerchief from her voluminous skirt, which sat a bit crookedly around her large waist, suggesting she had already undressed for bed when Lina had raised the alarm. She blew her nose loudly. When she was done, she added, her chest still heaving, "She drank a little when nobody was looking. I tol' her it won't do—you'll be discovered and dismissed, I said, but she didn' listen. Or maybe she didn' care no more. Poor soul ..."

I sent the chamberlain an inquiring look, but he raised his shoulders in a gesture meant to signify that he'd had no idea.

"Did you believe her to be in any danger?" I asked the cook.

She looked at me fearfully but answered firmly enough, shaking her head so vigorously that her cap, which she had not tied under her chin, tilted sideways. "No. Never."

I tried to make sense of it all as I waited for her to calm down again. At length, she put away her handkerchief and readjusted her cap. When I judged that she had her emotions under control, I asked, "What kind of mistress is Barbara Radziwiłł? Do the servants like her?"

Another glance at Opaliński.

"It's all right," he said. "None of this will reach the duke, you have my word."

His tone was soft, almost soothing, and it inspired trust. The cook seemed reassured.

"She's a grand lady," she started hesitantly. "But 'aughty. And can be snippy wit' the maids, impatient. Nobody really knows her well—she often locks 'erself in 'er chambers and won't see nobody but the duke, sometimes not even 'im, from what I hear."

Silence fell on our gathering as we contemplated that revelation, new to me, but, based on his look of studied indifference, not to Opaliński. In the distance, the tower clock struck three, its sound muffled by the stone walls. All of us in the small kitchen looked grim and hollow-eyed with exhaustion.

"Thank you," I said to the cook, then turned to the others. "I don't see what else we can learn tonight. We had better get some rest. Tomorrow"—I spoke to the chamberlain—"we should talk to the other kitchen staff and anyone else who knew Milda or shared her living quarters."

Doctor Nascimbene and the cook gathered to leave. Opaliński and I waited for them to step out into the corridor, then followed. Outside, we found two new guards and a night duty servant. She had a bundle in her arms that looked like a shroud. Two wide, plain wooden planks tied together—a stretcher for the body, I assumed—rested against the wall.

The servant's face was as white as the cloth she carried. I laid a hand on her shoulder. "It will be hard," I said, "but know that you'll be giving Milda the dignity everyone deserves in death."

The young woman nodded, head bent and eyes closed, and the tension around her shoulders eased just a little.

A few minutes later, I slipped into my chambers as quietly as possible. I needed a few hours of sleep to get ready for what I knew would be a very difficult day—or days—ahead.

10

September 10th, 1545
Thursday

I did not sleep much that night. I dozed off only to dream of a prostrate figure on the floor covered with a white shroud. Fearful of whose body I might discover, I nonetheless wanted to lift the cloth, but someone or something was restraining my arm with painful pressure. And when I finally wrestled it from that invisible grip and reached for the fabric, I woke with a gasp. My right arm was pinned under me and tingling unpleasantly—I must have fallen asleep on it and the discomfort had found its way into my nightmare. After that I lay awake, listening to rain pelting against the window pane.

At length I rose, lit a candle, and began to pace my bedchamber, turning everything over in my head. With some consternation I realized that even though it grossly interfered with my plans, the case had piqued my curiosity. It revived that long-forgotten excitement of solving a riddle composed of clues that would give me the true picture if I managed to figure out how they fit together. It injected a strange energy into my mind and made me come alive in a way few things had done in a long time.

I decided to accept Zygmunt's assumption that Barbara, not Milda, was the murderer's intended target. Even in the unlikely event that the maid had made a mortal enemy in her short life, he—or she, for since the winter of 1519, I had been stripped of any illusions that a woman was incapable of violence—would not have chosen poison as the weapon. Poison was a sophisticated and expensive tool, far beyond the reach of most people.

It was also known as "the Italian weapon." I shivered and wrapped my dressing gown more tightly around me. In recent years, the scar of the wound on my left arm inflicted by Helena's knife started bothering me when the weather turned cool and damp. I now felt the tightness and the pulsing sensation where Doctor Baldazzi had stitched it together. Pausing in front of the rain-streaked window, I gently rubbed the area, an action that usually provided some relief, and thought about the manner of Milda's death and what it could tell me.

The Italians' reputation for using poison as a method of getting rid of their enemies or opponents was widespread, even though plenty of others did, too. Why, even Helena, a Pole, had laced wine with belladonna before she gave it to Don Mantovano on the night she killed him. Although, I reminded myself, she had procured the herb from Doctor Baldazzi.

I pulled the linen coif off my head, let my hair fall loose, and ran my fingers through it, as if that could help me think. Perhaps our deadly reputation was justified, after all. A groan of frustration escaped me—I knew very well why I resisted the idea. If poison led to Italians, then Italians led to Queen Bona, and not only her estranged son would blame her. Scores of others, especially in Kraków, would agree.

I recalled my sister-in-law, before I left for Vilnius, sharing the rumor about Queen Elizabeth's young maid who had died under mysterious circumstances a few days earlier. I had dismissed the allegation of poison as a vilification spread by Chancellor Maciejowski's faction, but was there some truth to it? After all, the similarity of circumstances was uncanny. I had never believed the many accusations Bona had faced over the years—being a poisoner was only one of them—but I had to keep an open mind or I would never get to the truth of what happened to Milda.

❧

I met Chamberlain Opaliński, assigned to aid me in the inquiry, at eight o'clock. As we headed to the main kitchen, he informed me that the duke had ordered the entire cellar, not just his private wine stores, closed except to those with a special permit from now on. It was a sensible precaution.

The kitchen was a bustle of activity, delicious smells of frying eggs and baking bread whetting my appetite. Opaliński commandeered a table in a corner so we could interview each member of the staff. A maid arrived with fresh cheese, fragrant rosemary bread rolls, butter, and a jug of wine.

I studied the color and smelled the contents. "Malvazia," I announced, not without relief.

"The same the Master Cupbearer brought for the duke yesterday morning," the chamberlain said. "I spoke with him to confirm."

"So someone brought the Spanish wine and replaced the one the duke had ordered," I said. *But who, and why?*

"Do you think it was poisoned in the kitchen?" Opaliński asked as we buttered our rolls.

"It's quite possible." I reflected. "I suppose he could have done it elsewhere, but since he had to carry it and could have been asked to share it if he bumped into an acquaintance, my guess is he kept the vial hidden and didn't empty it into the flagon until he reached the kitchen."

The chamberlain scratched his neatly trimmed beard, puzzled. "None of the guards outside saw anyone who didn't belong in the kitchen the entire day, and the only person who came through with flagons of wine was the authorized cupbearer in the morning."

"Then he must have gotten in through that door from the outside."

Opaliński shifted in his seat. "He would have had to get through two sets of doors—from the main courtyard and the delivery door, both of which are kept locked."

I thought about that. "Unless he walked out of the palace through the terrace from the state rooms on the ground floor. As for the delivery door, the key was on the peg, but he could have bribed someone to duplicate it."

Opaliński considered the point, then shook his head. "Too risky. He could have been stopped and interrogated."

"Servants carry wine around all the time, and many noblemen do, too." I thought about that last, then conceded, "Although usually in goblets, not in flagons." I considered the possibilities once more. "He could have worn a disguise or done it late the night before, when there are fewer guards around."

"Done what?"

"Taken the wine to the delivery door and left it there. If there was no delivery during the day, nobody would notice it, and he could have gone back empty-handed to complete his scheme between eight and ten last night."

"Hmm." Opaliński chewed his roll and swallowed. Neither of us had touched the wine yet. "So, one way or another, he gained entrance through the side door under the cover of darkness, replaced the Malvazia with the Spanish—"

"Dumping it outside, most likely," I interjected.

"—then proceeded to poison the Spanish."

"That makes most sense," I said. "He took the vessel with him and left nothing behind that could be traced to a particular person." I felt a grudging admiration. Whoever did this had thought it through.

We finished the rest of our meal, then took a reluctant sip of wine. I suspected we each wanted to show the other that we were not afraid, and that in both cases that was not true. In fact, after that sip, neither of us drank anymore.

Throughout breakfast, we observed the kitchen staff. Many cast furtive glances in our direction. The subdued atmosphere and the puffiness of some eyes told me they already knew what had happened. And why would they not? One of their own had been slain, and the night-duty servants would have spread the news quickly. The duke wanted to keep the death as secret as possible—not unlike his father in 1519, when Helena went on her murderous rampage. It would not work this time either. Once the servants knew, the story—and the attendant rumors—would spread like wildfire.

For nearly three hours, we talked to each member of the staff separately, from the chief cook to the servants who scrubbed the pots and the floors. We learned that Milda had been a good worker but prone to fits of temper, confirming the image of a troubled young woman the duke's cook had already painted. But she did not seem the type to attract enemies, although her peers also admitted that since the new kitchen had been built, they had seen little of her. It seemed that nobody knew Milda closely or was on friendly terms with her. By the time we finished, I could only hope that talking to the dead girl's chamber-mate would yield more information.

When we left the kitchen, Opaliński headed toward the staircase that lead to the servants' quarters on the top floor, but I stopped him. "We should pay a quick visit next door." I pointed toward the private kitchen.

He understood right away.

Inside, we found the cook, alone and grim-faced, washing up after the duke's breakfast. She informed us that Barbara's food had been returned untouched, and that she, the cook, was still awaiting a new maid.

Opaliński assured her that one would be assigned by tonight, then we walked over to the delivery door. Nobody had paid much attention to it the previous night given that the key was in place on its peg; now it was of vital importance as the means of the murderer's access.

"When was the last delivery?" I asked the cook.

"On Saturday."

"Have you or anyone else opened this door since last night?"

She shook her head.

I took a breath and turned the knob. The door yielded. The chamberlain and I exchanged a glance. Over his shoulder, I saw the cook pause at the vat and stare open-mouthed.

"This door's supposta be locked."

We stepped outside into an overcast and chilly morning. The air smelled of damp leaves and wet earth, unmistakable scents of the approaching autumn. We were on the side of the palace facing the river. A cobbled road led from the door and ran the remaining length of the palace wing and then along the wall that enclosed the main courtyard. The path that once served as the main supply route ended at a gate in the courtyard wall.

"The food and wine for the main kitchen is brought in every Saturday morning through a door in the southern wing and undergoes a general inspection there," the chamberlain explained. "Then it's carried to the kitchen through an underground passage. The duke's food still comes through here after it's inspected again by guards who also act as tasters, drinking small samples from every one of the wine casks that come in from the outside."

A double inspection—triple, if you count Milda—and a round-the-clock guard in the kitchen corridor. I marveled at that level of security, fueled by Zygmunt's distrust of his own mother. Was he right to be so suspicious? Whatever the case, the person who wanted to kill Barbara had clearly found a way around it.

I bent to examine the lock but found no obvious signs of manipulation. Opaliński saw that, too. "It had to be a duplicate key," he said. "If the lock was tampered with, there would be marks on it, some scratches, wouldn't there?"

"I suppose," I said, although I had never seen a picked lock before. I looked along the palace wall that ran in the opposite direction from the cobbled road. It was just a grassy lawn that extended toward the corner of the palace, where it merged with the ducal gardens. Three floors above us were the windows of my lodgings.

"How difficult is it to access the gardens from inside the palace?" I asked.

He hesitated. "I wouldn't imagine it's difficult."

"Are the glass doors of the state rooms that open onto the terrace locked at night?"

"They're not," he said, and my certainty that the murderer had taken that route solidified.

"So you *do* believe he was inside the palace last night, and perhaps the night before?" Opaliński lowered his voice, casting a fearful glance over his shoulder, as if someone might be lurking there. "Is it possible that he lives here?"

I matched his volume, so as not to alarm the cook. "Lives or stays as a guest. The entire compound is walled, including the gardens." I swept an arm around. "I imagine trying to scale these walls would be troublesome, especially if you're carrying wine in the dark." Then I added, "But he may be gone already."

Near the beginning of the path, not far from the door, grew a clump of bushes where a flagon of wine could easily have been hidden, covered against the rain, in advance of last night's attack. The whole area looked like a place few people would stray into unless they wanted privacy. But no one would have sought that kind of privacy during the cold and damp of the last two days. I considered the grass, rendered soggy and flat by the overnight rain. I tried but failed to discern whether anyone had recently walked on it or poured the Malvazia out onto it; nonetheless, both seemed at least possible.

"If the killer had a duplicate key, why didn't he lock the door behind him when he left?" Opaliński asked.

"Perhaps he forgot, or Milda arrived early and spooked him. Impossible to tell. But I don't see any other way he could have gained entry."

Yet the point was well taken. The person we sought was not so clever and steely-nerved, after all. He may have covered his tracks inside but inadvertently left us a clue on the way out.

As we climbed the staircase to the servants' floor, Opaliński offered to have all of the kitchen staff interviewed again to see if anyone would admit to having given the delivery door key to a stranger to duplicate.

"I doubt that would be useful," I replied after some consideration. "Doing a search of their possessions for extra ducats they couldn't explain might, but only three people had easy access to that key: the cook, Milda, and the Master Cupbearer, given that the kitchen is always locked when not in use. Milda is dead, so that leaves the cook and the cupbearer, who I'm assuming has his own key to the kitchen?"

"He does," the chamberlain confirmed as we stopped at one of many narrow doors on the attic floor, its ceiling so low I could have touched it if I stretched my arm above my head. The narrowing down of the bribery suspects to two, one of them a high-ranking palace courtier, clearly troubled Opaliński. Leveling accusations at powerful people was always risky, and if the cupbearer proved to be innocent, we would pay a price. "Let's see what we can learn here first," he said with a note of desperation in his voice. I felt sorry for him.

He knocked on the door, the sound sharp and short.

After some moments, a wan-looking girl in a chambermaid's outfit answered. She, too, showed signs of tears. "My Lord Chamberlain." She curtsied, keeping her eyes on the floor. She looked terrified.

When she did not move, Opaliński pushed the door open, and the maid stumbled backward. She righted herself in time to prevent a fall and stood in the middle of the room, head hanging low.

"I sent a message this morning, instructing Oksana to remain here until we spoke to her," Opaliński explained as I took stock of the simple room. It had two wood-framed, narrow beds with a table for a candle beside each one and a shelf for personal effects. The shelf held two combs, a painted wooden casket that might hold a girl's trinkets, and a small book bound in cheap cloth, which I guessed was a breviary, although I doubted either of the maids could read. The only other items of furniture were a washstand with a chipped ceramic bowl and a pitcher, two chairs, and a linen chest. Unsurprisingly, the room was clean, and the two beds—one of which had not been slept in last night—made neatly.

The chamberlain opened the painted casket, but it contained nothing more than some hair pins and a couple of metal brooches that might have been purchased at a fair. He returned it to the shelf and went to the chest that stood against the wall. When opened, it revealed a change of work uniforms for each girl, two pairs of clean if much mended stockings, and two linen dresses.

I took one of the chairs and instructed Oksana to sit on her bed. Opaliński remained standing. "Do you have any idea who might have wished Milda harm?" I asked.

She shook her head without a word, and her lips trembled.

"Can you think of anything that might help us identify who did this to her?"

Again she shook her head wordlessly.

I took a breath, trying to contain my impatience. "Did she confide in you recently? Secrets, for example?"

"No. We weren't friends. She was sullen and bad-tempered. We didn't talk much."

I sighed. There was a good chance I would learn even less here than I had in the kitchen.

I was trying to think of a way to drag more information out of Oksana when I noticed her casting furtive glances toward Milda's bed. I followed her gaze. The thin blanket reached the whole way to the floor, even though on Oksana's it hung only half way down.

I rose and lifted the blanket. Stuffed between the floor and the frame was a bundle of sheets.

Oksana jumped to her feet and burst into tears, covering her face with her palms, like a child. "She begged me not to tell anyone. She said it was only for a few days."

"What was?"

Her tears turned into heaving great sobs that blocked her words.

I put a hand on her shoulder and guided her, gently but firmly, back to the bed. "Calm yourself, girl," I said. "We're here to find out who killed Milda. Anything you tell us can be helpful and won't hurt you. If you are innocent, you have nothing to fear."

It took a long while for Oksana to calm down. At last, she wiped her nose and eyes on her sleeves and said haltingly, "She 'ad a cousin, Jurgis, who fled his village … to look for work … He needed a place to hide until he could make his way south, somewhere he heard they was looking for laborers …"

Opaliński's lips tightened, and he frowned. It was a major breach of security for someone to sneak into the palace and lodge undetected. The captain of the palace guard had much explaining to do. But that was none of my concern. I asked

Oksana, before the chamberlain could be tempted to reprimand her, "When did he arrive?"

"Last Saturday."

The day the food was delivered to the palace. I looked at Opaliński and saw that he thought the same thing. The boy must have found a way to come in with the farmers who brought their produce to the palace. He might have got himself hired as a carrier and after his work was done scurried up the servants' staircase to Milda's chamber.

"And when did he leave?"

"This morning," she said.

"What do you mean, this morning?! He was still here when his cousin was killed?"

She nodded, fresh tears springing to her eyes. "When we learned she was dead, and then the messenger from my lord chamberlain came to tell me to stay 'ere, he decided to run."

I turned to Opaliński. "We must check with the guards if they caught anybody leaving who wasn't supposed to be here."

"I would have heard of it," he said. "Although they are more lax with people who leave than those who come in."

They seem to be lax either way, I refrained from saying. Instead, I addressed the maid again. "So you stuffed his bedding under Milda's bed?"

"I'm sorry, my lady. I didn't know what else to do!"

"It's all right," I said soothingly. Her little deception was the least of our worries. But something else puzzled me. "Why did Milda's cousin need to hide here, instead of going directly south to seek work?"

"It's against the law," she said fearfully.

I gave the chamberlain a quizzical look. He explained. "Peasants in Poland-Lithuania are prohibited from relocating without the landowner's approval, with the exception of women who marry." I had forgotten the oppressive conditions of serfdom in these northeastern lands. Opaliński continued in the dispassionate tone of a servant of state, "It benefits small and middling gentry, but magnates who possess tracts of empty land need every pair of hands they can get, which leads some laborers to abscond from the estate of a master they don't like and settle on a magnate's or a churchman's land. It's hard to find them and bring them back, and their new masters have no interest in giving them up to the law."

"You best find 'im and talk to 'im, my lord," Oksana said. "They often whispered to each other in the night. Milda might have told 'im something she wouldn't have told me. We weren't really that close, like I said."

I sighed. "He could have gone anywhere by now." The Duchy of Lithuania was far larger than the Kingdom of Poland and more sparsely populated, rendering those tracts of land the chamberlain had spoken of very vast indeed.

"He said he'd pay for a bed at an inn tonight and leave tomorrow mornin'," she added, but she did not know which inn he had in mind.

"We'll need a description of this young man," Opaliński said.

The maid frowned. Her scrunched-up nose told me the image in her head had not impressed her. "Thin and scruffy, yellow hair like a mop of straw, dirty rings 'round his neck." She dragged a finger across her throat. "Didn't go near the washbasin the whole time he was 'ere."

The chamberlain rolled his eyes. Oksana had just described most of the local urchins, although this one was somehow able to pay for a bed. Still, we would be looking for a needle in a haystack in a city that had as many inns and taverns as Kraków.

From Oksana's chamber we went to Opaliński's office, where I was glad to see refreshments laid out, for it was past two o'clock in the afternoon. A small but comfortably appointed office, it adjoined the duke's antechamber and offered a refuge from the beehive created by petitioners and courtiers awaiting an audience.

But not today. A few young men idled in the antechamber as we passed through, but their faces showed they had no hope of admittance to Zygmunt's presence.

"I told those who arrived this morning that His Grace was indisposed and wouldn't see anybody," Opaliński said, pouring us each a cup of warm cider. He gave me a look to signify it was only an excuse. "But a few stalwarts will linger, hoping to get noticed and favored for their dedication," he added, not bothering to hide the sarcasm.

I seated myself in a soft upholstered chair across from his desk and took a small fluffy pastry dusted with cinnamon and sugar from a platter. "How fares Barbara?" I asked.

"She's shaken. The duke hasn't left her side since last night."

"He seems very devoted to her."

The chamberlain nodded. "More than he ever was to his wife."

I studied him, trying to discern a deeper meaning behind his words. Did he disapprove of Zygmunt's treatment of the late Elizabeth? By all accounts, the duke had been inconsiderate and unkind, but it was also true that she had been foisted on him, although no more than he upon her. But Opaliński sounded matter-of-fact, and his mild blue eyes shone with wisdom and understanding. Lack of affection was common in arranged political marriages, and the chamberlain, experienced courtier that he was, must have seen his share of them.

"Until this Jurgis is found, there isn't much else we can do," I said, bringing us back to the issue at hand. On the way to his office, Opaliński had sent for the captain of the guard.

"So what do you think, Caterina?" he asked. Somewhere along the way we had switched to the familiar mode of address. "Was Barbara truly the target?"

"Yes," I said cautiously. "I think so. The duke's affair upsets many people, and some of the powerful would welcome her demise." I could not say anymore. I could not level such a grave accusation at anybody without solid evidence.

Opaliński did not have such qualms. "His Grace believes the orders came from Kraków."

"If he already knows who's behind it, why did he order me to find out?" I tried to hide my irritation.

"He wants to be sure." He raised a hand in a placating gesture. "He'll accept the truth whatever it turns out to be," he added diplomatically when I narrowed my eyes at him.

"So let's begin with what we know for certain. The Habsburg envoys brought the Spanish wine to the palace." I won't deny that I felt a certain satisfaction in pointing that out.

"That's true," he admitted. "Although the duke isn't the only person benefiting from Karl von Tilburg's generosity. The ambassador is known to share his wine with those whose favor he seeks. I wouldn't be surprised if he's plying half the court with it to secure pledges to back the imperial marriage suit."

He was right. Had not Zaremba received a flagon, too? Although I was not sure how *his* backing would help the Habsburgs. Perhaps they overestimated his status: Zaremba cut a fine figure, his clothes and bearing suggesting someone higher-born than a knight from the Lithuanian hinterland. But Zaremba had said the same thing as Opaliński: the ambassador was proud of his wine and shared it with many, any one of whom might have attacked Barbara. It seemed like a dead end, although I was not ready to let go of it yet.

"Besides," Opaliński went on, "using their own wine to poison Barbara would be too obvious, wouldn't it?"

"Perhaps that's what they want us to think."

He shook his head, as if he found it hard to believe. Then an idea occurred to him, "But if we're thinking of a German connection, what about the Hohenzollerns?"

"I'm afraid that after so many years in Italy, I'm not familiar with the finer points of your foreign policy," I admitted ruefully.

Opaliński threw his head back, calculating. "It was a decade or so ago. The Elector of Brandenburg appealed to the old king to grant him succession rights to the Duchy of Prussia. The king refused under pressure from Queen Bona. Perhaps committing this crime in the hopes that the queen would be blamed was the Prussians' way of exacting revenge?"

It was far-fetched but not impossible. "Perhaps, but the Habsburg ambassador is here and the Hohenzollern one is not. In any case," I added, "I believe His Grace should query von Tilburg."

Before Opaliński could reply, the door to his office flew open. I turned to see something that brought to my mind the image of a charging bull. The man who came through the door, nearly filling its frame with his broad shoulders, was red in the face, his bushy beard framing a mouth that quivered in barely suppressed rage. Rudy.

The chamberlain rose and bowed courteously but showed little alarm. If anything, a faint shadow of annoyance crossed his features. "My Lord Radziwiłł."

"I was halfway to Nesvizh when a messenger caught up with me to inform me of the attempt on my sister's life," Mikołaj Rudy barked. "What is the meaning of this?"

"It was most unfortunate, but your lady sister is safe, praise God. His Grace is with her."

"I know! Her chamber is locked!" Rudy, I guessed, was not used to having doors barred against him.

"As soon as His Grace comes out, I'll inform him of your lordship's return."

"Hmm." He grunted, although it sounded more like a growl.

Opaliński turned to me. "Have you met Pani Caterina Konarska from Kraków? She is helping me uncover the identity of the man who committed this vile act."

Helping him? But the moment I saw Rudy's glance slide over me, disinterested if not dismissive, I knew why Opaliński had said that.

Barbara's brother made a perfunctory bow in my direction before turning back to the chamberlain. "And what have you found so far?"

"We have only just interviewed—"

"It was that Italian witch! She will interfere in her son's and the duchy's affairs until her last breath," he spat.

I was shocked at the way he referred to the queen. Alluding to her death might even be treason.

Opaliński's face became even more of a courtiers' mask. "We are considering all possibilities."

"There is nothing to consider, my Lord Opaliński." Rudy paced the chamber like a caged bear, and I took a step back. His presence was suffocating—not just because of his physical size but because of the energy of his anger and the ambition he did not bother to hide. I wanted to run out of there.

As if in response to that silent wish, the captain of the guard appeared on the threshold. It was a good opportunity to leave. Before I reached the door of the antechamber, I heard Opaliński's voice give the captain his dispositions.

The search for Jurgis was about to commence.

As night fell and the waiting continued, I had one more thing to do—inform Zaremba that we would not leave the following day. I had not seen him since the previous night and had no desire to pay another visit to his chamber. Nor did I want to explain why I was postponing our departure. I decided to send a note via Rasa saying I was delayed, which I hoped would buy me time. Tomorrow or the next day, the culprit might be found—or at least identified, if he had already left the city—freeing me to return home to deal with the consequences of this strange turn of events.

I scribbled a few words and gave the piece of paper to the maid as she left for the night.

Then I went to bed, still entertaining a shred of hope yet unable to shake off an obscure sense of foreboding. But I was so exhausted that it did not prevent me from falling asleep quickly.

11

September 11th, 1545
Friday

The next morning, there was still no news regarding Milda's cousin. I therefore decided to go and see the route Barbara's would-be assassin had taken from the palace to the kitchen door. I wrapped my cloak around me, for the day, although sunny, was cool.

The state rooms on the ground floor of the main wing all faced the gardens. I stopped in the middle of the formal reception chamber. It was empty but for a guard at each end. The heavy velvet curtains were pushed aside, and the golden-white light of mid-morning poured through the high windows that doubled as doors, their tops crowned with graceful, gilded arches. One of those windows was open, and I moved toward it, ready to plead the need for fresh air should the guards question me. But they said nothing as I slipped outside.

I had glimpsed the gardens from the duke's audience chamber and the banqueting hall upstairs, but the sight that greeted me here was even more splendid. From the stone terrace that ran the length of the wing, I stepped down a graceful staircase into a Mediterranean-style garden, its center occupied by a fountain in the shape of a *syrena.* Half-woman, half-fish in a kneeling position, she held a sword and shield and thrust out her naked, voluptuous torso proudly above a tail covered in scales. It was an old Polish victory symbol that one of the Jagiellon monarchs must have commissioned for his Lithuanian residence. Water bubbled from the platform and trickled around it, giving the statue the illusion of floating. Around the fountain, paths of white gravel radiated in every direction, intersecting with concentric circles of the same stone. Between the paths lay immaculately maintained beds of flowers, past their prime—except for roses that still gave off a sweet scent—but still impressive in their array of varieties and colors.

I stood for a long moment, transfixed by the beauty before me. The lush late-summer aspect conjured an image of ripeness and fertility, although there were no fruit trees—only decorative oaks, maples, and cypresses along the perimeter and a variety of bushes trimmed into rounded or elongated shapes along the gravel paths. Most of the trees were still green, with only the first tentative bursts of color. In another month, the garden would look glorious in its full autumnal splendor. Inevitably, my mind traveled to Konary and its leafy estate. In our orchard, the hard little apples would be ripening into sweet, juicy fruit ready for plucking.

I thought about Sebastian walking among the trees, inspecting them while keeping an eye on the building repairs. I had not thought much about him in these last whirlwind days, but now I missed him. I felt ashamed of some of the things, innocent though they were, that had passed between me and Zaremba. Had my husband and I drifted so far apart that I would entertain the idea of an affair? Silently I promised myself that when I returned home, we would talk about everything that had remained unspoken between us for so long, and we would try again. Hopefully, it was not too late. The thought gave me a pang of anxiety, and I pulled the cloak closer about me.

Shaking off those thoughts, I took the shortest path, which ran left alongside the terrace, to the northeast corner of the palace. It ended where the lawn began, the same lawn I saw when I came out of the kitchen with Opaliński yesterday morning. I was now certain that the person we sought had reached the kitchen by this route sometime after eight o'clock on Wednesday night. Under the cover of darkness, there was little chance of being seen in this area. No one had legitimate business here at night. In fact, the grass, now dry, revealed a faint track leading up to the door. I followed it but could see no discernible footprints that might tell me something about the culprit's type of footwear, size, or, indeed, sex.

Disappointed, I turned to walk back but opted for the less direct route, taking one of the garden paths. The morning breeze had died down, the air was still and clear, and the sun had leached the chill out of it. When I returned to my chambers, I would send Cecilia and Giulio out for a walk. It would be the first real autumn and winter in his life, and I had ordered several warm doublets and jackets for him and a little marten coat. But today, I mused as I lifted my face to the sun and breathed in deeply, he would not need a coat. Today was a perfect late-summer day, perhaps the last of the year …

The sound of gravel crunching under someone's briskly stepping feet interrupted my moment of solitude. The person was approaching from the opposite direction, with a rapid pace that suggested a greater purpose than a morning stroll. My heart beat faster as I prepared for a palace guard to burst out and inform me that Jurgis had been found. I had scarcely had time to think when Maria appeared from around the bend. Her cheeks were flushed from exertion, and she was holding up the front of her red gown—a color I noticed she preferred—lifting it off the ground so I could see her silver satin boots and a bit of white stocking above them. She halted abruptly when she saw me.

"Caterina!" she exclaimed, all smiles. She seemed genuinely pleased to see me. "Where *have* you been?"

I made a quick calculation in my head. I had last seen her on Monday, after my first audience with Zygmunt August. It had been only four days, but so much had happened that it felt like months had passed. "I . . . I have been busy."

"How is little Giulio?"

"He is well, thank you."

She put her arm through mine. "Let's walk together."

"Oh." I said. "I thought you were in a rush."

Maria waved her hand. "I do a brisk walk every morning for exercise. It helps clear my head when I've had too much wine the night before." She winked roguishly at me. From up close, I could see that despite her cheery mood, she looked a little tired, and the skin under her eyes was puffy. I wondered what she had been up to these last few days—and nights. Most likely, not anything I wanted to know.

"Did you hear"—she lowered her voice, bringing it close to a normal volume—"that a maid from the duke's private kitchen was killed with poison?"

So much for secrecy. But at least the rumor was accurate for a change.

"I did." I kept my tone neutral, or so I thought.

Maria stopped abruptly, withdrew her arm from mine, and took a step back. Her face assumed an expression of pretend shock as her eyes shone with excitement. "His Grace didn't ask you to investigate, did he?" As I searched for a response, she exclaimed triumphantly, "He did! Oh my God!"

I neither confirmed nor denied it, but I admired her sharpness. On the road to Vilnius, she had told me she knew about my involvement in Helena's case from her aunt Giovanna, an admission that did not surprise me in the least. And now she put two and two together so quickly. Or perhaps my role had already leaked out.

My continued silence posed no obstacle for Maria, who did not need a partner to talk. She slipped her arm through mine again and resumed walking, half-dragging me with her. "Can you tell me anything? Was she badly contorted? Apparently, her lips and tongue were blue and covered with foam, and her uniform—"

"Maria"—I extricated by arm from hers—"I am not at liberty to discuss what happened. I hope you understand."

She looked momentarily disappointed but rallied quickly. "Do you have a suspect? They say the real target was Barbara—what a surprise!" She snorted. "What amazes me is that it took this long."

"I don't have any suspects."

"They say the queen paid someone to do it." She shrugged, implying that she did not put much stock in it, or perhaps did not care.

"Who says that?" I asked.

"Oh." She gestured vaguely over the tops of the trees in the direction of the city. "Some people I've talked to in the baths."

"Well, I haven't seen any evidence of that, so I can't say."

"The queen is too clever to have done it this way. If you ask me"—Maria paused briefly, then went on as I did not ask—"someone's trying to set her up to take the blame."

Opaliński and I had already speculated about that possibility, but of course I said nothing.

"It may have been one of the other kitchen servants!" she continued, her excitement mounting. "Word is they don't like their new arrangements, and they don't like Barbara because she's prickly and short with them, behaving like she's already grand duchess. And they have access to all the food and drink, so they could easily have evaded the duke's precautions."

I had already dismissed the theory of a disgruntled servant. None of them had the means to put together a plot involving a poison, and they stood to lose a lot more than they could gain if discovered. But that was not the case with many of the nobility. There was no shortage of powerful people who disliked both Bona *and* Barbara, for different reasons. The Habsburgs, for starters. Suppose they hired someone to get rid of the royal mistress by making it look like the queen did it, while paving the way for another Habsburg marriage? Using their own wine would be risky, but they could claim that someone had sabotaged *them* to spoil relations between the empire and Lithuania.

I wanted to share none of these thoughts with Maria. "It's worth considering," I said as I resumed walking, without linking arms with her this time. "By the way," I added, changing the subject, "have you seen Zaremba? We were supposed to leave for Kraków, but now the plans have changed."

The look she gave me had something calculating in it. "I was going to ask you the same thing. I haven't seen him lately." She chuckled, "To be honest, I thought he was with you."

"With me?"

"Oh, come! I see how he looks at you." She lifted her dark, perfectly outlined eyebrows meaningfully. "I thought the feeling was mutual. In fact, I thought that explained your recent disappearance."

"Of course not," I scoffed, more loudly than I intended. "I'm married!"

Maria threw her head back with a hearty laugh. "An impediment that has stopped few."

"Well, it stops *me*." I paused at the foot of the stairs leading up to the terrace. Irritated with the turn this conversation had taken, I wanted to be rid of Maria—the woman was only tolerable in small doses.

She must have noticed my reaction, for she said, in a tone both conciliatory and oddly coaxing, "Don't be cross, Caterina. There is nothing wrong with a little romance when you're away from home. But if you don't find that appealing . . ." She let the phrase hang between us for a heartbeat, then added, seeing that I would not take the bait, "Well, it's up to you." She gave me a pat on the shoulder and turned away in a whirl of crimson skirts.

"If I see him, I'll let him know you were looking for him," she said over her shoulder before she disappeared inside.

I rolled my eyes and followed at a slower pace.

With still no word from Opaliński, I went to supper in the banqueting hall early, before the biggest crowd gathered, which usually happened after seven o'clock on those nights there was a feast. The duke did most of his entertaining on Fridays, Saturdays, and Sundays, although since Barbara's arrival in his life these revels were said to take place more frequently.

It was Friday, but when I arrived, I saw a half-full hall and no musicians. The mood struck me as subdued, at least compared to last Sunday's festivities when I had first seen Barbara. The food, too, was less elaborate. No stuffed swans or sugar unicorns this time. Instead, there were platters of roasted duck, and the pungent smell of fish stew filled the air. Oranges, apples, candied walnuts, and bowls of quince dessert lay ready to lure the lovers of sweet things.

Most likely, this simplicity stemmed from Zygmunt's absence. I had no doubt that rumors were already circulating. These diners would amplify and distort the tales, then take them to the baths and into the town.

I sat next to a middle-aged Polish noblewoman married to a Lithuanian lord. Upon learning that I had come to Vilnius for a consultation with Doctor Nascimbene, she proceeded to regale me with a litany of her own ailments. I strongly suspected most of them were imaginary, given the woman's solid figure and the appetite with which she devoured her duck and chewed on slices of oranges before licking the juice off her fingers.

With feigned attentiveness, I listened to the miracles performed on her person by the Italian physician. I nodded occasionally as I scanned the faces around the hall. Eventually, she turned her attention to the person on her other side, leaving me free to study the diners. Was Milda's killer among us, partaking of the duke's generosity even as he or she plotted to destroy his happiness? I did not see any of the Habsburg emissaries—had they left the city, or would they arrive at the supper late, and which would be more suspicious? I found that I could not answer these questions. The killer had used poisoned wine from Spain, a Habsburg domain, and had carelessly left the kitchen door unlocked; other than that, I had few clues to go on. It was possible, I thought grimly, that our quarry's identity might never be known.

A commotion at the door alerted me to a new arrival, and I was surprised to see Rudy Radziwiłł. Why was he not with his sister, who, given the duke's absence from the public for the second day in a row, must still be unwell?

The duke's secretary Rotundus and the florid-faced courtier Piotr Frikacz came in with Rudy, and the three of them proceeded to the high table and took their customary seats, talking in low voices among themselves. Rudy showed no signs of yesterday's fury, and he surveyed the gathering with a pensive air. Apprehension had replaced last Sunday's confidence, robbing him of his air of a courtier about to reach the pinnacle of influence.

Or he was pretending admirably. I could not get Maria's words out of my head. *Someone is trying to set Bona up to take the blame.* What if Rudy had arranged this attempt on his sister's life? He would not have wanted to kill her, of course. He would have known about the taster, and he would have sacrificed the girl without a second thought—of that I had no doubt—in order to harden the duke's heart against the queen even further. The arrival of the Habsburgs in Vilnius might have pushed Rudy into action. What if they managed to persuade Zygmunt to make another political marriage? It would not necessarily mean giving up Barbara—he could still keep her as a mistress—but the Radziwiłłs' influence would be curtailed.

It made so much sense, and, if true, would be so outrageous that my breath caught in my throat when I tried to imagine how I would tell the duke about it. Would he believe me, or would such an accusation enrage him? He would have to accept it if I had proof, but, of course, I had none.

I left the food on my plate untouched and made my way out of the hall. I needed to share my thoughts with someone, and the only safe person to ask—the only one who might provide some insight into how to proceed—was Chamberlain Opaliński.

I climbed one flight of stairs, but as I turned toward the duke's apartments, a familiar voice stopped me in my tracks. "Good evening." Zaremba stood on the next landing up. With his sword buckled to his belt and his combination of black leather and velvet, his frame outlined by a torch mounted on the wall, I had to admit he looked fetching.

"Panie Zaremba." I inclined my head. I was glad of the dim light, for his presence still unsettled me.

He descended unhurriedly, giving me more time to compose myself. His steps echoed in the empty staircase. "I got your message last night."

"Yes. I'm sorry about the delay." Now that he was closer, I could see that despite his elegant attire, he looked tired. Dark circles under his eyes suggested he had not slept much, and his beard had grown into a stubble across his jaw. Again it occurred to me that he must spend his time in the baths or taverns or one of the city's many brothels. But that was none of my business.

When he did not respond, I made to go. "I have something I must see to."

"May I ask what? Perhaps I can be of help?" Under his courteous exterior, I detected a touch of impatience. He seemed eager to return to Kraków, although I did not know why. If he spent his time in brothels, he could not be that keen to deliver the new headdress to his wife.

"Thank you, but there is no need." Then I changed my mind. Since he would escort me home, he deserved some explanation for the delay. "There's been a death in the palace, and I'm looking into the matter for the duke."

He studied me for a few heartbeats, but his expression was hard to read. "An unexplained death?" he asked. "Do you mean a murder?"

I could not tell from his tone if he had already heard the news. Not for the first time, it struck me how he could make both his voice and his face inscrutable. "There is evidence of foul play, yes."

"Was the victim someone I would know?"

"I don't believe so. The girl who died was a kitchen servant."

"Ah." Silence again. "And the duke asked you to investigate?"

He sounded incredulous. Did he not know about my involvement in Helena's case? I fought off disappointment—quite illogical given how much I disliked talking about her and my part in her arrest. "Yes, and Chamberlain Opaliński is helping me." I felt satisfaction at correcting the record, if only to one person.

"And how are you progressing, signora?" he asked, his gaze narrowing. He was still skeptical.

"I'd rather not discuss it," I said coolly. My irritation rose—at the situation in which I found myself, at Zaremba's condescension, and at his persistent questioning. "But I can't leave yet. If you are in a hurry, however, you should go. I can travel with the courtiers."

"Her Majesty tasked me with bringing you back to Kraków, and I will." He inclined his head slightly, his eyes not leaving my face. It was a deep, penetrating look.

"Then I hope the delay will not be long," I said, taking a step back.

"Please keep me informed." He bowed.

For a moment, neither of us moved. Then he resumed his descent of the staircase, heading toward the banqueting hall.

"I will," I said as he turned to look at me one last time over his shoulder.

When he was gone, I smoothed my gown and ran a hand across my forehead to recompose myself. Then I walked to the door of Zygmunt's apartments, where the guard, already familiar, moved aside to let me in. Inside, the scene differed little from the previous day: a few stalwart courtiers talking in hushed tones, still expectant but with a creeping air of resignation.

I crossed the antechamber toward Opaliński's office and knocked. He bid me enter and rose from his table when I came in, a rare look of animation on his face. "Caterina! Good timing. I was just about to send for you. Jurgis has been found."

Moments later, we were on our way to the southern wing of the palace, where Jurgis waited for us in a chamber within the captain's headquarters. I considered sharing my earlier thoughts regarding Mikołaj Rudy with the chamberlain but decided it would be better to see what the boy had to say. For his part, Opaliński informed me that the search had taken so long because they had started at the cheapest inns in the poorest parts of town but found Jurgis in Under the White Swan, not far from the palace. It was one of the fanciest such establishments in Vilnius, where the best rooms had feather-stuffed mattresses and no fleas.

I was fully prepared for a cleaned-up version of the boy described by Oksana, the result of an older man's generosity. During my frequent travels of late, I had seen more than one handsome youngster pampered by a wealthy patron of particular tastes, whom he accompanied on a business trip or to a country estate while the patron's wife and children remained behind in the city.

I was therefore puzzled to find that Jurgis still fit the maid's depiction exceedingly well. Barefoot, with threadbare trousers and a shirt of indeterminate color that may once have been white, he cut a shabby figure indeed. His matted blond hair looked like it had not seen a comb since Easter. A golden fuzz covered his upper lip and had spread to his cheeks. I guessed his age at around fourteen. Like all peasants, he was tanned and, despite his thinness, well-muscled from hard work.

He was also terrified. His limpid blue eyes shifted from the captain to Opaliński to me like those of a cornered animal, as if he could not decide where the first blow would come from.

The chamberlain ordered the captain to leave us. I looked around for a place to sit but saw few options. The chamber contained a rough-hewn pine table and two hard chairs whose wood bore various greasy and suspiciously rusty stains, as well as cut marks. A bench stood against one wall, covered with a thin, dirty-looking blanket, and from that bench Jurgis rose when we came in. I had no trouble guessing that the place was used as an interrogation room.

Opaliński bade the boy to sit, but as we remained standing—neither of us wishing to take our chances with the rickety chairs—Jurgis sprang to his feet once more. Whether he did so out of respect or because he felt even more intimidated with us looming over him, it was difficult to say. But it took us a good quarter of an hour to persuade him that he was not going to be arrested or sent back home, and that we only wanted information that might help catch his cousin's killer.

"Don't know who killed 'er, I swear!" His fist struck his thin chest with a hollow sound. Then his eyes filled. "Don't know who'd do such a thing. She was a good girl an' an orphan, poor thing. What will my mum say when she finds out?" His voice was close to breaking.

"I don't doubt that she was a good girl," I said reassuringly. "I think, in fact, that she was not the intended target. Somebody wanted to get to Pani Barbara Radziwiłł through her."

The fear in his eyes redoubled. He opened his mouth, then closed it again. I sensed uncertainty in him, as if he were calculating whether to speak or hold his peace. He knew *something.*

"Had she talked to any strangers lately?"

His breath quickened, and a sheen of sweat appeared on his face, but he did not speak.

"If you know anything, Jurgis, you must tell us. Milda's killer committed a grave sin, one he must pay for. As her kin, you want to see justice done for her, don't you?"

I was thinking that I might have to jiggle his conscience further with a few coins, when he said, haltingly, "She … she said there was a man … at the market …"

I held my breath. "Yes?"

"Asked 'er about the duke's mistress."

My heart slowed. "Asked her what, specifically?"

Across from me, Opaliński fixed the boy with an intense look. He was so still I was certain he was not breathing, either.

"When she took 'er meals, what time she went to bed, things like that," he replied. "Said he was an ad … admirer."

The chamberlain and I exchanged a look. This was the first solid clue we'd had since discovering the unlocked delivery door. Now we knew that our suspect was a man, and that he had learned about Barbara's habits from the unfortunate maid.

"And your cousin gave this man the information he wanted?" Opaliński asked like a disappointed parent.

Jurgis nodded and hung his head, as if he himself had committed an indiscretion. But it was more than an indiscretion. It was treason, whether Milda had realized it or not. I wanted to be angry, but I could not, because I guessed her motivation even before Opaliński asked the next logical question.

"Why would she do that?"

There was a long pause during which the boy gathered the courage to say what we both knew was coming. "He gave 'er a silver talon."

Of course. An impoverished serving girl was an easy target, a perfect source of the information the killer needed. What made the whole incident so sad was that if his scheme had succeeded and Barbara had died, he probably would have killed Milda anyway to cover his tracks, perhaps making it look like an accident. The moment she accepted the payment, her fate was sealed.

"Did she tell you when that meeting happened?"

"On Tuesday."

I gasped. The day before she died! Opaliński, too, looked alarmed. Perhaps, like me, he had imagined the murder as the result of some complex, painstaking research and plotting of long duration. But now it appeared that everything had happened within the last few days. Suddenly, solving the crime felt even more urgent.

"Did she say what he looked like?" the chamberlain asked.

Jurgis screwed up his face, trying to recall. "Tall, with a funny black beard." We gazed at him expectantly. "An' 'e spoke like 'e wasn't from around 'ere," he added.

"You mean like a foreigner?"

The boy nodded.

"A German?"

He shrugged.

Not a helpful description, I reflected. A black beard excluded Rudy Radziwiłł, but with half the men in Vilnius bearded, it hardly narrowed the search. The foreign accent also argued against Radziwiłł. Unless it was someone acting on his behalf . . .

"Do you know where the money is now?" I asked. We had not found even a copper coin, much less a silver talon, in the maids' chamber. "Did she spend it all in one day?"

Jurgis's shoulders slumped, and he hung his head again. His reaction told me what had happened.

"You took it from her hiding place when you learned she was dead and had no more use for it," I said gently when he failed to answer. "And you used it to pay for your bed at the White Swan, didn't you?"

All he did in response was nod, still avoiding my gaze. I wondered if he kept the change or let himself be taken advantage of by the innkeeper. The latter, most likely.

Opaliński rolled his eyes with a *what-did-you-expect* look. Still, I was glad he took it in stride. It would have been harder to get any information out of Jurgis if the chamberlain acted like a typical royal interrogator, resorting to threats or torture to exact cooperation.

"Do you remember if that coin was Polish or Lithuanian or came from a different country altogether?" I asked.

Again Jurgis shrugged. He might never have seen a full talon before, and he almost certainly could not read.

"All right," I said. "I appreciate what you've told us so far, and I have just one more question for you."

He looked up, timid yet clearly affected by my acknowledgment. He seemed eager to please.

"Do you know if this man asked Milda for the key to the kitchen where she worked?"

He shook his head with a disappointed air. "She didn't tell me nothing like that."

I reached into the small purse I carried at my belt and pulled out a few silver pennies. "This should buy you a bed and a bowl of stew for a couple of days until you can make your travel arrangements."

"Thank you, my lady." Jurgis took them readily enough, which told me that he had indeed been cheated at the inn.

Shortly afterward, we sent him out of the palace into the dark September night.

It was almost ten o'clock when we returned to the chamberlain's office. The antechamber was empty, the courtiers having given up for the day. It had been a long one for me, too, but, strangely, I did not feel tired. The information Jurgis had given us, although it had fallen short of providing a firm lead, was intriguing.

"He wouldn't have had time to have the key duplicated, so he must have found another way to access the kitchen," I reflected as I bit into a pear from a bowl on Opaliński's desk. I had barely eaten anything all day and was hungry.

"For all we know, he has left the city and is out of our reach." The chamberlain sounded dejected.

"Why are you so sure?"

"You heard the boy. He was a foreigner, hired by"—a momentary hesitation—"someone to get rid of Barbara. If he has any sense, he left Vilnius the same night."

"Not necessarily." I threw my head back, swept up by the familiar thrill of reasoning my way through incomplete evidence. "If I were the assassin"—I took another bite, chewed and swallowed, then lifted up the pinky finger of the hand in which I held the fruit—"I would have waited to see if my target was dead. I wouldn't assume I succeeded just because I'd laid the groundwork. Things can and do go wrong—as we've seen."

"Hmm." Opaliński grunted.

"Speaking of laying the groundwork"—I really wanted to share my suspicions regarding Rudy Radziwiłł, but now that I was sitting just steps away from Zygmunt and Barbara's private quarters, I became aware of just how risky that could be—"I had an idea that might be controversial given ... the current situation."

He spread his arms. "Everything we discuss is confidential. And if we have solid evidence, the duke will welcome any news no matter how unpleasant it might be."

I doubted he would welcome *this*. But I leaned forward, lowered my voice to assure even greater privacy, and laid out my theory regarding Barbara's brother. Opaliński's eyes widened as I spoke. When I finished, he sat back and fell into a thoughtful silence.

"If true, it would be a grave allegation," he said finally, shaking his head. "Grave indeed."

"I know. And I have no evidence except for secondhand information about a 'funny black beard' from a peasant who spent the last week staying illegally at the palace." I could hear my voice pitching higher with the frustration of it. "But it fits," I insisted. "It would help protect the family's interests, push the duke farther away from his mother, and, who knows, perhaps even hasten the marriage—"

I broke off, but it was too late. What I said may have been common knowledge, but it was not to be spoken aloud, and certainly not in front of one of the duke's most trusted men.

But Opaliński only nodded, the slow and deliberate nature of the gesture all but confirming the rumors. "What about the fact that the man spoke with a foreign accent?" he asked.

"That can be faked."

"But why would Mikołaj Radziwiłł need to gather information about his sister's eating habits?" he countered. "I'm sure he's familiar with them, and even if not, there must be easier ways to find out than to stalk her maid at a fish market pretending to be German."

I had thought about that, too. "I grant you it seems illogical. But what if that was the point? Perhaps he set this whole charade up to avoid any suspicion falling on him. There's also a possibility he hired someone to remove himself even further from this. You know him better than I do, but already from my limited experience it's clear that he's ambitious and resourceful, and won't let anything stand in his way. Tell me I'm wrong."

"No." Opaliński shook his head. "Not at all." He let his courtier's mask slip for a moment. "Radziwiłł is clever, cunning, and ruthless. He always thinks several steps ahead. Though I still find it hard to believe, I cannot deny that he would be fully capable of devising a scheme like that." He exhaled heavily, looking unhappy.

"I understand how you feel," I said sympathetically. "But we can't dismiss this possibility simply because Rudy Radziwiłł is a great lord."

"And the duke's best friend, and Barbara's brother!"

"I know."

"If only you offered concrete evidence, Caterina, rather than an argument Socrates himself would be proud of."

"At least I'm offering *something*," I retorted, piqued.

"Your point is taken." He raised his palms in a placating gesture. "I have to admit"—he shook his head again, slowly, in disbelief—"I find this murder most puzzling." Then his face blanched.

"What?" I asked.

"You said earlier that if *you* were the assassin, you wouldn't leave until you made sure the job was done." I inhaled sharply as I grasped the implication before he finished his thought. "If you're right about that, he's still here—and he might try it again."

12

September 12th, 1545
Saturday

After that sobering insight, Opaliński summoned a servant to bring more wine, and we stayed in his office until well past midnight. We wondered what we could do to protect Barbara beyond her self-imposed seclusion and the measures the duke had already taken. In the end, we decided that Opaliński would inform Zygmunt first thing in the morning regarding my suspicions and our belief that Barbara might still be in danger.

Later, when our flagon was nearly empty, we fell into reminiscing about Kraków, where Opaliński had gone to university before spending time at the Faculty of Law in Bologna. It was a typical path toward a high-ranking career at court. Less typical—but not unheard of, especially in Poland—was his social background. The son of a cobbler, he had learned his letters and sums at a church school, but he would have inevitably followed in his father's footsteps had the priest not discovered the young Opaliński's talent for book learning. After tutoring in Latin and enough canon law, the boy had progressed far enough to apply, and gain admittance, to the university founded by the first Jagiellons.

I hoped the wine would loosen the chamberlain's tongue and allow me to learn more about Zygmunt and Barbara. But whether by virtue of his education or natural inclination, he avoided answering my most probing questions without making his evasiveness obvious. I found out nothing new, and I reflected that the duke had chosen wisely by keeping Opaliński in a position that required trust and discretion.

I woke up later than usual on Saturday with a headache that felt like the iron band a torturer might tighten around a prisoner's skull. I sat up with a groan. My body felt heavy, and I panted as I lifted myself out of bed. I was too old for that kind of drinking.

After using the chamber pot and splashing water from the washbasin on my face, I opened the window and stood in my shift in the cool morning breeze to relieve the flashes of heat I experienced too often these days.

The morning was bright but windy. White, feathery clouds scuttled across the sky, plunging the lawn below me into shade, followed by patches of sunshine. On the other side of the wall that separated the palace grounds from the river, the lazily flowing waters of the Neris sparkled silver. The stone of the wall glistened wetly, suggesting it had rained again overnight.

I was just closing the window when a knock on my bedchamber door made me wince as it reverberated through my aching head. I heard Cecilia's voice and bade her come in. She handed me a note on a thick cream paper, which I knew right away came from the chamberlain's office, although it bore no seal. I had seen a stack of them on his desk. I took a breath, hoping it was not bad news.

> *Dear Caterina,*
>
> *I trust you slept well. I have nothing new to report this morning, save that I spoke to His Grace of what we discussed last night.*

He invites you and your son for a walk in the gardens at two o'clock.

P. O.

I had more than enough time to break my fast with the cheese and bread left by Giulio and Cecilia from their own meal. Then I took my time, dressing carefully and pushing my hair into a hairnet of golden thread decorated with pearls, a gift from Sebastian upon our arrival in Kraków. I rarely powdered or rouged my face, but I did so that morning to hide the puffiness that stared back at me from the looking glass. I hoped Zaremba would not take it into his head to visit the gardens, and immediately scolded myself for the thought.

I arrived at the appointed spot by the *syrena* fountain just as the second clang of the tower bell faded. I was surprised to see the duke and his entourage already waiting. Anxiety seized me: a duke—who was also a king, I reminded myself—did not wait for anyone, least of all a minor noblewoman he had met only a few days earlier. Whatever he had summoned me to discuss must be serious. Perhaps my accusation against his trusted advisor and his mistress's brother infuriated him. I barely dared to breathe as I approached the fountain and dropped into a deep curtsy, straining my aging joints. I pressed my lips together to stifle a groan of pain.

With a quick upward flick of his palm, Zygmunt bid me rise, and I complied as fast as I could. "Good morning," he said simply, his face inscrutable.

"Good morning, Your Grace."

In my nervousness, I forgot that Cecilia and Giulio stood behind me until the duke's eyes traveled to them. I turned to see Cecilia frozen in a curtsy of her own with eyes downcast, and Giulio awkwardly executing a man's bow I had hastily taught him an hour earlier. He had forgotten my admonition not to look the duke in the eye and stared at him with a gaze of mixed timidity, curiosity, and excitement. I was about to apologize when Zygmunt smiled—a friendly smile that brightened his face, if only for a moment, before the somber cloud descended again. I remembered Bona's words that her son liked children.

"May it please Your Grace to meet my son Giulio," I said.

"I *am* pleased to make your acquaintance, young man," Zygmunt August said in Italian. "I trust you are feeling better."

"Yes, Your Grace." The little voice piped up.

The duke turned to his attendants—an armed guard and four young courtiers, of whom I knew only Piotr Frikacz—and ordered them to walk behind us at a distance. Then he moved down a nearby path lined with slender cypresses, and I fell in step beside him. Cecilia took Giulio and proceeded ahead of us, also out of earshot. Thus the two of us were assured privacy.

Continuing in Italian, the duke spoke first. "You have a fine boy, Signora Konarska." A wistful note entered his voice. He yearned for an heir, I saw. It brought to my mind the rumors that Barbara was barren, but I pushed the thought aside.

"Thank you, Your Grace," I said. "And thanks to your generosity, he seems to be on his way toward a full recovery now." I smiled as I watched Giulio skipping down the lane ahead of us, his joy at having escaped the confines of our chambers apparent in every movement of his slight form. Every few steps, he paused to pick up stray leaves that had already blown off the trees before resuming his capering.

"I'm glad to hear that," Zygmunt said.

We continued in silence for a while. The sky had become overcast and the wind blustery, tugging at the duke's Spanish cape and my headdress. I hoped the pins securing it in place would hold.

"Chamberlain Opaliński told me about your suspicions regarding Mikołaj Radziwiłł," he said finally, in what I recognized as his characteristic direct manner. His tone was calm, but with a steely edge.

I had to speak carefully. "It's only a theory, Your Grace, and one I didn't formulate lightly. I admit I have no proof, and so that's exactly what it is: a theory." I paused, then added, "You have tasked me with investigating Milda's death, and that's what I'm doing. You haven't put any restrictions on me, and I feel it's important to consider all possibilities, however uncomfortable they may be."

The duke contemplated this for a while. "I have no illusions regarding any of my courtiers," he said at length and with an honesty that surprised me, "but with regards to Mikołaj, I'll accept nothing short of iron-clad evidence. He was a friend to me even before I met Barbara. He supported me for the dukedom before most of the major noble families of Lithuania did so. He knows the strength of my devotion to his sister and would have no reason to test it in such a ... brutal way."

Thus Zygmunt August all but revealed his intentions regarding Barbara Radziwiłł. If he had shared his plans with Mikołaj, then perhaps the duke was right. Yet one of Radziwiłł's ambition might well have decided to ensure that a man of so fickle and inconstant a temperament as Zygmunt's did not change his mind, especially with the Habsburg envoys in town.

But I knew better than to keep pressing that line of argument on the duke without facts to back it up. My instinct told me that if I did, his patience and goodwill would soon run out. I also reminded myself that until I had proof, I needed to keep an open mind, for there were others who would benefit from Barbara's *actual* death.

"Then we must consider alternatives." I paused, and he nodded for me to go on. "Your Grace will forgive me, but"—I felt sweat break out at the nape of my neck and was glad of the cool wind. I had no idea how to speak to the duke about his private life in a way that would not be considered bold, impudent, or at least presumptuous. But speak of it I must. We could not avoid the matter forever—"your relationship with Pani Barbara has upset the marriage plans of royal families across Europe. Even now, the emissaries of Emperor Charles are here at the court, and although I don't know the nature or extent of their mission, I imagine they also wish to ascertain Your Grace's marriage plans."

I had expected a sharp reaction but was again surprised by his quiet, almost resigned, voice. "Yes. They have come to sound out my interest in another alliance with the House of Habsburg."

"Then perhaps they had a hand in what happened. The wine, after all, was theirs."

"I summoned Ambassador von Tilburg last night and questioned him about the wine," he said. "He swore on his honor he had nothing to do with it. He also vouched for everyone who's part of his mission."

"And Your Grace believes him?"

His hesitation was barely perceptible, but it was there. Still, he answered firmly enough. "They are consummate diplomats who wouldn't resort to such heinous methods—or at least such heavy-handed, obvious ones." His last words told me that Zygmunt was not a naïve man. He added, "I am not prepared to risk an international incident by accusing the emperor's men of a grave crime without evidence to substantiate my allegations."

Again, I could not dispute that. We walked for a while without speaking, passing our starting point and beginning a second circle around the gardens. The duke was deep in thought.

"Opaliński tells me that you believe the wine was poisoned in the kitchen just before it was to be sent up to Barbara's chambers?" he asked eventually.

"Yes."

"Then anybody could have done it, whether he acted on Habsburg orders or not." I nodded. "So it proves nothing. My mother could have been behind this."

I had been waiting for that, and the vehemence in his voice told me he favored that theory. Perhaps secretly he *wanted* it to be true. Was his hatred of Bona so deep? But it did not escape me that Zygmunt's own caveats regarding the heavy-handedness and obviousness of the method could also be used to counter his suggestion of the queen's involvement. For she was just as consummate a politician as any Habsburg, if not more. And, unlike with the Habsburgs, no obvious leads pointed in her direction.

Before I could think of a suitable answer—or a diplomatic evasion—the duke said, "Regardless of who masterminded this, we don't know who committed the actual murder. Until we capture that man, we cannot decide who sent him, and Barbara will remain a virtual prisoner in her chambers." There was deep concern in his voice, but also a hint of frustration. "She won't even take a walk in the gardens under guard for fear of an assassin's knife. How long can this go on?"

As we approached a bend in the graveled path, Giulio, who had been out of sight for a while, raced toward me. His left hand was full of brown and golden leaves, and with his right he held up a single flaming red one triumphantly, like a war banner. "*Guarda, mamma! Ho trovato una foglia rossa!*"

In his haste to tell me he found a red leaf, he ignored Zygmunt's presence, and I was mortified. I bent down and spoke in a low, urgent voice, pressing the hand with the leaf to his chest. "I'm talking to His Grace and you must not interrupt. Run back to Cecilia. I apologize—" I turned to the duke and broke off when I saw that smile on his face again.

Zygmunt stretched out his hand, and Giulio gave him his treasure, smiling back. "Why, your face is as flushed as this leaf," the duke said in a merry tone I had never heard from him before—as if he had forgotten his troubles for a moment. He twirled the stem, making a show of admiring the leaf, causing Giulio's cheeks to glow even more. "It's a good sign."

Again I could not help but recall the rumors about Barbara's barrenness, and what they might mean for the duke's hopes for a son. He must have heard the gossip, but he did not seem to care. He was willing to ignore the possible disappointment he faced if he went ahead with the marriage. A measure of his love, I supposed.

I took Giulio gently by the shoulders and was about to send him running ahead when we heard the crunch of feet on gravel. The steps sounded urgent. A moment later, Opaliński appeared in front of us, and, as if on cue, the wind died down, the sudden quiet ringing ominously in my ears. The chamberlain's face was drawn, and although he maintained his courtly composure, it was obvious he brought bad news. An alarmed-looking Cecilia had caught up with us at last, and I gestured for her to take Giulio away. Whatever Opaliński had to say, I did not want my son to hear it.

Opaliński bowed. He placed his right hand flat in the middle of his chest, over his heart, a gesture that did not succeed in stilling its slight tremor. "Your Grace, I was just informed of another poisoning. Somebody has tried to kill Pani Barbara at the Radziwiłł palace."

13

September 12th, 1545
Saturday

"Barbara?" My voice echoed hollowly as my eyes went to the gray stone turrets of the neighboring residence. It didn't make sense.

"Kolanka," Opaliński specified.

The significance of that name sprang from somewhere in the recesses of my mind—Kolanka was Barbara Radziwiłł and Mikołaj Rudy's mother, and her daughter's namesake.

Zygmunt's face blanched, and his gaze followed mine. He held out a hand to signal to the courtiers behind us to maintain their distance. "How is she?" he asked.

"Safe but distraught." Opaliński took a breath. "It was her parlor maid who met with an unfortunate end."

I saw a flicker of terror in the duke's eyes, although he fought to contain it. "I must go there immediately," he said.

"With your permission, I'll go with you, Your Grace," I offered.

Zygmunt bid his guard stay and dismissed the others, while I instructed Cecilia to take Giulio back to our chambers. Standing some distance away, he had not heard the news, but his wide eyes told me that he sensed something was wrong. I kissed him and told him all would be well, and that I would be back in time for supper.

It was a promise I would not be able to keep.

Along with Duke Zygmunt, Chamberlain Opaliński, and the guard I walked to the back of the garden. There we found the small door installed to allow the duke to meet with Barbara before their affair had become known. It was an inconspicuous oakwood door bound in iron and half-obscured by overhanging vines. The guard, who stood nearly six feet tall, had to bend his head to pass under the rounded top.

We stepped into the Radziwiłł palace garden. It was smaller than the duke's, but just as immaculately maintained. On any other day, I would have stopped to admire the charming miniature fountains scattered among the flowerbeds that represented nymphs and sea creatures trickling water into marble basins. But we hurried through this ironically peaceful landscape and headed for the rear of the palace.

None of us spoke until we reached the ornate doors that gave onto the terrace. There we were greeted by a man of dignified bearing, whose only sign of nervousness was the gesture with which he repeatedly smoothed his graying beard. He wore a light blue *żupan*, a long outer robe buttoned in the front and tied with a broad red sash around the waist, but no hat. A pair of bright yellow leather boots completed his outfit, which struck me as very Lithuanian, unlike most of the fashions worn at the court next door.

He executed a deep bow in the duke's direction, then Opaliński introduced him to me as the Radziwiłłs' steward, Dimitr Siemaszko. Before we continued on to Barbara Kolanka's apartments, Opaliński explained my role in the investigation of the murder of the kitchen maid. In response, the steward's lips, partially hidden by a generous moustache, widened into an uncertain but polite smile, and he inclined his head slightly.

The Radziwiłł palace was smaller than its neighbor, with fewer tapestries and none of the priceless artwork of the ducal residence. But it was a fine home, nonetheless, with airy corridors lined with gilded mirrors, ancestral portraits and armor, and doors framed by thick velvet curtains. What struck me most was the quiet. Perhaps it was the effect of today's terrible event, or maybe with the duke and Barbara in residence next door, the entertainment and social functions had shifted there.

As I examined the surroundings, Siemaszko filled us in on what to expect. "My lady fainted when Jovita was discovered dead in her dressing chamber, and it took us some time to restore her to consciousness. She shouldn't be unduly upset."

We nodded with understanding. Then I asked, "Why would a parlor maid drink wine in her mistress's dressing chamber?"

Siemaszko stopped short, causing the rest of us to do the same. He turned. "Forgive me. I should have explained this first. Jovita didn't die from a poisoned drink. She died from wearing a poisoned garment."

"What?" Opaliński's eyes widened in shock.

"Someone sent a ruff as a gift for Pani Barbara. Jovita found it in a box in the dressing chamber and put it around her neck, probably to admire herself in the looking glass. We can only guess what happened next, but at some point, she collapsed from the effects of the poison seeping through her skin and died while trying to tear the thing off her neck."

My heart sank, and not just in response to the gruesome scene painted for me. I took one look at the duke and knew what he was thinking. If poisoned drink was considered the Italian weapon of first choice, a poison-soaked object was a close second. Everyone had heard of sudden deaths at royal and princely courts after someone wore a pair of gloves or a nightdress received as a gift. The fact that such things happened in France and the Spanish lands—not just in Italy—was a nuance I doubted he would bother himself with.

"Is there any indication who the sender might be?" I asked.

Siemaszko spread his arms. "The package was addressed to Barbara Kolanka at the Radziwiłł palace but had no sender's name attached. My deputy interviewed all the servants—we don't have that many—but nobody saw it delivered. It's as if it appeared out of nowhere in the room off the side entrance, where incoming packages are stored before being distributed."

"Has anyone talked to the guards?" I looked around. I had not yet seen any.

"We have only two serving at a time. They are posted at the front gates, facing the street. We don't have any at the side door, though it's always locked." Then he added, almost apologetically, casting an anxious glance at Zygmunt whose brow furrowed when he heard that. "We don't have the same level of security here as there is at His Grace's palace."

Yet this killer was clever enough to have penetrated even the duke's defenses, I thought. The Radziwiłł house must have presented no obstacle at all.

We passed quickly through a small antechamber, where two terrified-looking maids dropped deep curtsies on seeing Zygmunt August, and entered what must have been Barbara Kolanka's sitting chamber. The heavy velvet curtains were half-drawn, and the room was dim with shadows. I could discern three round tables with bowls of fruit and sweetmeats, and upholstered settles such as a gaggle of women might use to embroider together while trading gossip. Fire burned in the grate, but no candles dispelled the gloom.

There were only two people in the room. A woman about my age slumped against the cushions of one of the settles, a lacy handkerchief pressed to her chest. Next to her, in a protective and solicitous pose, sat a younger man who rose upon our arrival, causing the woman's other hand to fall limply on the seat next to her. When he stepped into a patch of diffused gray daylight, I recognized Mikołaj Radziwiłł.

"Your Grace." He bowed, his face tight. "I appreciate your prompt arrival."

"Of course." The duke squeezed Rudy's shoulder in a fraternal gesture. "I have brought with me Signora Konarska, who you may remember is investigating the poisoning at my palace."

Barbara's brother looked at me from under his thick eyebrows, and it was clear he did not remember. When recognition dawned, his mouth twisted in a grimace that was hard to read—it may have been contempt or just annoyance. Without a word to me, he turned back to the duke. "We must find out who's doing this!" His voice was forceful and full of controlled anger. "I won't sit idly by while my family is targeted!"

Zygmunt raised his hand, signaling calm. "We are looking at the evidence. Patience, my friend."

I regarded him with a newfound appreciation for his composure. Barbara's mother, hearing the exchange, rose from the settle with more energy than I would have expected from her and ran toward Zygmunt, sobbing. "Your Grace! The villain who tried to kill my daughter has entered my home! None of us are safe! Protect us—I beg you!"

For a moment, I feared she would throw herself at him, but she fell to her knees while still a step or two away and sank to the floor in a billow of blue silk and silver brocade. Mikołaj Radziwiłł rushed to her side and lifted her onto another settle, where he held her as her shoulders continued to shake for some time before her crying subsided.

The duke sat opposite them and waited for her to calm down. Then he said, "Your daughter is well protected at my palace, and I'll send guards to boost your forces here. You need not fear any more attacks."

"What's the evidence?" Rudy spoke through gritted teeth, looking from the duke to Opaliński, but ignoring me. "Poison then, poison now. The Italian methods. This is coming directly from the other court—" He broke off as the chamberlain cleared his throat loudly in warning.

In Rudy's arms, his mother burst into tears again. He patted her back as if she were a child. "There, mother, under His Grace's guidance we will find who did this and bring him to justice. I promise you on my father's grave."

She nodded into his collarbone but continued to weep.

The vehemence in Mikołaj Rudy's voice sounded authentic, even if his overbearing approach was doing little to soothe his distraught mother's nerves. The duke remained silent even when Rudy all but accused Bona of being behind it. And the silence lingered after he made his vow, the only sound coming from the occasional crackling of logs in the hearth.

As unpleasant as he was, I discerned no signs of Rudy's involvement. I saw nothing but a son's concern for his mother's well-being and an eagerness to take revenge on whoever had tried to kill her. I watched my theory collapse because I could think of no reason why he would have organized a mock attempt on his mother's life. For one thing, the plot was too risky: while he could count on his sister's taster falling victim to any poison in food or drink, he could not predict that the maid would try on the poisoned ruff before her mistress did. This murderer wanted Barbara dead and, when his first attempt failed—seeing no other way to get to her, sequestered under guard as she was—decided to kill her mother. But why?

Barbara Kolanka stopped weeping and wiped her eyes with her handkerchief. Despite the redness and puffiness of her face, I could see where Barbara Radziwiłł got her looks. Kolanka was still an attractive woman, her slim figure with its generous bust and small waist much like her daughter's. The skin of her neck and cleavage, framed by a flattering rim of delicate lace, had lost some of the suppleness of youth, but it did not yet show the wrinkles and blemishes that come with aging.

"Is your maid still as she was found?" Zygmunt asked gently.

She nodded, then squeezed Rudy's hand. "My son told me not to have anything cleared before Doctor Nascimbene arrives"—her voice was soft and melodic like Barbara's—"and before Your Grace's men have had a chance to have a look at her." Her gaze shifted to me with a touch of uncertainty.

"Signora Konarska is helping us," the duke explained again.

I inclined my head, and Kolanka returned the gesture, although the puzzled look did not completely leave her face.

"We would like to see the poor girl now," the duke said, steeling himself. He rose when Barbara's mother pointed toward one corner of the chamber.

Steward Siemaszko moved in the direction indicated, and the three of us followed, leaving Kolanka and Rudy Radziwiłł behind. Siemaszko opened a door covered with the same brocade wallpaper as the rest of the chamber and therefore invisible to anyone unfamiliar with the apartment.

We entered a chamber that was quite unlike the one we had just left, mainly because it had no curtains at the windows and was bathed in light. The ambience of the elder Barbara's dressing chamber was very feminine, filled with vases of white and pink late-summer roses and autumnal chrysanthemums, yellow and orange. They were scattered on windowsills and tables, including the dressing table topped by a gilded mirror and covered with bottles of perfumes and jars of creams in amounts that could rival those of Queen Bona in the old days. A sweet fragrance hung in the air—scents of jasmine and orange blossom mixing with that of the fresh flowers.

Another death scene, even more incongruous than Milda's because of its luxurious surroundings, provided a sharp contrast to this finery. Jovita lay on her back in the middle of the floor, limbs splayed, eyes staring vacantly at the ceiling, her mouth twisted in a grimace of pain. Her left hand was extended, as if, in her final moments, she had flung something as far away from her as possible. Following the line of her fingers, I saw a small ruff resting under the chair of the dressing table. It was made of delicate, nearly translucent lace gathered in petal-like shapes, designed to fit snugly around the neck. It was a fine piece.

And it was deadly. The uneven ends suggested that the girl had taken no time to undo the buttons that secured it in the back; instead, under the force of what must have been searing pain, she had torn it roughly from her neck. She had not acted fast enough, however, for an angry red ring the same width as the ruff, a little more than an inch, encircled her neck. Pustules dotted the ring, and some had broken even before she died, oozing a yellowish fluid that had dried and crusted on her skin.

It was as terrible a way to die as Milda's poisoned wine, but it probably took longer. I shivered at the thought of what they must have suffered in their final moments.

A round box on the dressing table caught my eye. It resembled the one in which Zaremba kept the headdress he had bought for his wife, except in its color: a dark shade of blue, like the sky at midnight, instead of pale pink. A nod from Siemaszko confirmed that that was indeed the box in which the ruff had arrived. Holding it gingerly between my fingers and careful not to touch the rim, I looked it over for any letters or signs that would indicate its origin but found nothing. The box still contained several white silk wrappings; I took a bone-handled comb from the table and poked around but saw nothing underneath them.

"What time was she discovered?" I asked, turning back to Siemaszko. The wind had picked up again, moaning in the eaves somewhere above us.

"A half hour past eleven this morning," he replied. Almost four hours ago.

"By your mistress?"

He shook his head. "By me." Then he added, seeing my look of surprise, "Pani Barbara never rises from her bed before noon. Jovita comes—used to come—at eleven to prepare her attire for the day. This morning, my lady was awakened by muffled sounds that she attributed to a mewling cat somewhere in the garden. She called Jovita, but when she received no response and the crying continued, she rang for another maid. I was in the servants' quarters at the time and saw that the summons came from her bedchamber, so I decided to check on the problem myself since Jovita should have been with her." He paused for a moment, glancing at the body at our feet, the muscles of his throat working. "When I arrived, Pani Barbara told me about the noise and that it had stopped moments before, but she still hadn't seen Jovita. I went to the dressing chamber and found her"—he exhaled forcefully—"like this."

The wind rattled the window panes. The silence that followed the steward's words magnified the sound and gave it an eerie quality. I imagined something invisible trying to break into the chamber. Or maybe—I shuddered—something trying to break out. In some cultures, people open the windows of a room where someone has died to let their soul fly free. But the windows were closed tightly, and the cloying scent of the flowers mixed with that of death rendered the air heavy and oppressive.

I tried to concentrate on the present. I had no idea why the murderer had targeted Barbara's mother, but at least it shortened the list of suspects. Like it or not, I had to remove Rudy Radziwiłł from that list. Two possibilities remained: the Habsburg rulers of the vast territories in Central and Western Europe, who would like nothing better than to add the crown of Poland-Lithuania to their domains; or Queen Bona, who would spare no effort to prevent that from happening. And although either would benefit from Barbara's death, I could not say the same for her mother's.

Nor could I understand why they—whoever "they" were—thought they could murder the duke's inconvenient mistress with poison. It may not have been common knowledge that she used tasters, but one could find that out with a bit of work and a few coins. In fact, their agent had gotten to, and bribed, Milda—the very person hired to taste Barbara's food. The whole plot made no sense.

While contemplating the scene without drawing any conclusions, we heard voices in the sitting chamber. A moment later, Doctor Nascimbene walked in, his black robe billowing behind him. I felt a welcome breeze on my cheeks—an open window somewhere else in the apartment, no doubt. The old physician bowed to the duke, cast one glance at the body, and shook his head sadly but without much surprise—the expression of a man who had seen everything in his long life.

We watched as he checked Jovita's pulse at the wrist and the neck, pressing his fingers against the redness on her skin. Then he examined the eruptions, his unhurried manner telling us what we already knew—that she was beyond help. He rose slowly, gripping the back of the dressing table chair for support, and raised his other hand to forestall Opaliński who had moved to help him up.

"Poisoned clothing," he said when he finally straightened, panting a little. "I have seen this before, but not in many years."

The duke and I exchanged a look. Among the desolation in his eyes I saw a flicker of triumph: before Bona employed him at the court in Kraków, Nascimbene had worked as a medic at the court in Ferrara. The duchess at the time,

Lucrezia Borgia, was Bona's aunt and had her own reputation as a poisoner.

"The ruff is so small," I said, marveling at the dainty object. How innocuous it appeared, to have done so much damage! "Is it possible it killed her so fast?"

"It is," the doctor affirmed. "To make a garment suited for the purpose, the fabric is dipped in a vat of poison and dried. This is repeated several times to increase its deadliness. The skin around the neck is thin so the poison seeps in quickly and kills by paralyzing the breathing muscles, leading to suffocation."

Opaliński and Siemaszko looked queasy. I felt the same way. The duke, true to his reputation for piety—another contradictory trait—crossed himself.

"What are we to do with this ... item?" the steward asked, eyeing the ruff as if it might transform into some mythical creature and attack him.

Nascimbene pulled out a starched handkerchief from his bag. Slowly, he bent forward again, and this time the chamberlain stepped forward, took the cloth from his hand, and scooped the ruff up deftly, without touching it. The ruff ended up in a sort of sack, which he tied into a double knot, then placed on the dressing table.

"Have it burned outside to avoid inhaling noxious vapors," Nascimbene told Siemaszko.

"Can you tell what type of poison was used, *dottore*?" Zygmunt asked.

Nascimbene spread his arms. "I can only guess, Your Grace, but I think I know what killed your kitchen maid."

The chamber fell silent, and the air in my lungs thickened as a voice inside me whispered that I was not going to like what I heard next. The duke motioned the doctor to continue.

"St. Nicholas powder."

My hand flew to my mouth. Zygmunt gasped. But he did not lose his presence of mind; instead, he ordered Siemaszko to dispose of the poisoned ruff according to Nascimbene's instructions. The steward looked unhappy—most likely, he would have preferred to hand off the task to an underling—but he had no choice. The first question after the door closed behind him came from Opaliński, the only one among the remaining four of us without any Italian blood. "What's St. Nicholas powder?"

"A mixture of arsenic, lead, the root and fruit of belladonna, and the extract of cymbalaria, also known as toadflax," Nascimbene explained. I squirmed. Just the sound of those ingredients was unpleasant. "It has no scent and a taste that's easily masked by more pungent food or drink, and it's very deadly. A pinch—or a few drops, if it's liquified—are enough to kill a grown man. It's a popular poison in Italy"—he glanced anxiously at the duke, which showed how astute the old man still was, despite his frail appearance—"because belladonna and toadflax grow there commonly."

Nascimbene was right to fear the duke's reaction. Anyone with any connection to Italy had not only heard of St. Nicholas powder but knew that the poison was invented in Bari. Most Italians associated it with that place. And Bona Sforza grew up in Bari as the heiress to the duchy.

"Are you sure, *dottore*?" the duke asked, a muscle in his jaw twitching.

"As much as I can be, Your Grace," he replied. "I examined Milda's body again on Thursday morning in the mortuary chapel, after I asked the priest and his assistant to move her to a slab near a window. There was still some foam inside her mouth, and in the daylight I saw that it had a bluish tinge to it. The priest is much younger than me and has better eyes, so I asked him to confirm it, and he did. One doesn't often see that kind of discoloration with poisoning, and it gave me pause. I spent the last two days consulting my books, and this morning I finally found what I was looking for—the confirmation that St. Nicholas powder is a poison that produces blue-tinged foam in the victim's mouth."

I tried to take a calm stock of this information, but I already felt a tide of bitterness swelling in my chest. The clues increasingly pointed to Bona. The deaths of these innocents were bad enough, but I also had to consider the possibility that she had used me, sent me on a mission while plotting to have Barbara murdered should I fail. What if suspicion had fallen on *me*, as it surely would have if I had done what she sent me to do? Instead of walking around the gardens with the duke, I would now be chained in a jail, separated from my son, awaiting trial and execution. Could she really be so callous?

I tried to keep my emotions at bay. I could not risk anyone, least of all Zygmunt, noticing any change in me that might give him pause. "Do you think the same person killed both girls?" I asked.

"That's what it looks like to me," Doctor Nascimbene said.

Opaliński nodded agreement. The duke did not answer, but his face told me he, too, believed that.

But did the Habsburgs plan the crime—or Bona? I was not longer sure.

❧

Zygmunt announced he would stay with Barbara's family, leaving the doctor, the chamberlain, and myself to return to the palace by ourselves.

When we stepped onto the terrace of the Radziwiłł palace once more, the clouds from earlier in the day had dispersed and the sun returned. But it gave out less warmth at this afternoon hour, and the wind still whipped around us. Like this rapid and unpredictable chain of events, slipping out of everyone's control—perhaps even the killer's. And who was the culprit? After two deaths, we had yet to come close to identifying him. No matter who issued the orders, the murderer could be anybody callous and greedy enough to accept the assignment. There were many such men in this country, indeed throughout Europe.

As we made our way toward the back of the garden, I heard myself speak, and the words came out before I could stop them. "The duke blames Queen Bona for these murders." Perhaps it was a measure of my own growing anger, but I found relief in saying this. I knew that I would not shock these two inveterate courtiers. "At first I found it hard to believe, but now I'm forced to accept that it may, in fact, be true. And if so, God help us all. The damage to the monarchy will take years to repair."

Nascimbene sighed. "I can't deny the strength of the evidence, but"—he paused in thought—"Her Majesty is too clever not to predict that she would become the prime suspect in a poisoning. If she wanted to remove Barbara from the duke's life ... in this manner, she would have used a method less likely to attract suspicion."

A vague notion rattled in the back of my mind, and then I grasped it. "Like a riding accident." The two men gave me a curious look. "It's happened before."

I told them that when I first moved to Kraków with the queen in 1518, the court was reveling in a scandal involving one of the king's men. I could not recall his name, but he had been accused of killing his wife by tampering with her riding saddle to pave the way for marrying his mistress. Barbara and Zygmunt shared a love of horses, and they often hunted together. If a killer slipped something into her horse's oats or water trough to make the animal nervous and more easily spooked, most people would write off the death as an unfortunate accident.

The doctor and the chamberlain admitted that such a scheme would indeed make more sense than poison, leaving me to wonder how I got into the strange position of imagining more "logical" ways of killing someone.

After we passed through the door, Opaliński locked it behind us. As on the way over, he struggled with the lock, which must have become rusty with disuse since Barbara had moved into Zygmunt's palace. But after two or three tries requiring a knuckle-whitening force, I heard a click, and the key turned.

"The duke has his own," Opaliński explained as we moved away from the door. "By the way, Caterina, it looks like you were right: our man is still here—if not in the palace, then certainly in Vilnius, trying to complete his mission."

For a moment, I blinked at the non sequitur. Then I remembered suggesting last night that the assassin might have stayed around to see whether Barbara succumbed to the poison. And Opaliński warned me that if so, the killer might go after her again. But it never occurred to us that he would attack someone else. Did he have others on his list? Instinctively, I glanced around, as if he might be lurking behind one of the sculpted boxwoods, ready to strike at us, his hapless pursuers.

"I don't know what to think anymore," I admitted. "He may have hired someone to deliver that package"—I pointed a thumb behind me—"to the Radziwiłł palace, or he may have sneaked it in himself under cover of darkness, as he did before. He could have left the city by the time Jovita put that ruff around her neck, or he could still be here." I threw my head back in hopelessness and frustration. "There is no way to know."

"But why her mother?" Opaliński voiced the question that had been vexing me for the past four hours.

Again I tried to figure out why Barbara Radziwiłł's family would also be targeted. Again no clear answer presented itself.

"You assume that it's about the duke's affair, but is there any proof of that?" Doctor Nascimbene's words broke through my thoughts. He slowed his steps. "It looks personal to me. Have you thought about that?"

We arrived at the *syrena* fountain and stopped to let the old man rest. "What do you mean?" I asked. "What could be more personal than a love affair?"

Opaliński, familiar with court intrigue, was quicker than I. "The doctor has a point! The Radziwiłłs aren't popular among the Lithuanian nobility. Much of it is envy, I suppose: they rose swiftly over the last two years. Mikołaj Rudy recognized immediately what was at stake when the old king proposed to elevate his son to the duchy, and the Radziwiłłs didn't hesitate to back his claim. The move paid off handsomely—the duke has gifted him four hundred złotys this year alone, and he won't do anything without consulting Rudy. And there is an even greater reward still to come—"

He left the implication unspoken, but I knew he referred to the marriage. I wanted to say that still left the affair as a motive, but Nascimbene, who kept nodding throughout the chamberlain's explanation, got in first. "That might be reason enough to try to bring them down," he said, "but there is one other thing that's worth considering—the Radziwiłłs are Calvinists."

I did not know that. Calvinists were the strongest Protestant strain in Poland, but there were few adherents to Reform in Lithuania—its Christian population consisted mainly of Catholics and Orthodox, putting Barbara's family in a significant minority. Could religious hatred lie behind these crimes?

Opaliński's theory about resentment of the Radziwiłł family's success struck me as a more likely motive for murder than the religious difference. I had seen plenty of smirks and headshakes when Barbara arrived in the banqueting hall on my first night in Vilnius. And I recalled what Zaremba had told me when we were watching the pagan rite at Gornitsa—that Zygmunt August promoted an atmosphere of toleration in Lithuania and, just as in Poland, religious tensions here were insignificant.

I glanced at Opaliński and saw him open his mouth to reply, only to close it when the sound of footsteps alerted us to the approach of a palace guardsman. He walked toward us with his soldierly gait, and his face betrayed nothing of the news he carried. Yet his purposeful manner convinced me that we were about to have another crisis on our hands.

"My lord chamberlain." The guard came to a stop. "The captain has sent me to find you. It's urgent. It's about the boy Jurgis."

14

September 12th, 1545
Saturday

It was almost supper time, but instead of rejoining my son as I had promised, I again found myself in the captain's office on the ground floor of the palace.

The captain looked grim. He stood next to a stout man with the flushed, shining face of one who enjoys food and drink. He had made an effort to improve his appearance by slicking back his unruly, greasy mane with water, which still glistened in his hair. He wore a leather jerkin too small for his frame, and his stomach—covered in a stained apron—protruded between its unbuttoned flaps. His size gave the impression of physical slowness as he bowed in response to our entrance, but his small dark eyes were animated, the eyes of someone used to counting coin and looking for opportunities to profit. A female version of himself stood next to him—a few inches shorter, but equally chubby and florid-faced. She had at least changed into a clean apron.

I guessed their profession even before the captain introduced him as Ostafi, the owner of the Under the White Swan inn, accompanied by his good wife. The bad feeling I got when I had first seen the guard returned.

"Master Ostafi has come to inform us that the boy we brought here yesterday for questioning was found dead earlier today," the captain explained.

My mind reeled. Opaliński brought his hand slowly up to his forehead in a gesture signifying both disbelief and a sense that we were now dealing with a true catastrophe. For, whether he really cared about young Jurgis's life or not, this new development upended all of our theories. Unlike Barbara and her mother, the boy was poor, his life had no political consequence, and neither did his death. Nothing connected him to the Radziwiłłs.

Except his murdered cousin who had served the duke's mistress.

"When did he die?" Opaliński asked the innkeeper, his voice barely above a whisper.

The man shrugged. "It's hard to say exactly, m'lord. I remember seeing 'im return from the palace round about ten o'clock las' night, and I can't say I saw 'im again after that. I went to 'is room just after two this aft'noon to give 'im 'is daily bill and see if 'e wanted to rent for another night." He inhaled, the memory of the scene clearly upsetting him. "That's when I found 'im on the bed, already cold and mighty stiff with purple bruises on 'is neck." He drew his hand across his throat, and I could see beads of sweat on his forehead.

"If his body was stiff at two, that indicates he was killed during the night, perhaps even late yesterday evening," Doctor Nascimbene said from behind us.

The provision of those firm details by the innkeeper and the doctor's inference helped to anchor my scattered thoughts. "Did you hear any noises or commotion in his room last night?" I asked, assuming the investigator's mantle again.

The couple exchanged a glance, then the innkeeper said, "My wife 'ere told me a man 'ad come searching for a blond boy around midnight."

At first, I did not understand what he meant. "A blond boy?"

The innkeeper cleared his throat. "We get those types sometimes. Often they're just passing through the town, but some of 'em are from 'ere"—a nudge from his wife curtailed the digression before he said too much. "They come in," he went on, "and there's usually a boy or two can be found in the crowd as would be willing to ... entertain for a few coins. We don't force anyone, of course"—he raised two greasy palms in an adamant gesture—"but if they's willing ..." He left the rest unsaid.

In the silence that followed as we absorbed this, the wife looked away, at least having the grace to look ashamed.

I swallowed a queasy feeling. "And what made you think Jurgis was willing?"

The woman shrugged, still not looking anyone in the eye. "I didn't know what to think. He looked like he needed money, and since he 'ad paid for 'is room 'imself, I assumed that's how he'd come by it."

"So you sent that man to his room?"

"I says to 'im there's a blond lad in that there room, I says go and ask if he's willing—"

She went quiet, the stubborn silence of a stunted conscience that believed it had nothing to reproach itself for. It was all I could do not to shake her. Instead I asked, mustering my remaining patience, "Can you describe this man?"

When I first heard that she had seen him, I tried not to get excited. This killer was too clever to simply walk in and start asking questions that might attract attention. Either he sent someone else to do it, or he disguised his appearance. My caution turned out to be justified.

"I didn't see 'is face weel," she said. "'is hood was pulled down over 'is eyes. They all do that."

I fought to keep my disappointment at bay, when she added with a touch of triumph, "But I seen 'is eyes for just a moment as he was walking away. They was blue—and very cold." She puffed out her already large bosom, proud of her perceptiveness.

"Did he have a beard?"

She shook her head, and my heart sank. It meant that the man from the market and Jurgis's killer were not the same person. It was the first indication that we might be up against a team of assassins, and it made everything much more complicated. I glanced at Opaliński, who reciprocated with a dismayed look, leaving me wondering if he had come to the same conclusion.

"Anything that you remember about his attire?" I asked. "Did he wear a doublet or a Lithuanian robe?"

"Can't say, because he wore a cape. It looked funny, though." She screwed up her face. "I haven't seen one like that before. It was brown-like, but not really. It was"—she frowned even more, the effort of thinking obvious for all to see—"*marrone*!"

She looked very satisfied with herself. There were lots of Italians in Vilnius in those days, the duke himself was half-Italian, and no doubt the two innkeepers thought themselves very worldly for knowing a few words of our tongue. I was appalled by her smugness and lack of remorse for her inadvertent role in Jurgis's death.

I glanced at Opaliński, who shook his head to indicate that he had no questions.

"I sent two of my men with a wagon to bring the body here in case you wished to examine it," the captain said.

But it was another hour before they returned and carried Jurgis to the chapel. The priest said a prayer over him, then we waited in the sacristy while rain lashed at the windowpanes and the doctor worked. When he rejoined us, it was to confirm that Jurgis had been strangled and that there were no other signs of violence, or of a carnal act, on him.

In that moment I realized that a small part of me had hoped that perhaps the innkeeper's assumption was correct and the death the result of an illicit encounter in which the boy had agreed to participate. But Nascimbene's verdict stripped me of that illusion. Milda's cousin died because he knew of her meeting with the mysterious man at the market.

But how did the killer know about it? Judging by how terrified Jurgis had been during our interrogation, and how much it had taken for us to get information out of him, Friday must have been the first time he had ever told anyone. If so, there were only two people who were familiar with Jurgis's story—Opaliński and me.

My insides were gripped by an icy chill. Was it possible the chamberlain was in cahoots with the assassins? I could not bring myself to look his way, worried that he would read my suspicion.

"Thank you, *dottore*," I said, trying to keep my voice even. "I think that's all I need to know." I was not quite sure what I meant by that, for Nascimbene's examination shed little light on the case. I think I just wanted to excuse myself from the company without making it obvious.

As I moved to leave the chapel, Opaliński offered to walk me back to my chambers. I declined as politely as I could, my heart pounding. I no longer knew whom I could trust and with whom I was safe. Back in the palace, I kept to the main corridors, cursing the lights that had been dimmed for the night. At the Vilnius court—unlike at Wawel—guards were few and far between. I wondered that they remained so scarce even in the wake of the murders. In places I saw not a single soldier. Perhaps the garrison was too small, and all available hands were needed to protect the duke's apartments and the Radziwiłł palace.

I walked quickly, glancing frequently over my shoulder and keeping away from darkened doorways so as to give myself a chance to run should anyone jump out of the shadows.

When I finally made it to my chambers, I locked and bolted the door, my pulse beating fast.

As I leaned my forehead on the door, waiting for my breathing to slow, I remembered Helena's case and realized that, just like then, nothing here was what it seemed.

15

September 13th, 1545
Sunday

I woke up feeling even worse than the morning before, although I had not had wine last night. I had no energy, and a dull headache pressed against my temples. Outside, the sky was leaden gray and low, and although the rain had stopped, it looked like an unpleasantly damp day. I ran a hand over my forehead and was relieved to find it cool. With three deaths in four days, and the investigation stalled, coming down with a chill was the last thing I needed.

I lay for a long time staring at the wood-paneled ceiling of my bedchamber. Had I really arrived here only a week ago? It seemed like months, but no. It had been seven days, and in that short time, three innocent young people had been brutally killed, and two prominent noblewomen had narrowly avoided the same fate.

How many times had I run through the short list of suspects? I could no longer remember. And my frustration mounted each time. By all appearances, either Bona or the Habsburg envoys were responsible for this. There were enough clues—the Spanish wine, the poisoned ruff—to point in either direction, as well as a motive to support either case. Yet these were savvy and sophisticated players who would not have left themselves exposed to such obvious suspicion.

But it *had* to be one of them, and that morning I was more inclined to place the blame on the imperial envoys, because it was clear to me that Jurgis had been killed because we interrogated him. If the killer acted on the queen's orders, he would not have had enough time to report this development and receive new dispositions—unless he had broad discretion to act. That, however, was not how Bona operated. No matter the project—big or small, important or trivial—she took control and made the decisions herself. Delegation of responsibility made her restless and irritated. More than once, I had heard her express frustration with the representatives who governed Bari and Rossano on her behalf. She was forced to accept the situation, but she did not like it. I found it hard to believe she would give free rein to someone in a matter as sensitive and consequential as this one.

But if the Habsburgs wanted to get rid of Barbara and her mother, who did they use to carry out the scheme, and was Opaliński a part of it?

The last thought made bile rise to my mouth. With no answers to these questions, I got out of bed and sluggishly pulled on my dressing gown. I had skipped supper last night, but I was not hungry. Once again I hoped I was not ill, because I needed a clear mind to come up with a plan of what to do next.

Although I heard someone racketing about in the sitting chamber, Rasa had not yet come to make up the fire in my grate, no doubt informed by Cecilia about how late I had returned last night. It did not take long for the chill to seep into my bones, so I called the maid in, and as she busied herself with the wood and kindling, I decided to do what Maria had suggested days ago—go to the baths. It was mid-morning, and there were no messages from the duke or, to my relief, the chamberlain. Sitting in my lodging, mulling over everything that had happened, seemed pointless. Perhaps with luck I would catch some gossip at the baths that would provide a key to unlocking this mystery.

I forced down some bread spread with comfits in an effort to recover my energy, then made my way to Maria's chambers. They were on the floor below mine, where the titled guests' lodgings were located, although hers were relatively small and at the end of one of the corridors. She was a Sforza relation, but a distant one and low in terms of noble rank. Zygmunt, like his mother, respected hierarchies.

I knocked on the door and waited. I was quite certain she would be in, for she had a habit of staying up late and sleeping late. I knocked again, more loudly, and, after a minute or so, heard a noise on the other side. It could have been someone shuffling around in a haze of sleep, but I thought I also heard whispers. Finally, the door opened, and Maria appeared. She was still in her negligee—satin and lace and feathery trimmings—her hair streaming in black coils around her shoulders. But despite her state of undress, she was alert, as if she had woken a while ago.

Her face broke into an uncertain grin at the sight of me. "Caterina! How good to see you." Then the grin was replaced with a frown of concern. "But you look tired!"

"I am." I hesitated, then decided not to say more on that score. "Can I come in?"

Now it was Maria's turn to hesitate, but only for a moment. "Of course," she said, stepping aside. "Pay no attention to the mess. I told my maid not to come in this morning." Her voice held a peculiar note, somewhere between guilt and defensiveness but very subtle, as if she were about to be caught red-handed.

It did not take me long to realize why. At the foot of a settle in the middle of her well-appointed sitting room was a pair of man's boots, and I saw a cloak bundled on the seat. A belt with a sword lay on the table, and although one sword looks much like another to me, I recognized the other items immediately. The boots were made of tan leather, and the right one had a small bulge at the level of the big toe. The russet cloak was familiar, too. I had last seen it on Wednesday evening resting over a chair in Zaremba's chamber.

Her gaze had a hint of challenge in it, as if she expected me to judge her. But she was amused, too, as I could see from the roguish glint in her eyes and the hint of a smile. She was Maria d'Aragona, after all. I suspected the high color in her cheeks came from the night's exertions rather than embarrassment. The Marchesa del Vasto was not the type to blush.

Before I had a chance to say anything, the door to the bedchamber opened, and Zaremba stepped out. Maria studied me for a reaction, but as I had already guessed the identity of her lover, I managed to keep my face neutral. My gaze strayed toward the clothing on the settle. When I met Zaremba's eyes again, an unspoken recollection of a similar moment in his own room passed between us, and his face hardened. The expression lasted so briefly I wondered if I had imagined it; then he made a small bow, to which I replied by inclining my head. He turned to Maria, as if he wanted to say something but hesitated to do so in my presence. Feeling like an intruder, I took a step back toward the door.

Maria made a gesture as if to detain me, but I was already over the threshold and in the corridor. She followed me out, closing the door behind her. "You have been so busy I had to occupy myself somehow. Otherwise, I would die of boredom!"

Although she lowered her voice, I had no doubt Zaremba could hear every word if he put his ear to the door. I was momentarily embarrassed for him, although that feeling passed quickly.

"Die of boredom, Maria?" I lifted my eyebrows incredulously. "We have been here *a week*. You can attend banquets, ride to the countryside, and so much else."

I recalled my reason for coming here. "Why, you even have your baths," I added. To my dismay, my voice took on a whiny quality. I felt a prickle of tears under my eyelids: after yesterday's events, reclining in a hot bath seemed like the most luxurious thing in the world, and now it was not going to happen.

She saw my eyes fill and misinterpreted it. "I thought you weren't interested in him." She looked mortified. "I asked, surely you remember!"

I sighed impatiently. "Of course I'm not interested. That's not the point."

"Then why are you angry with me?"

I stopped. Yes, why *was* I angry? Why did their relationship matter to me? Did I even want to know? I took a breath, but no words came out.

"In any event," Maria went on, "baths and banquets aren't the same thing. Is it possible that after so many years of marriage you have forgotten the taste of–"

She broke off as I turned away with a grimace. "Not only are you flaunting your affairs, but you mock me for reasons I don't understand," I shot back over my shoulder.

"I'm sorry, Caterina!" She sounded genuinely apologetic. "I didn't mean for it to sound that way."

Without looking back at her, I waved a hand to dismiss the subject. I was almost halfway down the corridor.

"Why did you come to see me, anyway?" she cried. "Are you getting ready to return to Kraków?"

I turned around. "Actually, I was hoping we'd go to the baths, but I see you're busy."

She ignored the sarcasm. "That's an excellent idea!" Her face brightened. "Let's do it! I'm finished here anyway." She motioned with her head toward her door, rolling her eyes. "You've come just in time to rescue me."

Despite my irritation, I had to bite back a laugh. Maria brought her hand to her mouth to stifle a giggle, and for a moment we fought down our mirth. I felt my anger dissipating.

After all, what did I care about Zaremba or about Maria's affairs? I had more important problems on my mind. I had to catch a killer, and I had to bring my son home safely. Nothing else mattered.

❧

An hour later, a hired carriage clattered down the main street, carrying us toward the Turkish baths. The Sunday traffic was lighter, but a number of people and carts nonetheless wended their way through the muddy streets. Church bells tolled in various parts of the city, their unsynchronized sounds discordant, like a quarrelsome conversation. Maria, as I had expected, wanted to know the latest on the investigation.

"At least tell me if it's true that there was also an attempt on Barbara's mother," she pleaded when I tried to remain mum. "I heard it last night in the banqueting hall."

There was no point in denying it, although the speed with which the rumor had spread astonished me. Barely twenty-four hours had passed since Jovita's body was discovered.

"What are you going to do?" she asked when I confirmed it, withholding the news of Jurgis's murder, of which she seemed unaware. Apparently, nobody cared enough about a peasant boy to make him the subject of court gossip.

"I have no idea," I said honestly, and my look of resignation must have been such that Maria put her hand on mine comfortingly. "For all we know, the culprit has left the city—or is getting ready to commit another murder."

Maria shook her head gravely, for once at a loss for words. What I did not tell her was that I carried with me a tiny hope that I might hear something useful at the baths.

We arrived at our destination in a fashionable part of Vilnius, home to middling nobility and host to a small community of Italian artists. Maria explained that the nobles liked to hire them to fill their houses with paintings and sculptures in the French and Italian style.

Despite Maria's assurances, the baths surprised me. I had expected a seedy and suspect establishment, little better than a tavern or a brothel, but this building radiated opulence. Silk hangings decorated the corridors, and ceramic tiles in geometric white and blue patterns, similar to those in the ceiling panels of the ducal palace, lined the walls of the lounge areas, pleasantly warm after the chill outside. In every room, silver incense burners gleamed amid flickering oil lamps set inside holders of delicate painted-glass latticework that brought to mind oriental designs. The distribution of the lamps, suspended from the ceilings on thin iron chains, provided enough light to move around but also offered shadowy areas for those who wanted their identity hidden. I wondered how many of those figures resting in anonymity were highly placed court officials wanting to avoid being pestered for patronage.

Not all of the visitors were so private, however, for I also recognized courtiers from the banqueting hall engaged in subdued conversations in better-lit areas. I strained my ears as we passed for any indication that they were talking about the murders, but I could not make out much.

I released a relieved breath when our changing-room attendant handed us two sleeveless linen shifts along with our towels. We were not to bathe naked! Good that I had resisted the urge to turn back when we stepped down from the carriage and faced the stone building that held the baths. Almost giddily, I slipped the shift over my head behind a silk partition.

With our hair bound up and secured under the towels to form a headgear that resembled a small Turkish turban, Maria and I made our way through the corridors where platters of fruit and confections were placed at intervals for the visitors' enjoyment. In the *caldarium*, the bathing chamber, almond flower- and jasmine-scented steam rose from the water in the center pool, surrounding the lamps suspended above it with yellowish halos. Water also trickled into carved basins in each of the four walls, like small fountains, its sound magnified by the enclosed tiled space, as if we were in a cave. There was something mysterious and adventurous in that sound, and I immediately liked it.

The chamber, a third the size of the banqueting hall in the palace, was not very busy; most people came in the afternoon and evening, Maria informed me when I expressed surprise. The investigator in me was disappointed, but Caterina Konarska could not help but rejoice. The trickling water, the faint notes of a harp that floated in from behind one of the doors, and the murmur of voices promised the relaxation I craved. Only a handful of men and women lounged in the pool. As we descended the tiled steps into the water, one of the women came out and headed for a lounge chair, where a beaker of wine and a plate of fruit awaited her.

Of those remaining, three formed a small circle and spoke in low voices, leisurely splashing the water with their palms. The rest soaked by themselves, one older man appearing to have fallen asleep on the underwater bench. Someone who could have been his son or nephew hovered nearby, presumably to make sure he did not slip under. None of them paid us any attention as we made our way to the empty side of the pool. I was grateful for that, for I felt self-conscious with my arms bare in public. Maria showed no such discomfort, of course, as she waded confidently next to me.

I'd had no idea how tired I was until I immersed my body in hot water. Being enveloped in a wool blanket next to a blazing hearth on a winter's night paled in comparison, because here the warmth permeated quickly to my very core, deeper than skin and muscle. On the bottom of the pool, I felt a warm current flowing over my feet, and I recalled hearing that baths such as these were typically built over a stream. The fresh water flowed over large underground firepits, heating it to this blissful temperature. I marveled at the ingenuity of the idea as I tilted my head back to rest it on the edge of the pool. A moan of pleasure escaped my throat.

Next to me, Maria chuckled. "And to think that less than a week ago you were scandalized at the idea."

"I wasn't scandalized." I rolled my head from side to side. "Well, maybe a little. I imagined men and women running around naked, engaged in all kinds of—"

"Oh, you have a vivid imagination, Caterina!" She laughed. "Although there *are* separate chambers for men and women, where one can bathe naked if one wants to."

"Hmm." I closed my eyes, reveling in the lightness of my body. "Ten years ago I might have tried that, but not now."

"That again!" Maria scoffed. "You still have an alluring figure, you know." She looked down at the shift clinging to my body, and my first instinct was to immerse myself more deeply. But I resisted it; instead, I looked down and had to admit that perhaps she was not entirely wrong. My breasts were still firm enough, and I had so far avoided gaining excessive weight around my waist, although I was by no means as slim as I had been when I had first arrived in Poland in my late twenties.

"You've never told me how old you are," Maria said.

I lifted one sardonic eyebrow in her direction. "Fifty-three."

She sat up. "No!" She clucked her tongue. "I cannot believe it! Same age as Bona, but nowhere near the number of wrinkles, not to mention—" she traced an exaggerated arc with her palms around her midsection in an allusion to the queen's girth.

"She had a tendency toward chubbiness even when she was young."

"Still." Maria sat back again, shaking her head. "You're lucky. I hope to look as good when I'm your age."

Leisurely tracing semicircles under the water with my arms out in front of me, I thought about whether I would have had the courage to bathe in the women-only chamber. Then Maria spoke again, her voice a whisper in my ear, "But just so you know, there's also a mixed-sex chamber where one can swim naked."

I gave her an incredulous look, and she nodded with that mischievous smile of hers, eyes glittering in the light of the lamps. "But I've never been in it."

I looked away so as not to betray the grave doubt I had as to the veracity of that statement. When I did so, I caught sight of a man walking out of the pool. His shift clung wetly to his body, revealing the musculature of a soldier, and his straight bearing seemed to confirm that profession. It brought Zaremba to my mind, and the thought sent heat to my cheeks and to the area I wish I could say was the pit of my stomach, but it was lower.

"I still can't believe you chose Zaremba, of all the men at court," I heard myself say.

"Why?"

Yes, why?

"Well, for one, he's married."

Maria turned her head slowly in my direction. Then she burst out laughing so loud the other bathers stared at us. "*What* are you talking about?"

"He has a wife in Bar."

"He does not!" Tears of mirth were glistening in her eyes. "He hasn't been married and never will be. He says his heart belongs to the army. He's a soldier through and through."

I struggled to hide my confusion. "But he told me he was married–"

"Did he?"

"Yes. Last Wednesday. Why would he lie?"

She scratched her forehead, sending a trickle of water down her smooth skin to disintegrate over her eyebrows. "I have no idea. He tried to seduce you, and mentioning a wife doesn't seem like the best way to accomplish that. It makes no sense."

"No."

"Are you sure you didn't misunderstand?"

I shook my head, thoroughly perplexed. "He had a box in his chamber, which he said contained a headdress for his wife."

Maria gave me a surprised look, and I knew she was not responding to news about the box or the wife. I hastened to explain. "I went to speak to him about organizing our trip home after Giulio's visit to Doctor Nascimbene. That's all."

"That's really odd," Maria thought for some moments. "Perhaps he bought it for a woman and called her a wife for your benefit, not wishing to look like a libertine."

"Does everyone think that because I have been married for twenty-five years, I have forgotten the ways of men?"

She snorted. "Yes."

I gave her a half-smile. "Well, I have not."

"It's all in jest, Caterina." She squeezed my hand, then brought it up to the level of her eyes. "Look, your fingertips are all wrinkled." She lifted up her other hand and examined it. "As are mine. Let's get out and have some wine and grapes. Like they did in ancient Rome!" She laughed, the earthy, carefree sound that was her most endearing quality. Sometimes I envied her zest for life, this *gioia di vivere.*

Our banter continued over the refreshments, but during the carriage ride back to the palace Maria's chatter eluded me because Zaremba and his lie returned to my mind. I dismissed her idea that the headdress was for a lover whom Zaremba called a wife in order not to offend my sensibilities.

Too much had passed between us by that time. But if that was not the case, then who was the headdress for?

The carriage rolled through the streets, past people hunched over or hooded to protect themselves from the misty drizzle that had developed when we were in the baths. It was still only mid-afternoon, but it seemed later because of the steely, low clouds. A thought was pressing at the back of my mind.

Then a single question exploded like a flash of lightning in my head: Was it a headdress?

I sat upright, blood draining from my face.

Maria paused her monologue, of which I had long since lost track, and gave me a quizzical look. "Are you all right?"

"That box in Zaremba's room . . . I never actually saw what was in it. I assumed it was a headdress, but it could have been—"

"What?" Maria frowned. Then she narrowed her eyes. "Why are you so interested in it, anyway? You have gone white."

A terrible thought occurred to me, actually two terrible thoughts, neither of which I wanted to share with Maria—for her own safety, if my guess was correct.

"It's nothing." I waved my hand. "I don't like people lying to me. Besides, I'm still light-headed from the baths. I'll be fine." I turned to the window, doing all I could to hide my trepidation and my impatience and willing the carriage to go faster as it made its way in fits and starts around the traffic clogging the streets. In my head, I was frantically formulating a plan.

By the time we reached the courtyard, I knew what I must do. The thought made my throat dry and caused my heart to pound furiously. I declined Maria's invitation to go to the banqueting hall, no doubt in search of more gossip, telling her I needed to check on Giulio.

At the first floor landing I bid her a hasty goodbye and raced up the stairs the moment I was sure nobody could see me. The rush of blood to my head brought a sudden terrible clarity to my mind as the pieces fell into place. Things that had not made sense before now fit together, and facts I had previously not considered significant assumed the weight of evidence. I was panting by the time I turned onto the final flight of stairs.

I was holding the front of my skirts up and gazing at my feet to avoid tripping, so I nearly collided with the figure at the top of the stairs. The first thing I saw were boots—tan leather. I looked up to find Zaremba in front of me. With a cry that sounded more like a whimper, I took a step backward and almost lost my balance. He grabbed my arm and steadied me but did not let go once I regained my footing. His fingers dug into my flesh, but I was so terrified I did not feel any pain. Nor did I try to extricate myself. It was as if everything inside me froze, and I was incapable of the slightest movement.

"Why such hurry?" He smiled, but his eyes remained watchful. "Is everything all right?"

I swallowed. "Of course. I . . . I spent too much time in the city and need to check on Giulio." I made a supreme effort to collect myself for my son's sake. I needed to get to him as soon as possible, or he might be in grave danger.

Zaremba considered me for a few moments; as usual, I had no idea what he was thinking. I forced an answering smile. "It's been a busy afternoon."

I pulled my arm away, making sure the movement was not too sharp, and he let go. I gathered my skirts and walked past him on weak knees, maintaining enough distance to run if he reached out for me again. "I'll see you tonight at the banquet. It's going to be a big one—it's Sunday." I tried to keep my voice light, but even I could hear the false note.

"I look forward to it." He bowed, but his eyes and their scrutinizing gaze never left me.

I felt them on my back as I walked down the corridor and turned out of his sight. Then I ran as fast as my heeled boots would allow. My hands shook too much to handle the key, and I began banging on the door like a madwoman, images of my son being harmed as punishment for my involvement in the investigation running through my head. The man I had searched for—and found, I believed—had no qualms about endangering the lives of innocent bystanders.

The door opened, revealing Cecilia's alarmed but unbloodied face. I staggered with relief. "Where is Giulio? Is he all right?" I pushed past her into the sitting chamber.

"He's reading," she replied.

I wheeled around and gripped her by the shoulders. Her eyes widened in renewed alarm. "Listen to me, Cecilia," I said, my voice tight. "Take Giulio and make your way out of the palace, but without haste, as if you were just going for a stroll."

"But—"

I cut her off. "Outside the gate, you will hail a carriage immediately." I dropped my grip on her shoulders and beckoned her to follow me to my bedchamber. I lifted the lid of a trunk where I kept my purse and counted out four silver talons. "You will ask the driver to take you to the Turkish baths."

"To the baths? Whatever for?"

I raised a hand to calm her. "Opposite the baths there is an inn called The Lamb and Bell." As Maria and I left the baths, I had the presence of mind to survey the area as we waited for our hired carriage. The inn across the street—its sign showing a white lamb's head with a red bell around its neck—seemed clean enough and, being located in a good part of town, looked like a good place to hide away. "You will go there and wait for me. I'll join you by nightfall. Ask for a room. We will spend the night there."

Cecilia looked so scared I feared she would start crying. I made an effort to keep my voice calm and even. "I can't explain at the moment, but I need your help to get Giulio away from the palace. If you run into anybody on your way—even someone you know—tell them you're taking my son for a walk. Say nothing else. Do you understand me?" I squeezed her hand.

She nodded, blinking.

"Good." I attempted a smile. "Everything will be fine. We'll be on our way home soon." In the back of my mind, I had the desperate thought that the next merchant convoy for Kraków would not leave until Friday. I would have to find another way to get us out of Vilnius, but I could not worry about that then. I had other things to attend to first.

"Just do as I say, and we'll be all right," I repeated, trying to express an assurance I did not feel.

"What about our things? Should we not pack first?"

"Don't worry about that. I'll send for Rasa to help me." I made my way out of the bedchamber. "Put on your cloak, and I'll get Giulio."

My son was curled up on his bed absorbed in a book with gold leaf-edged pages, which I immediately recognized as the gift from Zaremba. I ran up to him and snatched it from his grasp as if it, too, was tainted by poison. Giulio sat up, stunned, his hand reaching instinctively for his possession before falling into his lap.

"What is it, *mamma*?"

I took a deep breath. The last thing I wanted to do was frighten him. "Cecilia will take you for a nice walk right now, darling."

"But I don't want to go for a walk." His face twisted into a grimace. "I want to read my book." He reached out his hand again.

I put the book on the table. "Remember Doctor Nascimbene told you to get more exercise?" The old physician had said no such thing. "You must go outside at least once a day to get some air. Now get up and put your cloak on."

"But I don't want to!" he whined. "It's cold out there."

"Just a bit chilly, darling," I said, summoning my patience. "Nothing your cloak won't keep away." I picked up the wool garment, and suddenly I saw it again, plain as day: Zaremba's cloak thrown over the back of a chair in his chamber on Wednesday night and, just this morning, on Maria's settle. Its strange, indefinable hue that could have been red or brown or a mix of both, depending on the light. *Marrone*—the innkeeper's wife's voice rang out in my head again. *Chestnut.* He was the only man I knew who possessed a cloak of that color.

I turned back to Giulio, who was sitting on the edge of the bed, eyeing the book with a sulky expression. "Put this on right now and go to Cecilia. She's waiting for you." My voice had an edge that made him rise without another complaint.

He shot me an anxious look as I wrapped him in the cloak, and I grasped him in a tight embrace, kissing the top of his head. "Listen to what Cecilia says and don't talk to anyone, stranger or not, do you hear me?" I waited until I felt him nod against my chest. "Good boy. I will see you very soon." I held him at an arm's length and looked him in the eyes. "I love you—never doubt that."

"Ti amo anch'io, mamma."

"Go." I swallowed a knot in my throat and pushed him gently toward the door so he would not see the tears that threatened to spill from my eyes.

They did only when I heard the door close, but I had no time to weep. I set out to work quickly. I opened the trunks and proceeded to throw our clothes, boots, and hats into them.

I left Zaremba's book on the table, vowing I would buy Giulio a replacement as soon as we were back in Poland. I tried to keep all other thoughts out of my mind, but I could not stem the flood of recollections that rushed over me as I went about my work: the door of the house at Gornitsa that Zaremba had supposedly opened with a key he suddenly remembered he had; the small amount of Spanish wine he reluctantly offered me on Wednesday night and his comment about the Habsburg envoys sharing it around at the court; the headdress bought for a wife he did not have, in a box that probably contained another item of clothing altogether . . .

The obviousness of the solution was maddening, given how long it had taken me to figure it out.

When I finished packing the trunks, I sat at the table to write a note to Rasa. I was about to direct her to have our luggage sent to The Lamb and Bell, when it occurred to me that I should not give away our hiding place to anyone. I did not know if I could trust her, I did not know if I could trust anyone anymore. I would have to leave everything behind, except the clothes on our backs. But it could not be helped. Possessions can be replaced, lives cannot.

I tucked the blank sheet inside my bodice. Once I made arrangements for our journey back to Kraków, I would write to Opaliński—no, directly to the duke, for the chamberlain might be Zaremba's accomplice—explaining my discovery and the trail of evidence that had led me to it. I would beg Zygmunt's forgiveness for leaving so suddenly, but I would not disclose where I was staying. By the time he read the letter, I would be on my way home.

With one last regretful look at the packed trunks, I threw my cloak over my shoulders and headed for the door. It was still light out; if I were lucky, I would be reunited with Giulio and Cecilia in time for supper.

I opened the door and collided with a solid bulk that barred me from taking another step.

My cloak, still unclasped, fell to the floor, and my hand flew to my mouth to stifle a whimper rising deep inside me. I knew I would not be seeing my son tonight.

Or perhaps ever again.

16

September 13th, 1545
Sunday

"Are you going somewhere?" Zaremba asked. He had changed out of his elegant black doublet into a padded gambeson with a thin chain mail shirt over it. His sword was buckled at his side. He looked ready—if not for battle, at least for a confrontation. My heart lodged in my throat like a stone.

"Yes," I managed through the stiffness of my jaw muscles. I took a step forward, hoping against the odds that he would move aside, but I collided with him again, as if he were a brick wall. I kept my eyes at the level of his chest so he would not see the fear that tightened its coils around me like a snake. Yet I doubted my ability to hide anything from him—the moment I bumped into him on the staircase an hour earlier, he knew I had guessed his deadly secret.

It was his turn now to take a step forward, forcing me to retreat deeper into the chamber. He closed the door behind him, the sound echoing ominously in the silence.

I was trapped.

Zaremba swept his eyes around the surfaces empty of day-to-day knickknacks. "You *were* on your way out." His gaze rested on the open trunk filled with toys. I offered up a silent curse for my hasty and pointless packing. "And not coming back, I see?"

"I have to go to Giulio." I made a move to go around him again, but he grasped my wrist, lifting my arm in a restraining gesture. "Please," I begged, forcing myself to meet his unblinking gaze, blue and cold.

I was looking into the eyes the innkeeper's wife had seen last Friday night.

He pushed me back, gently but firmly, guiding me toward the settle. "I wish I could, Caterina." His voice was low and distant. He did not seem upset or angry, but then he rarely showed any emotion. He sat opposite me and studied me for a long while, and I had no idea what was building up inside him and what it would make him do to me. But I could not allow myself to think about that. "I wish I could," he repeated.

I made an effort to meet his eyes again. "Then do that, Jakub." Somehow I managed to sneak a note of warmth into my voice in hopes of reminding him of the camaraderie we had once enjoyed—and the kiss we had nearly shared.

In response, he only shook his head. "I can't. I'm sorry."

Anger rose inside me and jostled for space with the fear. Both threatened to make me lose whatever control I still had over my nerves. "You have no right to keep me from leaving the palace."

"Why *are* you leaving the palace?" His tone was still calm.

I swallowed. "What I do around Vilnius is none of your business."

"*I* think," Zaremba said emphatically, "that you're trying to go back to Kraków." He cocked an eyebrow. "Is your investigation finished then?"

I could not respond. He would not believe me if I lied, and if I told the truth . . .

"Is it?" His voice grew a shade louder, and an edge of warning crept into it. I was sure he would have shouted the question at me, if he were not afraid of attracting attention.

"Yes." I held his gaze. "But you already know that. That is why you're here. To stop me from revealing the truth."

Zaremba's face was inscrutable. "And what *is* the truth?"

I wanted to take a deep breath, but my chest would not cooperate. Tense moments passed, during which I tried not to contemplate the terrible danger in which I found myself. At least I had managed to get Giulio to safety. When I could no longer delay, I said quietly, for my lungs still did not supply enough air, "The truth is that you tried to kill Barbara Radziwiłł and her mother but instead murdered three innocent people in cold blood. That's what I know. What I do not know is who paid you to do it."

He expelled air through his nose, a sound that may have expressed derision, or perhaps incredulity at the depth of his failure. "Tell me." He cocked his head. "When did you put it all together?" Whether he realized it or not, I glimpsed something approaching admiration in his face. He saw me as a worthy adversary. "When you saw my clothes in Maria's sitting room this morning and remembered the one thing missing from that picture—the box similar to the one you found in Kolanka's apartments? Or had you already guessed the truth?"

If only I had guessed! Lives might have been saved. I cursed myself again for my blindness to the clues that had been right in front of me since before we even arrived in Vilnius.

"I wish I could say that." I did not bother to hide my bitterness. "I wish I could say that when it became clear someone had broken into the kitchen without leaving a trace, I thought of you. Even yesterday afternoon as I watched the chamberlain struggle with the lock of the garden door, something bothered me about it, but I couldn't think what." My voice rose in vehemence. "But now I know: while I could see the key in Opaliński's hand, that night in Gornitsa you blocked my view with your back and refused my offer of a lantern because you *had no key*. Instead, you were picking the lock with some"—I gestured in the direction of his boots, into which he had reached just before he supposedly found the key, pretending to adjust a buckle—"spy instrument you probably always carry with you."

"Very good, Caterina." He smirked.

"I wish it had occurred to me," I went on, ignoring him, "that you wanted to leave for Kraków on Friday rather than Saturday so as to get out of Vilnius as soon as possible—but only *after* you'd had a chance to assure yourself that your assassination was successful. Yes, the evidence was there all along"—I breathed out in frustration—"but I didn't realize what it meant until only a few hours ago, when Maria told me you were not married."

Zaremba made another derisive sound. "The flesh is weak. Had I not succumbed to her charms, I doubt you would have ever found me out."

"Don't be so sure," I said defiantly, my pulse quickening again. I had to keep him talking. Perhaps Maria would stop by for a visit and alert the guards to my plight. I also had to avoid the temptation to look at the door, which Zaremba had inadvertently left unlocked.

"Who are you working for?" I asked before he had a chance to speak again. "Queen Bona?" My voice trembled. If Zaremba's actions were a betrayal of our budding friendship, Bona's involvement would be doubly so. For what kind of a person would exploit the desperation of the mother of a sick child as a cover for an assassination plot?

Zaremba blinked, seemingly surprised, then shook his head.

A small relief lessened the pressure in my chest, before I reminded myself that I could not trust anything he said. "The Habsburgs then?"

He shook his head again, faint amusement curling the corners of his lips.

Frustration tugged at me. "Don't tell me the Hohenzollerns put you up to it," I blurted out in disbelief.

He laughed then. "No, Caterina, *nobody* put me up to it." His laughter died suddenly, and an ominous cloud crossed his face. "I was working alone."

I stared at him.

"I see you don't believe me."

That was not an option I had ever considered. I ran frantically through all the known facts again and found myself unable to decide whether he was telling the truth. "So the Spanish wine the ambassador sent you was not for the purpose of poisoning Barbara?" I asked, incredulous.

"He really did send it to me as a gesture of friendship, nothing more." Zaremba looked amused. "Although I'm not so vain as to believe that my personal charm was responsible for such generosity. Rather, I suspect it was my work for Captain Pretwicz, who has German blood and has been an advocate for the Habsburgs in Kraków. It's also true," he added, "that von Tilburg likes to share his wine, which worked perfectly for my purposes as a cover." He paused, then corrected himself, "*Almost* worked."

Thinking back on it, it made sense. On Wednesday night—tired and rough-looking because he had just committed a murder—Zaremba told me the Germans had sent him a flagon. He must have used half of it to replace and poison the duke's wine, and he was deep into drinking the other half when I arrived at his chamber. He offered me less than half a cup—and only after I asked him—not because he wanted me gone, but because he had little left. He may also have worried that I might link him to Milda's death through the wine, so he made sure to mention the ambassador's habit of sharing the drink with others.

"How did you manage to bring the wine down to the kitchen without being seen by anyone?"

"You forget that I'm trained in the art of clandestine operations." His face assumed a look of wounded pride, although he may have been mocking me. "I've spent years tracking the enemy through woods and grasslands. I know how to move quietly. Compared with the vastness of the borderland steppe, this palace"—he waved his hand with a deprecating gesture—"with a few snoozing guards, presented no challenge, especially after dark."

The satisfaction of having guessed that last part early on was again clouded by the fact that I should have seen him as a suspect sooner. When I was watching the bonfire ritual at Gornitsa, I had not heard him approach until he was right behind me. He moved soundlessly, like a cat, through that dry autumn grass that would have rustled under anybody else's feet.

"Didn't you care that the duke might have drunk that wine, too?"

"As a spy," he replied with a touch of impatience, as if annoyed at having to repeat himself, "I know how to gather information. The duke doesn't drink after seven o'clock, except at a banquet. My goal would have been easily accomplished had that silly girl not decided to help herself to the wine while she was at it."

I felt the stab of anger at the callous way in which he referred to Milda's death, but I swallowed it down. There was no need to ask how he had found out that Milda was Barbara's kitchen maid: his espionage training and a few well-placed coins.

"Why did you do it?" I asked him then. "Kill all these people, try to kill Barbara?"

His reply came without hesitation. It was as if he welcomed the opportunity to unburden himself. "It's an open secret that the duke plans to marry Barbara as soon as the old king is dead, which won't be long. It's a reckless scheme"—he repeated what he had already told me at Gornitsa—"that will bring no beneficial alliance to strengthen our borders, especially in the south where we are constantly threatened by Tatars." He fell silent, although I had a distinct sense that he wanted to say more.

"Queen Bona would agree with you on that," I said cautiously.

"Probably, but she did *not* direct me," he said emphatically, "if that's what you're implying. I already told you: nobody did. I'd planned the whole thing myself even *before* Captain Pretwicz selected me to escort you to Vilnius. The queen requested one of his men, someone from outside court circles, to protect you on this sensitive mission, and I volunteered." He smiled briefly, then grew somber again, "I really hoped you would succeed in persuading the duke to break it off with Barbara and my intervention wouldn't be necessary—"

He broke off as voices rang out in the corridor. Hope flared in my chest like a bright lamp, and I felt a scream forming in my throat. But before I could utter it, Zaremba put a finger to his mouth and bent down to reach into his boot, his eyes never leaving me. I gazed fascinated as he plunged his hand inside and withdrew the hilt of a small dagger. He did not pull the weapon out fully, just enough for me to catch a glimpse of a steely, cold blade. The catlike gesture and his gaze were eloquent in the warning they conveyed. The sound died in my throat. We sat quietly, listening to a group of women laughing and talking as they passed by my door, until their voices grew fainter and eventually faded. Then it felt like we were alone in the castle.

But even as my hope of a rescue waned with each receding footstep, Zaremba's last statement echoed in my mind. I felt a touch of pity for him, which disconcerted me. He was not a cold-blooded murderer—or at least had not been from the beginning. I could even credit him with noble intentions. But I needed to keep any sympathy at bay, because it might lead me to blame myself even more for the loss of three lives as a result of the failure of my mission. I knew I was capable of that; it had happened before, with the murders at Wawel. I needed to remind myself that I was not the one who had slipped poison into wine and soaked a ruff in a deadly substance. He had, and he must pay for it. If I could find a way to get out of this chamber alive, I would ensure he did.

He had fallen into a pensive mood, his gaze straying to the window, where the drizzle had thickened and become a kind of mist. Soon, it would be dark. My eyes went to the door, and I forced myself to look away. I needed to buy more time.

"After you murdered the kitchen maid, you still tried to get close to me." It took me a moment to form the words, such was the humiliation I felt. "So you could seduce me." He turned his gaze from the window, and I met it. "I've been wondering why, and I think it was so you could keep up to date on the investigation while deflecting any suspicion from yourself." The memory of his lips just inches from mine rose unbidden, and I could hear his voice in my ear, calm and even, not thickened with emotion or desire. It was all a ruse, and it nearly led me to make an unforgivable mistake.

I felt a sudden, desperate urge to go home to Sebastian, to confess everything and beg his forgiveness. Would I ever see him again? I dared not think about that, lest my self-control slip entirely. Instead I said, enunciating every word, "You hoped to use my feelings to cloud my judgment, so I would be less likely to suspect you." I could not keep scorn from my voice, but also a certain satisfaction. Knowing that I had resisted him was a small blessing in this dire situation.

"I had no idea you were the one who solved Helena Lipińska's case all those years ago until Maria told me about it the day we arrived in Vilnius," he said. I remembered him staring at me with unease after last Sunday's banquet, our first evening at the palace, and now I understood why. "I must confess, it was rather inconvenient, but I couldn't back out. Instead I came up with a contingency plan."

I looked away in disgust. He had tried to use me, just as Bona had used me. I was nothing but a pawn to them. Yet it also occurred to me that he could have killed me at any time during the past week. Perhaps he had kept a discreet eye on me and, seeing how stumped I was, did not think much of my chances of unmasking him. That he turned out to be wrong was bittersweet, for I had played into his hands and given him this one last opportunity to dispose of me.

Outside, the light was fading, and mist clung to the windows, intensifying my sense of entrapment and isolation. The old scar on my arm twinged. In another hour it would be suppertime, palace residents and guests heading for the Sunday banquet, and Rasa would arrive for her evening chores. If I lived that long, would she be able to help me, or would she become another victim? How many more lives would Zaremba's folly consume?

"We need light," I said. "I can get candles out of the trunk."

He hesitated. "But only one." Then, before I had the chance to move, he rose, placing himself between me and the door. "I'll get it."

"They are all the way at the bottom," I said.

He went over and dragged the trunk across the floor toward me, then gestured for me to look. I removed a few items from the top, placing them on the settle next to me, then plunged my hand in and rummaged around until I found it—the thickest of our remaining candles, with the most wax left on it.

I lighted it, willing my hands not to shake, and placed it on the table between us. One glance at Zaremba's face in the new light told me that he was getting ready to end our encounter, but I also saw that despite his bluster he had not yet gathered sufficient courage to take that step. My reprieve would not last long, for he was a desperate man. I needed to keep his mind away from that path.

"Can you tell me the truth?" I asked quietly.

His head whipped up. "The truth about what?" His eyes narrowed. "You have already guessed the truth, and I have confessed everything to you."

"Not everything. I want to know your true motivations, the *real* reason behind these murders," I pressed. "Many people aren't happy with this affair, but you are the only one who has killed to stop it. Surely, your concern about border security wasn't sufficient to disregard the laws of God and man in this way."

I held my breath. I had taken a risk with my question: it would either infuriate him and hasten my end, or it would cause him to open up to me. I had already glimpsed the weight of this burden on his conscience, or whatever was left of it.

After some moments, the surprise melted from his face, and his gaze turned inward. Silently, he stroked his chin, where a new reddish-blond beard was growing, and there was a sadness about him I had not seen before. He was revisiting something painful.

"My father was a knight who had dedicated his life to the defense of the southern border," he said at length, and my mind traveled back to that night at Gornitsa. That was the first time he had mentioned his father's service, and it had brought up an unexpected emotion. Now I was about to learn why. "I grew up moving with him and my mother from one posting to another, living in a succession of garrison towns," he continued. "It was a difficult life, full of danger and constant change, but I loved it because I was proud of my father's role in keeping the encroaching Moldovans and Tatars at bay." He paused, and the muscles of his jaw worked. "In the summer of 1522, we'd been living in a small outpost, an old wooden enclosure in the Vinnytsia region, for several peaceful months. It wasn't a place where anything was expected to happen, but Mikołaj Firlej, who was Crown Hetman at the time, liked to rotate his troops among the different locations as a signal to potential attackers that we had a strong defense."

He hunched and lowered his head. His fist closed around a section of his chain mail, and for a moment I thought the iron links would snap. But then he let go, smoothing them into place with a sharp gesture. He took a deep breath and went on, "One night we were awakened by a sudden clash of weapons; screams of men, women, and horses; and the otherworldly howls of a band of raiders who had burst out of the surrounding forest. My father didn't even have time to put on his armor; he just ran out in his shirt with a sword in his hand, yelling for us to stay inside our quarters. My mother fell to her knees and started to pray, while I slipped out and climbed the stairs to the top of the inner wall. I could see that the invaders had already broken into the outer ward, cutting down any living creature in their path with their curved swords."

From his gaze, now fixed somewhere on the wall behind me, I could guess that the hellish scene was playing out in front of him again. Across the span of more than twenty years, the terrified youth was recounting the horror he had witnessed that night. "The swordsmen were backed by archers whose skill was such that they could shoot with precision from atop galloping horses. Many of the archers were shooting flaming arrows. That was the key to their success—there weren't enough of them to defeat us on their own, but the old wood of the central tower and the outer buildings was like a tinderbox, and the arrows set it ablaze in no time.

"I ran back to our house, but it was already on fire. I tried to find my father, but he was in the tower with the other defenders, and soon the damage to the wall was such that gaps began to open, through which the Tatars poured into the inner courtyard. I ran for one of the gaps to escape, but a raider slashed at me with his sword." He absently fingered the scar that ran from his temple to his collarbone. "I fell and he moved on, assuming I was dead, but I crawled through the ruins and out into the safety of the forest. From there, I watched the fire against the midnight sky as it consumed the outpost and burned it to the ground.

"At dawn the Tatars rounded up the few survivors, mainly women and children, tied them together with ropes, and marched them away. I'd heard enough stories to know that those who managed to live through the journey would be given as slaves to the khan or his cronies, or sold off to the Turks in Istanbul. It was then that I made a vow to my parents—whose bodies were still smoldering among the ashes—that I would devote my life to protecting our borders from those barbarians."

I shivered, and not just because of the chill in the unheated chamber. "What a terrible thing to have lived through at such a young age." I said through the tightness in my throat. "Nobody should see their parents die like that."

He buried his face in his hands. When he looked up again, his eyes were blazing. "And I have kept my promise!" He banged a clenched fist on his chest, as if he were in a confessional. "I joined the defense forces as soon as I turned sixteen the following spring and eventually came to serve under Bernard Pretwicz. I moved with him to Bar when the queen made him *starosta* there. I have served with him for years in defense of that border. I've been wounded, almost killed twice, but that region has never been safer. But now"—his voice cracked—"all this loss and work and sacrifice is for naught because Bona's pampered milksop of a son has taken a fancy to that Radziwiłł harlot."

I stared at him. My horror at what he had experienced as a youth mingled with equal horror at the pain he had inflicted on others. Yet I saw how the past haunted him. The words had poured out of him. He must have thought them, perhaps even spoken them to himself during sleepless nights, countless times, until they became an obsession, an incantation that had overtaken reason and led him to hatch this disastrous plot.

"Destroying Barbara is no guarantee that the duke will marry a suitable princess," I pointed out.

"But at least there would be hope!" Zaremba raised his voice in desperation. "Perhaps someone can find a way to persuade him to seek an alliance to take on those savages—and the Turks, while he's at it, instead of bankrupting the country by paying them off! Do you know that the new treaty with Khan Sahib Girei has cost the treasury two thousand red złotys and a further thirteen thousand in luxury cloth? Do you?"

I had no idea but also no reason to doubt what he said. That kind of appeasement was in line with Zygmunt's personality and ruling style. Yet foreign policy did not matter to me right then. I was tempted to refute Zaremba's self-justification, but in the end I refrained. I recognized the futility of arguing with him. He was a grown man, set in his ways and so wrapped up in his cause, which he approached with the fervor worthy of a religious zealot, that I would only waste my breath on such moralizing.

"I understand why you fear for your country's future," I said, choosing my words with care. "I even understand why you might see Barbara as a threat to the promise you made your parents. But I cannot see any reason why you wanted to kill her mother as well."

"It's simple, really." He threw his head back, as if to shake off the weight of the dredged-up memories. "I had failed when it came to the daughter, and the duke boosted the already tight security around her. I would have had to abandon the project altogether, but fortunately I was prepared." I winced at the word "project" used to describe a murder plan, but he did not notice. "I'd brought the poisoned ruff with me as an alternative means to kill Barbara, and now decided to use it against her mother. It was easy. I only had to carefully repaint the pink box in which I kept it, and which you had accidentally seen in my chamber. Slipping it into the Radziwiłł palace was no challenge, either. But to answer your question"—he held out his palms in an explanatory gesture—"Kolanka's death was supposed to intimidate the family so that, in fear for their lives, they would return to their country estate and leave Zygmunt alone to focus on what's important for Poland-Lithuania."

At that, I could not help but laugh aloud. Even I, whose acquaintance with the Radziwiłłs and with Lithuanian politics was superficial at best, understood that they were not so easily cowed. Lithuanians were a stubborn lot—a trait compounded, in the case of the Radziwiłłs, by boundless ambition, great wealth, and an unending hunger for power. Rudy would sacrifice his own mother for a chance to climb higher up the ladder. As for the duke, many courtiers in both capitals, as well as the queen herself, believed that Zygmunt would put his personal interests above those of the Crown any day, especially when it came to Barbara.

Zaremba's naïveté was stunning. He was no criminal mastermind, I realized, but a man lashing out blindly to avenge a wrong that no court or judge could redress.

"What's so amusing, Caterina?" he asked angrily. "Perhaps you do not fully appreciate the mess you have gotten yourself into?"

"Oh, I do," I assured him. I cast around for another distraction, and some instinct told me to bring the conversation back to him again. "Much more so than that poor boy Jurgis you throttled to death. Don't you feel any remorse about *that*?"

He paled, and I saw that my words had hit the mark. Earlier, he had spoken so casually about Milda's death. Was it possible that he identified more with the boy, almost the same age he had been when his father died?

"That was unfortunate," he said through clenched teeth. "That was *not* part of the plan. But I had no choice. The boy knew about my encounter with his sister at the market, and I couldn't risk him being called to testify before a judge, if it ever came to that."

"Snuffing out a life like that"—I snapped my fingers—"just to tie up a loose end."

"To protect myself."

"Wait." I paused. "You said 'sister,' but Milda—that was the maid's name, by the way"—I added emphatically—"wasn't his sister."

"Who was she then?"

"His cousin. He came to stay with her at the palace for a few days last week." Then I asked, "How did you even know about him? Did she tell you at the market?"

"I didn't know about his existence until the night I had to silence him." Seeing my perplexity, he explained, "After I'd met you on the stairs—it seems to happen a lot to us"—he attempted a joke, but I did not oblige him by laughing—"well, after I'd met you on Friday heading for the duke's apartments, I had a feeling something important had transpired in your investigation. After I'd bid you goodnight, I didn't go downstairs. I waited on the landing until I heard the doors of Zygmunt's antechamber close, then went back up and hid behind a door curtain until you and the chamberlain came out. I followed you at a distance to the guards' quarters, where again I waited. Finally you came out, along with the captain and the boy. The child was blond, like Barbara's maid. I assumed he was her brother, or why would you have brought him in? I was afraid she'd described me to him, so"—he shrugged to signify helplessness—"I had to do what it took to stop him from talking further. I followed him out of the palace and to the White Swan."

The enormity of our inadvertent role in Jurgis's death notwithstanding, I had to admire Pretwicz for having chosen and trained Zaremba as a spy. He had managed to avoid detection not just by me and Opaliński but also by the captain of the guards, a military man himself. And the guards he passed on the way as he followed us did not see anything suspicious about him, either, that would have warranted stopping him for questioning. In that, at least, he had outwitted us all.

"But you weren't wearing your chestnut cloak when I met you that night!" I suddenly remembered the White Swan landlady's description of this outer garment.

"Well observed." He inclined his head in a mockery of gallant acknowledgment. "I didn't have time to fetch my cloak as I followed him out, but once I knew where he stayed, I returned to the palace for it so I could hide my face under the hood. Then I went back to the inn to ensure his silence."

I fought down repugnance. "You should know that Jurgis didn't know your true appearance," I said. "Milda had only mentioned a 'funny black beard.' My guess is it was fake—you'd colored it before you met her and then shaved it off."

His expression turned sullen. "I bought a dye from a hag in the street who promised I'd be able to remove it easily. I applied it with a comb in an alley, and after I met the girl I sneaked into a tavern yard near the market to wash it off in a bucket of water"—he twisted his mouth in disgust while rubbing his fingers, presumably to indicate the messiness of the process—"but it wouldn't come off. So I went to a barber."

"She also told Jurgis about the foreign accent," I added, "but I foolishly assumed it was German, while in reality it was Polish. Still, either piece of information would hardly have counted as identifying evidence before a judge, so you killed that boy for no reason."

His face darkened, and for a moment he looked pained again. It was more satisfying than if I had punched him. But before I could relish the effect fully, my heart leapt at a sound outside. With baited breath I strained my ears, but all was quiet again; it seemed to have been one of those groaning noises that large buildings sometimes make as they settle.

"How did you know you'd find me here alone?" I asked to keep him talking.

"You're a mother, Caterina." He smiled with a touch of condescension, as if that were a weakness. "After our brief encounter earlier on your way back from the baths—yes, Maria told me where you were going this afternoon—I realized you had guessed the truth. And I knew your first instinct would be to protect your son. No more than ten minutes passed between the moment you disappeared into your rooms and Giulio's and Cecilia's hasty departure."

Of course. How many times did I have to be reminded that spying was in his blood? I could only be grateful he had chosen to go after me right away instead of harming Giulio first.

Silence fell, thick and sinister. Zaremba studied me, his eyes distant and cold again. Time was running out. I cast around for more things to ask, and although there was something in the back of my mind, one last question mark, I could not think of it. Fear had taken hold of me again, stronger than ever. It was completely dark outside, the banquet must be about to start, but nobody was coming. It occurred to me that perhaps he had killed Rasa, too. I needed to get away from that chamber, with or without help, if I wanted to see another day.

"Jakub." However much it pained me, I again addressed him by his Christian name. "I want to join Giulio and Cecilia. They are waiting for me. I want to leave this town and forget everything that's happened."

He rose from his chair and came to sit on the settle next to me, pushing aside the items I had taken out of the trunk earlier. He took my chin between his thumb and forefinger, and the only reason I did not pull away was because everything inside me stiffened. But I felt his touch on my skin—gentle but firm, as it had been earlier when he pushed me away from the door. It was the touch of a man capable of violence, if he deemed it necessary. He stroked my cheek with his calloused soldier's thumb, and I shut my eyes tightly. I did not want to see his face, and I did not want him to see my terror.

"For what it's worth, I admire you." His voice was strangely caressing. "And you are still a beautiful woman." A few days earlier, such words would have given rise to a shameful stirring in my blood, but not now. My body was paralyzed by fear, although, oddly, my senses sharpened. I strained my ears again for any sound of footsteps, but although I could hear the wood creaking and the gusts of wind rattling the shutters, no human sound reached me.

"Please let me go," I said plaintively. "I won't tell anyone." I knew how hopeless it was to appeal to him this way. I would not have believed me, if I were him. He had nothing to gain and everything to lose from doing what I asked.

"I like you," he repeated in the same wondering tone as before. Was there a note of regret in his voice, or did I imagine it? "But I can't let you reveal what you know to anyone *ever*." His voice became so soft it was barely audible. "Only one of us is going to leave this chamber alive, and I intend it to be me. I may have failed to kill her this time, but I'm not done yet."

His hand slid slowly down to my neck. My skin prickled as his fingers wrapped around my throat. Any moment now, he would start squeezing.

My hands began to shake. "And how"—my voice trembled as I struggled to get it under control—"are you planning to get away with *this*?" My breathing was shallow and fast now, and I could not slow it. The panic I had kept at bay this last hour was threatening to engulf me. I could see my body being thrown into the Neris under the cover of darkness, reemerging bruised and battered the next day, downriver in some rural settlement, never to be identified. I would be buried in a village cemetery, and my family would never know what happened to me and would have nowhere to go to pray for me.

The thought caused a surge of defiance I did not think myself capable of anymore. It pumped new strength and determination through my veins. My life had been threatened before, when I was a young woman and had only myself to think about, and I fought back. Now I had two children, one of them a young son whose health had begun to improve at last. I was not going to let Zaremba take me away from him as he had taken those other people from their families. I would not go meekly to an anonymous grave.

With that singular goal banishing every other thought from my mind, I crashed my palms into his chest, a guttural cry of indignation rising from somewhere deep inside me.

My earlier stillness must have put him off guard. He let go of my neck and glared at me, stunned, for a few heartbeats. It gave me just enough time to jump from the settle and run for the door. But the table and the blasted trunk stood between me and freedom, and that slowed me down, costing me precious seconds as Zaremba recovered. I had barely cleared those obstacles when he grabbed for me, his face contorted in fury. He raised his right hand and brought it down on my head, striking me in the left temple. The force of the blow sent my headdress flying, pulling my hairnet with it, and my hair tumbled out and spilled around my shoulders. I raised an arm to protect myself from the next strike as my legs buckled. The edges of my vision darkened, and I seemed to be looking at the world through a tunnel. My ears rang as if every church bell in Vilnius had begun tolling frantically inside my head at the same time.

I do not know how long my daze lasted, but it could not have been very long. Before another blow came down, one that might well have killed me, I became aware of a commotion in the chamber. It took some time for my eyes to focus and for the noise in my ears to abate. Only then did I take in the scene that was unfolding in front of me.

Two palace guards restrained Zaremba, each gripping one of his arms. Someone had brought in a lamp or candleholder, dispelling the low light. I watched Zaremba trying to wrench his limbs free, pulling and yanking, but the guards held fast. At length his struggle subsided, but they maintained their vigilance. He continued to tug at the restraints every so often, his chest working from the effort and his rage at being thwarted. The wild gaze he fastened on me told me I was the target of that rage.

Still grasping him firmly, the guards looked toward the door for further instructions. I wanted to know who gave them their orders, but I could not turn my head for the pain. Any movement threatened the resurgence of the clanging bells. The other man must have spoken, for the guards pushed Zaremba forward roughly, then paused again. A moment later, Chamberlain Opaliński appeared, one of my scarves from the open trunk stretched between his hands. I had the bewildering thought that he was going to strangle Zaremba and wanted to shout in protest, but I could not produce any sound. Then Opaliński proceeded to tie his captive's wrists behind his back in a complicated knot, and I closed my eyes in relief, my head dropping onto my chest with a stab of pain.

Heavy steps shuffled out of the chamber, and I thought I was alone. Then I felt arms gripping me, a gentle but firm touch that made me whimper in protest as my scrambled mind imagined that Zaremba had broken free and returned to finish me off.

"It's me, Piotr." Opaliński's voice came as if from a distance through the lingering din in my ears. He lifted my head, his gaze full of worry. "What in God's name happened here?"

I tried to speak but could not. Had the blow to my head rendered me mute? Had I escaped with my life, only to be rendered an invalid? Hot tears welled in my eyes.

"Let's get you to the settle." He braced himself to lift me. He was not a big man, and in my weakness I must have been a heavy burden, but at length he guided me there, putting a cushion behind my back. "Stay here, and I'll find someone to bring you wine."

I gripped his hand, unwilling to let him leave me, but he misunderstood the gesture. "Better yet, I'll get Doctor Nascimbene."

A sharp cry from the doorstep made me wince. Alarmed, Opaliński looked over his shoulder, then his face relaxed and he beckoned to someone I could not see. "Come here, child."

Rasa's scared face appeared before me, and I almost wept in relief. She was alive! She tried to speak, but her lips wobbled too much.

"Fetch the Italian doctor, then a pitcher of wine and some cloths and water!" he commanded. When she did not move, he gave her a gentle push on the shoulder. "Go!"

"Zaremba ..." I managed hoarsely when she was gone.

"Can you tell me what happened?"

"Do ... do not let him go ..." The effort redoubled the strength of my headache.

Opaliński nodded, but I could see that he did not understand the situation. His solicitous expression told me he suspected Zaremba had made advances I had spurned.

I gripped his hand again. "He killed them ..."

The chamberlain's eyes widened, and I blinked to confirm that he had heard correctly. "He wanted to kill Barbara." I closed my eyes.

"Are you sure?"

I nodded. "He's dangerous."

Opaliński inhaled sharply. "Do you have a piece of paper?"

I reached for the sheet I had tucked into my bodice, the movement reverberating painfully through my body. The quill and ink were still on the table. He sat down and scribbled a note, then went out, and shortly thereafter I heard pounding on a nearby door, then again somewhere farther down the corridor. But the banquet was already underway, and no one answered.

He returned after what must have been at least ten minutes. "I finally found someone to take a message to the captain to guard Zaremba closely."

Another ten or fifteen minutes later, there was a knock on the door, and Doctor Nascimbene walked in, followed by Rasa with a tray holding a bowl, a jug, and a goblet, and two folded linen cloths. Opaliński took it from her and sent her away, then explained the source and nature of my injury. The old physician opened his bag and pulled out some bandages and vials.

Opaliński turned to me. "I must alert the duke to what has happened. I'll be back."

"One more thing," I said, heartened to hear that my voice was steadier. "I sent my son and his nurse away to the Lamb and Bell inn to wait for me. Would you send someone to bring them back?"

"Of course."

After he was gone, Nascimbene poured wine into the goblet and added several drops of some mixture, then handed it to me. I took a few sips, cringing at the strong medicinal taste.

"Who would have thought he was the one." The old man shook his head as he dipped the cloth in the water bowl. "Such a decent-seeming man, a knight."

"We are all capable of evil, *dottore,* regardless of our status and accomplishments." I flinched as he touched the cloth to my sore temple.

"*È vero.*" He nodded sadly. *It's true.*

He put some ointment on the cloth and dabbed it onto my skin. It had a pleasantly cooling and analgesic effect. As he gently rubbed off the excess, he gave me an anxious glance. "So who was he working for?"

I knew he feared the same thing I had—that it was Queen Bona, Italian like us, who was the mastermind.

"He claims he did it all by himself," I said.

"And you believe that?"

I thought for a long moment. "I do."

He let out a small sigh. "So it's over."

"Yes." I made a weak attempt at a smile, and he smiled back.

We were both wrong.

17

September 14th, 1545
Monday

Whether from sheer exhaustion or the three cups of the wine mixture Doctor Nascimbene made me drink, I slept all night and had no dreams, at least none I could remember. At eight the next morning, I was sitting with another cool compress pressed to my temple, where a dark bruise had blossomed overnight. I told Giulio I had fallen and struck my head. I was propped against thick velvet cushions on a gilded-frame chaise longue in a new apartment, a luxurious set of rooms on the same floor as Duke Zygmunt's.

The fire in the large, ornamental hearth blazed brightly as I told Opaliński and a scribe he had summoned everything that had happened the previous afternoon and evening. I also explained how the clues fit together, painting the picture of a murderer who worked to protect the legacy of a father who had given his life to ensure the safety of the nation's borderlands.

"There was no team of assassins, after all." I rested my head on the cushions. It still felt thick and achy, but thankfully the ringing in my ears had gone away. "Zaremba acted alone. He dyed his beard before he talked to Milda, then shaved it off so he had no beard when he went to kill Jurgis. I'm sure the White Swan landlady will be able to identify him."

The scribe's quill scratched softly as he took down my final statement. When he was done, Opaliński bade him leave us. As the clerk folded his portable desk, put away his writing implements, and bustled out, I marveled again at the rescue the chamberlain had effected the previous night, which was nothing short of miraculous. What brought him to my former chambers—the reason I was still alive—was that the duke had summoned me earlier in the day. But I left for the baths without telling Cecilia, so she was at a loss to explain my whereabouts. She promised to inform me of the summons as soon as I came back, but then forgot in the chaos that followed my frantic return and her departure for The Lamb and Bell. By suppertime, when I had still not appeared before Zygmunt, Opaliński and two guards went to my lodgings to fetch me. For that, I could not thank him enough.

"On Saturday, after we learned of Jurgis's death, I thought you might have been the killer," I said when we were alone again, "or at least working with him."

Opaliński showed no surprise. "Let's just say I would not have accepted any wine from you that night, either."

I lifted my eyebrows. "Queen Bona's secret weapon?" I pointed a finger at myself.

He laughed briefly, almost embarrassed.

We were silent for a long moment, but it was a companionable silence, filled with happiness that neither of us need fear the other. We had become friends, the chamberlain and I, during this past week, and a betrayal of such magnitude would have devastated me.

After a while, he asked, "Are you satisfied that the queen had nothing to do with it?"

I nodded.

"And the Habsburgs?"

"If Jakub Zaremba was working for the emperor, he would have said so," I said firmly. "A man going down has more to gain from exposing his master than protecting him to the end. It would offer at least some hope of saving his skin."

"Unless he's afraid that his skin would then become the target of his master's wrath," Opaliński countered.

"But at least he would have a chance to run and hide. Taking all of the blame will bring him nothing but certain death." I still remembered the tales my late first husband, a judge in Bari, had told me about the defendants who came before his tribunal. "That's why desperate men often throw accusations even at those who are innocent, yet Zaremba did none of that." I spread my arms, removing the compress as I did, and winced in pain. "Perhaps there really is no one else." I pressed the cloth to my temple once more.

Opaliński considered this. "Perhaps you're right. We searched his chamber early this morning and found nothing that linked him to a third party. The only evidence of his crimes is some empty vials that Doctor Nascimbene believes contained the poison." He shook his head. "Pretwicz will have a fit when he finds out. Zaremba is one of his top men in Bar. This could affect the captain's standing with the queen."

I shrugged. Bernard Pretwicz's standing with the queen did not concern me.

"The duke won't like it, either," he added ruefully.

I grasped his meaning: Zygmunt would have welcomed the opportunity to accuse Bona of murder. I laughed then, a soft staccato sound at first, rising to a full-throated, unstoppable torrent of hilarity worthy of a madwoman. Opaliński watched me with concern, but did not interrupt me until I spent myself. I sank farther into the cushions, letting my arms fall limply by my sides, and breathed deeply until I was certain the fit had passed.

Opaliński reached for the goblet with Nascimbene's wine concoction and handed it to me. I took only a small sip, for it tasted strongly of valerian and I did not want to sleep all day. I needed my mind clear to make arrangements to return home as soon as the duke released me from my duty, which I hoped would happen today. In fact, Opaliński had announced that Zygmunt planned to talk to me this morning.

As we awaited the ducal summons, the chamberlain helped himself to some of the bread and cheese a maid had brought for my breakfast. I had taken nothing, my stomach getting queasy at the very thought of food. We talked for a while about the confusing trail of crumbs we had followed over the past few days. It made me feel a little better that someone else had seen what I saw and failed to grasp its significance immediately.

"You were right that the assassin would not leave Vilnius without making sure his victim was dead," Opaliński admitted.

"One of the few things I was right about," I scoffed. "I should have seen the answer much sooner—"

"You can't blame yourself, Caterina," he interjected. "In the end, you were the only one who put the pieces together. And if you made a few wrong assumptions along the way—"

"A few?" I put down the compress again and sat up. "Let's see—" I extended my thumb and was about to start listing my failures when the door opened. A palace guard stepped in and stood aside at attention, then Zygmunt August walked into the chamber.

Opaliński scrambled to his feet and bowed. I wanted to follow, my breath catching as I tried to swing my legs off the chaise longue, but the duke put out a hand to indicate that I should stay seated. I fell back but remained upright against the cushions.

He took an empty chair near the hearth. The room was warm, but he wore a cloak trimmed with sable. Despite his swarthy complexion, his face appeared pale against the dark cloth. The events of the past week had greatly strained him, I saw. But they had strained me, too; indeed, they had almost cost me my life.

"Last night Chamberlain Opaliński told me what happened to you, signora." Zygmunt leaned forward, resting his left elbow on a knee draped in a grey silk stocking. His voice expressed sympathy and concern. "I trust you are better today."

"I am," I replied, wondering if that was true. Perhaps physically. "I am well looked after, thanks to Your Grace's generosity."

"You deserve no less for having found the killer who violated the safety of my family and my household."

I did not miss the reference to Barbara and her mother as "family." I glanced at Opaliński and saw that he, too, had noticed. I lowered my head in acknowledgment.

"I saw the scribe's notes. It sounds like this man acted alone."

"That's what he claims, and we have no proof to the contrary," I said.

Tense silence hung over the three of us as Zygmunt mulled this over. "Then we must accept it as the truth," he said after what seemed like a long pause. But he did not look happy—or convinced. Opaliński was right: the duke really wanted to declare his mother a villain. What would he have done then, I wondered?

"Unless evidence to the contrary emerges," Opaliński added unexpectedly, proving that he, too, remained skeptical. "I believe Signora Konarska asked this question already, but I wonder—in light of this latest development, does Your Grace still have complete trust in the imperial ambassador? He's trying to arrange a new marriage with the House of Jagiellon, and in that he shares a motive with Jakub Zaremba, who confessed that he hoped for a more strategic alliance than that with the Radziwiłłs."

The duke's eyes narrowed, which made him look more like Bona than ever before. "I trust him," he said. It was the same thing he had told me on Saturday. Again he could not quite disguise the reluctance in his voice. He rose and began pacing the chamber. "I *cannot* risk a diplomatic feud by accusing Charles's envoys of trying to murder my ... trying to murder Barbara."

So Zygmunt was realistic enough to entertain the idea of Habsburg involvement, yet he was afraid to confront them. How like his father!

He stopped at the window and gazed at the gardens below, their autumnal colors muted in the dull gray light. Then he wheeled around. "How do you know my mother didn't order it? She hates Barbara, and she doesn't care about my happiness. All that matters to her is her own pride—and power." Though he strove to keep his voice level, I caught a glimpse of the spoiled, whiny boy underneath. "It would have been awfully convenient for her if this scheme had succeeded."

I decided not to cite the crudeness of the method, which would so obviously point toward the queen; I knew that would not convince him. Instead I said, "Last night, Zaremba told me he wants a war not just with the Tatars but also with the Ottoman sultan." Although not the most politically savvy person at the court, even I knew that was a policy Bona staunchly opposed. She had always pushed for an alliance with the Turkish empire, and those unfortunate camels at Wawel were just one proof of the cordial relations between Kraków and Istanbul.

The duke's deflated look told me he could not rebut that argument. I had another to hand, one that would answer a question that had been on my mind since our meeting in the early hours of Thursday morning. "Your Grace sent for me after Milda's death, even though I came from Her Majesty. Surely, if you truly believed her to be the culprit, you would not have done so?"

The corners of his lips curled in a small smile that quickly dissolved into his customary mask of polite detachment. "That night I called for you solely on the strength of your reputation. A few days earlier, you stood before me first and foremost as a desperate mother pleading for help for her son, and I found it hard to believe you capable of murder. But still," he raised a finger, "I had to reassure myself as to your mission here."

My heart skipped a beat. "My mission?" Had he somehow found out what Bona had sent me to do on her behalf? Would it come to haunt me after all? I folded my hands in my lap, conscious of the unpleasant dampness between my fingers.

"Your mission to seek a cure for your son," he specified. "I needed to make sure that was the only reason you came to Vilnius. So when I invited you to walk with me in the gardens on Saturday, I ordered the captain of the guards to search your chambers for any evidence that you might be in possession of a deadly substance."

"Oh." So he *had* considered me a suspect, after all.

"I had no choice, under the circumstances," he added, looking momentarily sheepish.

"Of course," I said graciously. "I had nothing to hide."

"So it seemed. Still, I had my chamberlain keep an eye on you."

Opaliński sent me an apologetic look, looking embarrassed. I felt a stab of disappointment, but I understood his position. When you serve the powerful, your will is not always your own.

"I am pleased that Chamberlain Opaliński had no cause to report anything alarming to Your Grace," I said, perhaps a bit too coolly.

"No, indeed." Zygmunt paced the chamber again. "But that doesn't mean the queen had nothing to do with it. She has many people with not a shred of conscience in her pay."

"There is no evidence that Zaremba is one of them."

"Who supplied this man with the poison?" he asked, as if I had not spoken. "St. Nicholas powder was invented in Bari, my mother's hereditary duchy. I am certain she's familiar with it. And a poisoned garment," he added in the same breath, "is another popular assassination method among the Italians."

"And the French."

He waved his hand. "The point is that it looks like too much of a coincidence. What did Zaremba have to say about that? If he didn't get it from the queen or someone acting on her orders, where did he obtain it?"

"I didn't ask him," I admitted. That was the question that nagged me throughout my encounter with Zaremba the previous day, the one I had forgotten under stress. "It's crucial, I grant it. With Your Grace's permission, I'll go and talk to him again."

I did not relish the idea—in fact, the thought made me nauseous—but I needed to know the answer. Otherwise I would not have absolute faith in my conclusions.

"You don't look fit for another face-to-face meeting with him," the duke said skeptically. "I can have someone else question him about it."

"I'd rather do it myself. He may be more inclined to talk to me since"—I searched for the right words—"we developed a rapport over the last few weeks. Besides, I think it will be good for my peace of mind." I was not sure the last was true, but I wanted to hear the answer from Zaremba directly. I hoped that seeing him in jail, where he was powerless to do any more harm, would help me put this ordeal behind me. "I should be able to do it tomorrow." I put the compress aside, trying to sound livelier than I felt.

He considered my offer for a while. "You have my permission," he said eventually, then turned toward the door. Opaliński rose to his feet.

"Your Grace," I said before he stepped outside, "I would also ask your leave to return home."

He nodded. "When you feel strong enough to travel, I'll give you a carriage and armed escort to take you all the way to Kraków. I'm in your debt—we both are," he added, his face softening. "Barbara left for Nesvizh this morning to recuperate in the country for a few weeks. But she sends her heartfelt thanks to you, Signora Konarska."

A lump rose in my throat, and I could only incline my head in acknowledgment. Not for the first time, I marveled at this complicated man who was generous, caring, and loyal but could also be stubborn, suspicious, and selfish. For all his animosity toward her, he was his mother's son through and through.

When the door closed behind him, I pressed my hands to my eyes. So much death and suffering. Could it all have resulted from one man's determination to keep his vow to his father, or was there more to it?

I had one more chance to find out.

18

September 16th, 1545
Wednesday

I stood in the square of bluish light that seeped through a small window near the ceiling of the jail cell, which was larger than I expected. I heard the clatter of horses' hooves on the cobbles outside and voices calling to one another as the palace staff went about the day's business. But in the cell the silence was so thick that those noises seemed distant, unreal. Somewhere nearby, water dripped from the ceiling, the regular plops on the ancient stone enhancing the eerie hush.

Three days had passed since Zaremba ambushed me in my sitting room as I prepared to flee the ducal palace. The bruise at my temple still throbbed, a constant reminder of his attack. Now he sat on a straw-filled pallet that bore stains and smudges with origins I preferred not to contemplate. His beard was growing out, but even so Ostafi's wife had recognized him immediately as the man who had come looking for a blond boy at her inn on Friday night. His shackled wrists and the iron clamp fastened around one of his ankles and chained to the wall kept him from approaching me. I stood beyond his reach, yet my heart beat nervously. I took deep breaths to still my anxiety as we gazed at each other, both of us defiant.

"Have you come to gloat?" he asked eventually, breaking the silence. A smirk lifted one corner of his mouth. He did not look angry or defeated or penitent. If anything, he seemed satisfied. I saw at best a hint of disappointment—like that of a man who had done his best to accomplish a goal but was thwarted by circumstances beyond his control. Serenely resigned.

"No." I shook my head, only to regret the motion when the ache in my temple intensified. "There is nothing to gloat about. There are no winners here, only losers. A part of me still hopes that this is a bad dream from which I will awaken and laugh and be relieved. That you haven't done these terrible things. But each morning I realize anew that's not the case."

A shadow of emotion crossed his face, but it disappeared in a flash, and the smirk returned. "Is that what you've come to tell me?" He lifted an eyebrow, accentuating the sarcasm. "If so, you could have saved yourself a trip. I'm not interested."

"That is not why I came."

"Then why *are* you here?" he asked with a touch of annoyance.

"Because there is one more thing I need to know."

"More questions?" His expression went from indifferent to slightly amused. "What now? You want to find out why I attempted to kill Barbara with poison, even though she had a servant to try all of her food and drink?"

"That was *not* my question, but it's a good one." It was one of the many smaller puzzles of this story.

He laughed briefly, a self-deprecating sound. "Believe it or not, I had no idea. That was one thing Milda failed to tell me. I didn't find that out until after I was arrested. I assumed she would take the tainted cup to Barbara, and that would be the end of it."

Fighting disbelief, I opened my mouth, but no words came out. They were not meant for him, anyway, but for one who was no longer there to answer. Had Milda, despite her simplicity and inability to resist the temptation of silver, withheld that piece of information on purpose, as a last vestige of loyalty to her mistress, or had she considered it unimportant, failing to sense the danger?

The truth of the girl's motivation lay forever beyond my reach, but Zaremba's admission further exonerated Bona. She had an excellent network of spies throughout Poland and Lithuania and would never have sent anyone to do her bidding who was incapable of gathering the best intelligence. Despite his boasting, Zaremba was not as good as he thought.

"Even to someone as inexperienced in the ways of espionage as I am it seems an elementary mistake," I said, unable to deny myself the satisfaction of pointing that out.

His face darkened, but then he spread his palms, and because his wrists were bound together, he looked like a priest pointing to the host during Mass. "I accept that. I failed, and I'm paying the price. Anything else?" He assumed an air of indifferent expectation, like a bored person who might as well engage in conversation for lack of anything better to do.

I suppressed my irritation; this man who had almost killed me did not even have the decency to talk to me respectfully. "Who gave you the poison you put in Barbara's wine?" I asked. "You say you acted alone, but the duke believes his mother sent you. Your information will clear up that misconception."

Zaremba shrugged. "I don't care what he thinks, and I don't care about his relationship with his mother. He's a traitor who will trade our security for a permanent spot in a harlot's bed, and the queen raised him to be that way."

"For the sake of the country you claim to love so much, you must divulge the names of everyone who helped you with this scheme."

He laughed softly, raising his shackled wrists and wagging a finger at me. The iron chains rattled. "You're cunning, Caterina. You have a knack for spotting a weakness and exploiting it. It's a dangerous trait in a woman. When your husband finds out about the trouble you almost got yourself into, he will regret letting you go so far away from home. If he is wise, he'll never do that again."

I bit my lip to hide my irritation and impatience. After all I had undergone at his hands, I refused to listen meekly while he pontificated. "Tell me who supplied you with the poison," I said coolly. "Then I will leave, and I promise you will never hear from me again." It was a vow I fully intended to keep.

He studied me for a long moment, as if considering my pledge, his gaze sweeping from the bottom of my skirts to the top of my headdress and back. It made my skin crawl and humiliated me, reminding me of the flirtation in which we had engaged. A flirtation that, on his part, was nothing but an act of cold manipulation. I gathered the sides of my gown, getting ready to leave, resigned to yet another failure.

"I'll tell you for the sake of our brief friendship," Zaremba said, causing me to pause mid-turn. "You may not believe me, but I cherished it—until the moment you found me out."

My chest became so tight it trapped the air inside it. I was about to have the truth, with all its implications.

"An Italian courtier in Kraków gave me the poisonous powder."

My heart sank, and a sudden chill assailed me. But it had nothing to do with the dampness of the cell.

"Which courtier?" I whispered. "What's his name?"

"*That* I do not know."

I stared at him. "What do you mean?"

"I'd spent only a week in Kraków before we set out for Vilnius." His voice was emotionless, matter-of-fact. "By the time I arrived, I already had a plan. I had chosen poison because it's a woman's weapon and would be harder to trace. Once in Kraków, I needed to procure a vial, so I made inquiries. I let it be known that I was interested in something Italian, which would make it even harder to tie to someone like me—a man serving in Lithuania's southeastern hinterland."

I was horrified beyond words by his pride in his own cleverness, as he added in a boastful tone, "I was well prepared on *that* front." But if he expected acknowledgment from me, he was disappointed.

"In any case," he went on, "I was soon put in touch with a man who is known, in certain circles, to trade in the substances I sought. He is said to supply them to anybody who will pay."

I had a vivid image of two cloaked and hooded figures holding a brief conference in the feeble light of a lantern, making their deadly transaction. "Let me guess," I said, "you met him in some dark alley, and he refused to give you his name. You did the same."

He smiled. "Something like that."

"How do you know he was Italian?"

"He spoke like one," he said. "He spoke like you."

I winced.

"Of course, he wasn't as attractive." He chuckled. "Although he wasn't bad-looking, either." He screwed up his face in a show of trying to recall the man's appearance. "Olive skin, small dark beard, black eyes women can easily lose themselves in, and dressed like a fop in those ridiculous puffy breeches." He made a wide circular motion with his tied wrists, presumably to indicate the size of said breeches. Then he paused and peered at me. "Are you all right?"

I struggled to gather my thoughts. Could it be? "And you have no idea what his name is?" I managed after a while.

"No, but"—he raised an index finger with a mysterious air—"I know *who* he is."

The painful pressure returned to my chest. I knew what he would say even before he said it.

"He serves Her Majesty. When I went to the castle with the letter of introduction from Captain Pretwicz—before my encounter with the dealer in poisons—he was there, hovering next to her chair. When we met a few days later, I recognized him even though his hood obscured his face."

There could be no doubt. He was talking about Gian Lorenzo Pappacoda.

"Did he recognize you, too?" I asked.

"I don't know. His eyes were drawn to the gold in my hands. He was counting it like an old miser as I held up my lamp for him. That was when I got a good look at his face."

"Dear God."

"Do you know him?"

"I met him once," I said. "I didn't like the look of him." I recalled Pappacoda's curiosity about my mission to Vilnius, a curiosity he tried to disguise under the nonchalance of an idle courtier. I remembered something else in his expression, too—wariness and a certain resentment. It surprised me because we had never met before, but now it made sense. My reputation for solving Helena Lipińska's case was known at Wawel. Bona might have mentioned it to him or in his presence when she hatched the plan to send me to Vilnius to plead with Zygmunt.

Once more in the throes of grave doubt, I asked Zaremba, "How can I be sure the queen had nothing to do with this, if you're telling me you got the poison from one of her trusted men?"

He lifted his shoulders slightly. "I sought him out, not the other way around, and the queen's name was never mentioned." Then he added, matter-of-factly, in an eerie echo of my words two days earlier, "I'm going to die, Caterina. I have no interest in protecting anyone."

"When you were looking for the poison, did you mention to your contacts why you needed it?"

"I did." Again he could not help the boastful tone, and I could see how long he had lived and breathed that plot, how proud he still was of it. "It would have come out anyway," he added, "once the news of Barbara's death reached Kraków."

"Weren't you afraid someone might take that information to Wawel before you secured the poison?" I asked, even as I wondered how many people would have worried about Barbara's safety. Probably not many.

He smiled indulgently, as if explaining something perfectly obvious to a child. "We are talking about unsavory characters who do illegal things. They have many lives on their conscience. The last thing they want to do is attract attention to their activities."

I suppressed a shiver at the thought that a man like Zaremba—a polished courtier and a distinguished knight—would mix in such foul company. Then again, Pappacoda clearly did as well. Who knew how many well-born, sophisticated royal confidants lead such secret, shameful lives?

"I had better go." I prepared to leave, wanting to get as far away from Zaremba as possible. "I wish you strength for what lies ahead, and I hope you find peace." I had said the same words to Helena the last time I saw her alive. I still had no more certainty as to what awaited us beyond death than I had then.

He did not respond.

As I walked to the door, I thought about the possible implications of this latest revelation and what I would tell the duke and Opaliński. If I revealed Pappacoda's involvement, it would only strengthen Zygmunt August's belief in his mother's guilt. I wondered why I cared so much about that. Was it a simple matter of fairness, or was it because, as the mother of a son myself, I felt for Bona and the suffering that this estrangement caused her?

There was another, even more serious aspect to consider. If Bona had not ordered Zaremba to kill, then Pappacoda was a traitor. His actions endangered her interests, both political and personal. A servant who put his own gain above duty and loyalty to his sovereign had no place in the royal household.

I remembered the immediate dislike I had taken to Pappacoda, my sense that he was a calculating and devious man. Time had proven me right.

As I emerged into the cool air of the courtyard, I took a deep breath. The atmosphere of the jail and the interview with Zaremba made me want to take a hot bath to scrub off the taint. But I consoled myself with the thought that in two more days I would be on my way home.

There I had one more task to perform: warn Queen Bona.

19

September 18th, 1545
Friday

I awoke early on the day of our departure from Vilnius to supervise the final preparations for the journey. This time, we would travel under the protection of ducal guards, not in a merchant convoy. After the terrible events of the past nine days, I buzzed with excitement at the thought of home. I hugged and kissed my son every time he crossed my path and sent Cecilia to check our trunks again, brewing Giulio's herbal mix myself.

The duke had released us to leave two nights before. On Wednesday evening—exactly one week after the attempt on Barbara's life and a few hours after my last meeting with Zaremba—Duke Zygmunt invited me and Opaliński to dine with him. In the opulent surroundings of his private apartment, I looked through the windows at the moon-silvered ribbon of the Neris and trembled to think its waters might have carried me away if things had gone differently. While we ate, the three of us reviewed the evidence again. Regarding the source of the poison, I said Zaremba did not know the identity of his supplier, which was true enough, for I had been careful not to mention Pappacoda's name. I added that there were plenty of Italians in Kraków with knowledge of herbs and their many applications, both salutary and harmful. But, reserved as ever, the duke listened more than he spoke. Even now, on the morning of my departure, I still could not say with certainty if he believed that nobody stood behind these murders.

The day dawned cool and bright, despite the unbroken layer of white clouds that hid the sun and gave the sky a bleached-out quality usually found on a scorching summer day or in the depths of winter. The castle clock tolled eight by the time our trunks were loaded and secured to the roof of the carriage. A blue-and-yellow vehicle pulled by four sturdy but graceful bays, the carriage proclaimed its association with royalty through doors emblazoned with the image of a crowned eagle on a red background with the gilded initials SA, for Sigismund Augustus, intertwined on its breast. I had not traveled in anything so fine since I left Bona's service to return to Italy as a young woman.

Giulio and Cecilia were already inside the coach. Maria climbed in behind them, a slow and cumbersome process because of her wide skirts, which fluttered in the stiff breeze. I waited, pulling my cloak closer around me against the chill and shifting impatiently from foot to foot. When I heard quick steps descending the palace stairs and a voice calling my name, I shielded my eyes with one of my gloved hands and turned toward the sound. The chamberlain was hurrying toward me. In his haste, he had not donned a cloak, and he held his cap to prevent it from flying off his head. He looked dismayed. My chest constricted painfully.

"Signora Konarska," he panted, addressing me formally in the guards' presence. "I have something to tell you. In private." He jerked with his head toward the entrance.

I glanced at the carriage, where Maria had at last taken her seat, her movements making the cabin sway gently. I held up my hand toward her, signaling that I needed another moment, then followed Opaliński.

When we were out of everyone's earshot, he lowered his voice and turned his back to the carriage and the guards. "You need to know that"—he lifted his cap and ran his hand through his thinning hair—"Zaremba killed himself last night."

My throat went dry. I could not produce any sound, so I just shook my head.

"He was found hanging in his cell shortly after dawn."

I put my hand over my mouth.

"I'm sorry," Opaliński said. "It doesn't seem like justice."

My gaze traveled to the far end of the courtyard, where the jail was located in a basement. One of the small windows close to the ground opened on the cell I had visited two days earlier, where Zaremba had now taken his own life. But I was not angry, as the chamberlain supposed. I was, more than anything, sad. Now that he was beyond the reach of human justice, what I remembered was the boy who witnessed his father's terrible death and was scarred for life. I had lost my father as a young woman, too, and I understood his pain. I also understood—even if I did not condone his actions—his fear that his father's death would be rendered meaningless if Zygmunt married Barbara.

I looked toward the carriage and saw three inquiring faces. They were impatient to be on their way, as was I, but I could not leave just yet. Not without saying a final goodbye.

"Where is he now?" I asked.

"He's been moved to the chapel." Opaliński said.

The chapel was next door to the administrative building that held the prison. "I'd like to pay my respects," I said.

The chamberlain looked surprised. He opened his mouth, then nodded. "I can take you there."

I returned to the carriage and told my companions that I needed to do one more quick thing before we left. A moment later, Opaliński and I were walking briskly toward the chapel, where Milda's body had been moved last week, and where her killer's corpse had also found its way.

I had only visited the sacristy before. Now I went inside the chapel, whose interior was surprisingly light. Its large windows without stained glass admitted more of the daylight than many churches I had seen. Instead of underground, the usual location of such places, the mortuary lay behind a closed door to the right of the main entrance. The chapel was empty, and our steps echoed on the stone floor as we crossed the nave. Opaliński opened the side door. The mortuary was small, with only two stone slabs permanently affixed to the ground and room for perhaps two more makeshift tables, if necessary. On one of these slabs, a body rested under a shroud.

I knew that if I hesitated, I might not be able to continue, so I walked over to the body and moved to lift the shroud off its face. As I did so, I heard Opaliński take a sharp breath. "I have seen corpses that met a violent end before, you know," I said with a note of irritation.

He looked chastised, but his air of misgiving did not lessen.

I lifted the shroud and swallowed hard. Shocked, I took in Zaremba's face, swollen and red, his lips also swollen with a bluish tinge. The skin of his neck bore the unmistakable mark of a rope—a thick gouge of darker coloration running under the lower jaw.

I said a quick prayer for the repose of his soul. About to cover the grisly sight, I paused. How had he gotten his hands on a rope? I had not seen a rope in his cell two days earlier. Even that filthy mattress did not have a sheet that could have been torn into strips for the purpose.

I put that question to Opaliński.

He shrugged, but a small frown creased his forehead. "I'm not sure. Perhaps he bribed someone?"

I cast my mind back again, remembering Zaremba wearing only his shirt and breeches, no purse at his belt. Nor would the guards have allowed him to bring money into the jail. They would confiscate anything of value at the time of his arrest.

I noticed something else that bothered me. I leaned closer and peered at the groove on his neck. "Do you see that?" I pointed to red scratch marks clustered closely toward the center, around his Adam's apple.

"Yes," Opaliński said cautiously.

I considered the marks once more, then lowered the shroud so I could see Zaremba's hands. His wrists bore purple bruises from the chains that had bound them for four days. I lifted the right hand, and, sure enough, there were small bits of skin and dried blood under the fingernails.

Opaliński gave me a questioning look.

"I'm afraid Jakub Zaremba didn't take his own life."

His look of puzzlement deepened.

"He was the one who left these marks," I said. "He was clawing with his fingers at the noose tightening around his neck."

Opaliński's face drained of color. "Are you sure?"

I covered the body. "Almost certain. You should have Doctor Nascimbene take a look at him to confirm, but I would be *very* surprised if he disagreed with me." Then I asked, "What did the guards who found him say?"

He thought back. "That he was hanging from one of the bars at the window and was already dead when they cut him down. They were ordered to bring him here directly."

I thought back on his chained ankle and bound wrists, which would have restricted his range of movement. He must have been released from those chains to "kill himself."

"Does the duke know?" I asked.

We walked out of the mortuary and back into the chapel. "I informed him as soon as I heard, at seven o'clock this morning. He was angry at first," he added, anticipating my next question, "then he said it will at least spare us the spectacle of a trial."

And any uncomfortable questions that it might raise, I thought. Aloud I said, "It's convenient then."

He froze with his hand on the door knob, his eyes darting this way and that as if he feared we had been overhead. But the chapel was as quiet and empty as before. Too late, I thought about the accusation implicit in my words. People had lost their lives or freedom for less. But when Opaliński spoke, his voice was calm, if firm. "He didn't order it, Caterina; he's not that kind of man."

"What about Mikołaj Radziwiłł?"

"Why would he do that?"

"To avenge the attempt on his sister's and mother's lives." But even as I said it, I did not believe it. Rudy Radziwiłł was too proud to concern himself with someone like Zaremba. Besides, he would not imperil his career by going behind Zygmunt's back to take revenge, which, in effect, would suggest that he had no faith in ducal justice. No, it was unlikely that Barbara's brother had a hand in this.

That left only one possibility.

The Habsburgs. Again.

And as before, I had no proof. Only a hunch, a vague but persistent feeling in the pit of my stomach that there was more to this story than met the eye.

But I was done with it. The task the duke had given me was completed, and it was time for me to return home.

"I must go. The others are waiting for me," I said, and Opaliński opened the door. We stepped out into the courtyard, shading our eyes against the glare of the white sky. "But you must convey my findings to the duke. There should be an investigation. Whoever did this has robbed Zaremba's victims of justice and prevented the whole truth from coming out."

"So you think he was silenced, like young Jurgis?"

"Yes. There is almost certainly someone else behind this. Someone whose identity might have been revealed if he had lived to stand before a judge." Someone who might be Pappacoda's paymaster as well.

Opaliński took a handkerchief from his pocket and wiped his brow. "Then he *was* working for someone?" He was breathing faster. For a moment I regretted leaving him behind to deal with whatever happened next.

"It looks like it. And protected them only to be betrayed," I said. *The fox was outfoxed.*

"But it wasn't Queen Bona," I added. "There hasn't been enough time for her to learn of Zaremba's arrest and order him killed. Whoever did this is here, in Vilnius, and following this case closely."

"Ambassador von Tilburg?" He looked incredulous.

"Not personally, no, but perhaps someone from his entourage or a hired assassin. I can't think of any other explanation. If the duke orders an inquiry into who went into Zaremba's cell in the last twenty-four hours and on whose authority, he may well discover a clue that has eluded us."

We arrived back at the carriage. "Thank you for all you have done, Caterina," Opaliński said as we parted. "And I'm sorry for what you have endured."

I put a hand on his arm. "I hope you and the duke and Barbara will find a way to put it all behind you."

"I wish the same for you," he said, squeezing my hand. "I will write to you."

"Please do."

"Godspeed."

When the carriage clattered through the gate and out of the courtyard into the main street, I exhaled, but I could not relax as much as I hoped. Zaremba's death only raised more questions, and not just about the forces behind his actions. If he worked for the Habsburgs, why had he so doggedly protected them, even going so far as to claim that he relished the idea of using their wine so they might be blamed for it? I had searched in vain for a solution to the riddle since last Sunday, and it remained the only inconsistency in the Habsburg theory that I otherwise believed to be strong and compelling.

As the fine houses of old Vilnius gave way to the cheaper, shabbier construction of the outskirts, I pondered the uncomfortable reality of leaving behind an incomplete case. I had done everything I could to warn Zygmunt, yet I was aware—and the thought gave me a stab of shame—that my determination to depart before I fully recovered from my injuries was dictated in large part by a fear that I might be given a new assignment, one far more dangerous than the first. Zaremba had been a formidable opponent, but the Habsburg machine would grind me to a pulp. Against the considerations of justice, I had weighed—and chosen—my family's safety.

Only one thought assuaged my guilt: I would soon meet with the queen. Alerting her to a possible Habsburg conspiracy carried its own risk—for just as Bona was believed to have spies in Vienna, it was an open secret that certain courtiers in Kraków received an allowance from the emperor—but I would do it. Although I had no solid proof, I considered it likely that Pappacoda was working for the Habsburgs—and perhaps other powers as well, if Zaremba was correct about his mercenary nature. The queen would dismiss Pappacoda from her service and banish him from Poland. As the *de facto* ruler, she would order an investigation, if not into the events in Vilnius, at least into the extent of the Habsburg network in Kraków in order to expose and dismantle it once and for all.

I put my arm around Giulio and hugged him to my side so hard he gasped and laughed. For the first time since I plunged into the middle of this case, I thought that something positive might come of it, even if the authors of the Vilnius conspiracy went unpunished. One day soon, I would bask in the glory of having contributed to ridding the Crown of German spies.

20

Konary
October 1st, 1545

The journey back took longer, because Zygmunt's men would not stop overnight at Bona's estates. At times, we detoured for several miles to find lodging that belonged to the duke. The days continued chilly and overcast, but we were lucky: rain held off for the most part, and that would have slowed us down even more. At last, the ancient walls of Kraków, with Wawel sitting proudly on its hill, emerged on the horizon at three o'clock in the afternoon on the first day of October.

We reached Konary at dusk. I invited Maria to spend the night before going on to the castle, but she declined, although not without greeting Sebastian effusively, her eyes assessing him with the discretion of an expert. She chattered nonstop, allowing my poor husband only a "yes" or a "how interesting" in response, and I was filled with terror that in the flood of words she would let something embarrassing slip. When we moved off to say our private goodbyes, she kissed me on both cheeks and spoke in my ear in a voice that, for once, was mercifully low. "I understand now how you were able to resist Zaremba. You're a lucky woman, Caterina." I let out a mighty exhale of relief as the carriage rounded the corner of the driveway and disappeared from sight.

Giulio's reunion with his father was joyful, and over the supper the three of us shared, I told Sebastian about Doctor

Nascimbene's diagnosis and his prescribed cure. The genuine happiness I saw in him—coupled with his observation that, despite the rigors of the journey, Giulio had filled out and had more color in his face—made me feel that the ordeal had been worth it. We talked about taking our son to visit our neighbors to acquaint him with other children so that, come next spring, he would have friends to play with outdoors. It was the first time in what seemed like years that we had been able to discuss his health so openly, and the first time that we had talked about a future for him. I realized then that we had both lived with the unspoken fear that Giulio might not have one.

After Cecilia had taken him off to bed, Sebastian and I sat before a lively fire in the main hall, and I told him the news from Vilnius. I had only managed to write him a short letter that Sunday morning before I set out for the baths where a casual conversation would set off a chain of events that almost cost me my life. I wrote again after Zaremba's arrest to tell him I would be returning home soon, but I left out the details of what happened. Now I told him everything, from my visit to Zaremba's chamber on the night when Milda had died to my discovery that his suicide had been staged to cover up another crime.

As I was recounting the events of that fateful Sunday afternoon and evening as Zaremba's captive, Sebastian came to sit next to me on the settle and held me, gently stroking the fading bruise on my temple. My voice caught at times as I told him of the attack and the last-minute rescue by Opaliński and the guards. But it was strong and determined when I shared with him my plan to warn the queen about the Habsburgs and Pappacoda.

"I heard that name at Emilia and Leon's house last week," Sebastian said, referring to a gathering at our in-laws' to celebrate the betrothal of their eldest daughter. "I didn't pay much attention, but it didn't seem as though the guests liked him. Someone referred to him as a 'weasel.'"

"I can see that," I scoffed.

"He sounds like a popinjay, hanging about to anticipate the queen's every wish and to please her."

"That's the exact impression I had."

He gazed into the fire, his expression pensive. "It's strange, though. The men the Habsburgs have in their pay are believed to be highly placed. Like Stempowski—remember him?"

For a while we reminisced about the events surrounding the murders committed by Helena Lipińska. Stempowski—then the Grand Chancellor—had been the official investigator on that case, designated by the old king. He turned out to be quite inept at that task, but he did excel at promoting German interests at court. As such, he was one of Bona's mortal enemies. One of her greatest regrets—according to Lucrezia—was that the evidence of his allowance from Vienna had not surfaced until after his death.

So Sebastian had a point—Pappacoda did not fit the profile of a Habsburg agent. Was it possible that Zaremba's purchase of the poison from him was purely coincidental? But if so, why was he murdered? I rubbed my forehead, frustrated with how this case kept going in circles.

"Whether he's in their pay or simply doing this unsavory work on the side for extra coin," I said, "it behooves me to alert the queen. His allegiance is clearly elsewhere, even if it's only to gold, and he shouldn't be allowed near her." I felt buoyed with optimism again. "She values loyalty, and the story I have to tell her will surely change her mind. She'll send him away. Then Milda, Jovita, and Jurgis will get a small measure of justice."

He cupped my chin in his hand. "I admire you," he said. "I have since that winter of 1519. If anyone in Vilnius could have solved this case, it was you. I only regret not being there with you—"

"Don't," I said, touching his hand. "Neither of us could have known what would happen." Gratitude flooded me. "You have always believed in me. It's a rare husband who allows his wife to travel alone and conduct her own affairs. You have no idea how much I appreciate it."

He kissed me softly. "That's because you are no ordinary wife."

After a moment, I drew away. I had a confession to make. Without it, any honesty and openness we would work to reclaim would be incomplete. "I can't let you think that without admitting something I am deeply ashamed of." I lowered my head but went on before I lost my courage. "Zaremba tried to seduce me when he realized I might be investigating the murders, and for a brief moment, I went along with his flirtation." I was unable to meet his eyes, even as I became aware of how still he had become. There was an expectation in that stillness, and I knew that the future of our marriage teetered on its thin edge. My next words would decide its fate. I forced myself to meet his gaze. "Nothing happened," I said. "If it had, I would never forgive myself, nor would I dare ask your forgiveness."

The tension in his face eased, but he looked sad when he said, "I haven't always been the husband you needed by your side, especially these last few months, but all I ever wanted was to keep our family safe and provided for."

"I know." I wiped the tears that were flowing freely from my eyes. "I know."

"My goal, since we came back to Poland, has been to make this place"—he swept an arm toward the darkened window, in the direction of the estate buildings—"the home that you and Giulio deserve."

I nodded, smiling through my tears but still unable to speak.

"It's nearly complete," he added, his mouth close to my ear, "so we can start again."

Later that night, as we lay in each other's arms, reacquainted with the intimacy we had allowed to drift away from us, he whispered in a voice that was already soft with sleep, "I can't wait to show you around Konary tomorrow. I think you'll like what we have done."

I stroked his arm, then ran my hand down to his, intertwining our fingers. I raised them to my mouth and kissed his knuckles, tasting the roughness where the skin had been scraped raw and healed over during the months of work he had done alongside the hired men. "And the apples?" I asked. "Are there any apples left in the orchard?"

"Yes. The reddest, sweetest, most succulent apples we've had in years." His voice turned slow and dreamy as he laughed softly into my hair, and a few moments later I heard his breath settle into the easy, regular rhythm of sleep.

I was home.

21

Kraków
October 3rd, 1545

I wrote to Lucrezia the next day to ask for an audience with the queen, with no witnesses. Her reply arrived via the same messenger before evening, summoning me for the following morning. I left Konary with Sebastian, who was going to wait for me at his sister's house, at dawn.

"Are you nervous?" he asked as our carriage wobbled on the uneven track.

"Oddly, I'm not," I replied, knowing that he meant my failed mission to plead with the duke against the marriage to Barbara. "I'm lucky to be alive and back with you. That's all that matters to me." Then I added, giving voice to a decision I had made on the way back from Vilnius, "If I incurred the queen's displeasure, I'll accept any chastisement, then put it behind me. If she never asks anything of me again, I'll consider that a blessing."

But my defiant words masked hope that the news about Pappacoda would mitigate her disappointment with me. It might not be what she sought, but Bona valued intelligence; in fact, she paid men large sums to keep her informed on domestic and foreign affairs. I was about to make a contribution of my own.

"One thing is certain," I said as we emerged onto the high road to Kraków, wider and less rutted, "I'm done with what you once called 'the excitement of court life.'" I closed my eyes and leaned my head against the leather headboard. "Oh yes, I am."

❧

Lucrezia waited for me outside the entrance in Wawel's inner courtyard, wrapped in a cloak to keep out the chill of the autumn morning. I was struck by the change in her appearance since August—she was thinner and more sallow. I asked about her health, and she shrugged her shoulders, saying "fine," then looked away when she saw my skepticism. She had turned to lead the way up the stairs when a soft, mournful braying sound reached us. Without pausing or looking back, Lucrezia said, "That's one of the two remaining camels."

"Two?"

"Yes." Her voice was flat. "One died at the beginning of September."

We climbed to the second floor and entered the queen's gallery. I could not hear the animal's plaintive sounds anymore, but its echo stayed with me. Somehow, it fit the subdued atmosphere of the castle, the hush that permeated its ancient corridors. I could not help feeling that with Zygmunt August in Vilnius and the old king confined to his bed, things had slowed down in Kraków, as if the court held its collective breath and waited to see what would happen next. I did not doubt, however, that Bona was as busy as ever.

And informed.

When the doors closed behind Lucrezia and we were alone, the queen said without preamble, "You fell into the middle of quite a mess in Vilnius, didn't you, Caterina?" She was dressed much like the last time I had seen her—in dark velvet and a white linen cap, and again I was struck by the contrast between the luxury of the gowns she liked to wear in her youth and the austere, widow-like style she preferred now.

"Yes, Your Majesty," I replied. "It was very unfortunate."

I had written to her a few days before I left Lithuania, informing her of my role in helping to apprehend Zaremba. It was before he died, but she knew about his demise, too.

"We must trust in divine justice now," she said, and I wondered if she truly believed in it, "but I would have wanted to see restitution in this world, too." Then she asked, a mix of eagerness and contempt in her voice, "The Habsburgs were behind it, weren't they?"

I knew then that it was Opaliński who kept her abreast of developments in Vilnius. As I suspected, he acted as her eyes and ears at her son's court. "It's very likely, but there is no firm proof."

A grimace twisted her lips. "Of course." She drummed her fingers on the armrest of her chair. "Conniving and underhand, the whole lot of them—that's how they build and maintain and expand their power." The intense concentration on her face told me that she was thinking of ways to prove their culpability, but I doubted that even her agile mind could come up with one. Their tracks were too well hidden. The only possible path was to investigate Pappacoda.

"The poison Zaremba used was St. Nicholas powder," I said, and she nodded grimly.

"Of course, they would choose that," she said through gritted teeth. She was well aware of the slanders that circulated about her. "I wrote to my son and stated categorically that I hadn't known this man Zaremba from Adam before he showed up here on Pretwicz's recommendation. He took advantage of my friendship with the captain and deceived us both!"

I heard hope in her voice, and it made me sad. I was certain Zygmunt would not believe a word she wrote. Most likely, he would throw the letter in a blazing hearth without reading it.

"I told His Grace that Your Majesty's and Zaremba's interests weren't the same beyond opposition to the marriage and that Zaremba wanted a war with the sultan—which the emperor does as well, but you never have."

Her features softened. "Your loyalty is very much appreciated, Caterina. You are one of the few people I have always been able to count on. It's a pity you didn't choose to stay at the court after you married," she said, as if the circumstances of my departure in the summer of 1520 had not involved two dead men and a kidnapping victim.

I did not know how to answer, but she continued, words pouring out of her. "There are few men left that I can confide in and rely on, especially now that Bishop Gamrat has died—succumbing to his failing health, *poverino*, on the very day you left for Vilnius! Do you know that he was the only one of my advisors and secretaries, in all my years here"—she swept out her arm, encased in a black sleeve—"who never betrayed my trust? Not once. And now he is no more." Her voice thickened and she paused, reluctant as ever to show emotion.

"You have my sincere condolences, Your Majesty." I inclined my head and kept it that way for a few moments to give her time to compose herself.

When I looked up, her face had again assumed its familiar expression of stubbornness and intensity. "That toad and traitor Maciejowski, who is Crown Chancellor but takes his orders from Vienna the same way Stempowski once did, is the most likely candidate to replace him as bishop. But I will do all I can to prevent that from happening!" Her right palm curled around the end of the armrest.

I did not doubt she would try, although with her power so diminished it was anyone's guess as to whether she would succeed.

"My son doesn't always listen to reasoned arguments, especially from me." She returned to the business at hand.

There was only a touch of bitterness in her voice, tempered with a newfound hope. "But perhaps this whole sorry business with Zaremba will finally make him see the folly of his plans regarding that woman. It is, quite literally, driving his subjects to madness. Surely that will persuade him?"

"We must hope," I replied, knowing it was in vain. "But there is something else I must convey to Your Majesty—something I haven't shared with anyone."

Lowering my voice—for it would not surprise me if Pappacoda was listening through a keyhole, with or without the queen's consent—I told her of my last meeting with Zaremba and his claim that he had procured the powder from her favorite courtier. "I withheld this information from His Grace, as it would only have confirmed his suspicions of you," I concluded, "but it shows the danger of continuing to put your faith in that man."

When I finished, the queen's brow was deeply creased and her lips pinched into an owlish look. "What proof have you of this?" she demanded.

"None," I replied honestly. "Just as I have no direct proof of the Habsburgs' involvement. But I have little doubt. Zaremba described Signor Pappacoda's appearance quite accurately and said he had seen him here in this chamber." I gestured toward the left side of her chair, where Pappacoda stood the last time I saw him.

"I cannot imagine Gian Lorenzo would do such a thing." Bona shook her head. "Why, he barely leaves my side!"

I spread my arms. "I don't see why Zaremba would have lied about it."

"He may have been mistaken or been an agent himself. The man was a raving maniac, after all."

I wanted to respond that there had been nothing raving or maniacal about Zaremba, that he had been clear-headed and calculating the whole time, but the thought gave me pause. Had Zaremba lied to me about this, too—to protect himself against being labeled a traitor in addition to a murderer—and had obtained the poison directly from the Habsburgs? Was Pappacoda, an Italian close to the queen, simply a dupe?

"The members of the court dislike him, true, but that's because they hate *me*." Bona pressed a clenched fist to her bosom, as if she begged for understanding. "They always have!" I saw again how lonely she was, how starved for sympathy and affection, and that her isolation heightened her suspicions of everyone around her. "I have received scant recognition or gratitude for all I have done here." She pointed diagonally toward the corner of the chamber, in the direction of the city, and, presumably, the rest of the kingdom. "Instead, whenever I find someone I can trust, they try to destroy him."

"Why not order a discreet investigation, then?" I suggested. "If it yields nothing, we will know that Zaremba lied."

"But that's exactly what they want, isn't it?" She threw her arms out, exasperated. I wondered who "they" were. Her husband's advisors? Her son's allies? The pro-Habsburg faction? Bona had fought with all of these groups, whose membership often overlapped, at one time or another during her quarter of a century as Poland's queen. "They want me to turn against the few who have remained loyal to me and to spend my time suspecting and investigating my supporters while my detractors take over the reins of power."

As she spoke, her voice rose in pitch, and when she finished, a ringing and poignant silence wrapped us in its folds. The castle seemed deserted, and the idea of Pappacoda lurking in the shadows unsettled me. I yearned to flee the palace, which I barely recognized as the place I first saw in the spring of 1518. Then it was a beehive of political activity, a vibrant court full of music and foreign visitors, and my only concern was keeping an eye on the amorous intrigues of a gaggle of adolescent girls. I felt exhausted, as if I had run many miles, pushing myself along the way to manage just a bit more, then a bit more again, until I had nothing left.

"I believe it to be my duty to inform Your Majesty of the possibility that one of your men may have acted in a harmful way," I said. *Now it is up to you what you do with this information.*

I did not speak that last part aloud, but Bona seemed to understand. "I thank you, Caterina, and I want you to know that I'm aware of the risk you have taken in coming to me with your conclusions. The people we are up against are not to be trifled with. You can rest assured that nobody here in Kraków will learn of your involvement in Zaremba's arrest from me, nor will I share your"—she hesitated—"other concern. Your safety is important to me."

She turned to a cherry wood table next to her chair, where, among the bowls of sweetmeats, lay a small velvet bag tied with a string. It tinkled softly when she lifted it and handed it to me. "This is a token of my appreciation for what you did in Vilnius and for arguing so forcefully to clear my name." She must have heard that from Opaliński, too. "There is still time to dissuade my son from making this mistake; there is still time," she repeated softly, with an inward gaze, as if speaking to herself.

I bowed. When I was almost at the door, I heard, "Caterina!" and when I turned, the queen asked, "And how fares your son?"

Incredibly, I had completely forgotten about that. "He is much better. I thank Your Majesty once again for making it possible for us to see Doctor Nascimbene."

"We are glad then, we are glad." She said it in that same inward way, and I wondered if the "we" she used was the royal one, or whether in her mind she was speaking both for herself and Duke Zygmunt.

I bid goodbye to Lucrezia and decided to walk the short distance from the castle to my in-laws' house in St. Jan's Street. As I descended the cobbled road from Wawel Hill, I fervently hoped I had set foot there for the last time.

The new purse at my belt was not heavy, which pleased me. Although I had completed my task, I did not consider the results a success. I was still full of doubts, and the only two people who could lay them to rest showed no willingness to do so. Mother and son, so deeply at odds with each other, were like two peas in a pod—caring and generous, but also headstrong and stubborn. Once they made up their minds, they did not change course. If a link existed and remained undiscovered between the Vilnius murders and the Habsburgs, it would be because of the obstinacy of the two most powerful people in Poland-Lithuania.

The queen had dismissed my warning because she saw Pappacoda as a faithful servant and believed—perhaps correctly—that she lacked such people around her. And perhaps he *was* faithful, and Zaremba had made common cause with the Habsburgs, who for different reasons also wanted Barbara dead and Bona blamed for the murder. I wrestled with the frustration of never learning the full truth and of seeing justice denied to the victims.

But I could not put my life and my family's safety at risk by continuing on this quest alone. I had done my duty by informing Zygmunt and Bona of a possible conspiracy, and the matter was now out of my hands.

As it happened, the truth did not remain hidden forever, although it did not come out for another twelve years. And when it did, it happened in the worst possible way.

EPILOGUE

Bari, Kingdom of Naples
July 1560

Before I tell you of the terrible crime committed in this town three years ago, I should mention that I was disappointed if not surprised when, some weeks after my last meeting with Queen Bona, a letter arrived from Chamberlain Opaliński. In it he informed me that after an investigation, the details of which he did not provide, Zaremba's death was ruled self-inflicted and the case closed.

I wrote to Doctor Nascimbene then, but he died in January of the next year, 1546, and my letter went unanswered. Thus I never found out whether the investigators consulted him and, if so, what medical opinion he gave, although I believe that, like me, he would have recognized a murder covered up as suicide. And there is always a reason for that kind of deception.

The reason was finally laid bare for all to see when Queen Bona—recently arrived in Bari from Poland, and still healthy and robust in her early sixties—came down with an unexplained stomach illness and died in November 1557. At that time, King Philip II of Spain, the son of the late Emperor Charles and a notorious spendthrift, owed her 450,000 ducats plus interest. Many at Bona's new court immediately suspected that rather than repay the sum, the king had hired an assassin to dispatch the queen.

This suspicion was strengthened when it transpired that two days before the queen's death, when she was already gravely ill, Gian Lorenzo Pappacoda had brought a scribe to her bedside to take down her last will and testament. In it she supposedly left her duchies of Bari and Rossano to King Philip and large sums of money to Pappacoda himself. Bona's doctors, one of whom subsequently died under mysterious circumstances (as did the scribe who assisted in the drafting of the fraudulent will), found evidence that someone had been adding small amounts of St. Nicholas powder to her food for days. When these revelations reached the queen's Polish heirs, they wanted to put Pappacoda on trial, but the traitorous courtier fled to Spain.

While the exact details of the Vilnius conspiracy of 1545 will always remain unknown, it is clear to me that Gian Lorenzo Pappacoda, a man of no loyalty and in the pay of the Habsburgs, played a central role in it.

As a Habsburg agent, he knew all about Vienna's desire to get rid of Barbara and see Bona blamed for the crime. When the queen came up with her own plan to stop the marriage—which she almost certainly shared with Pappacoda, starved as she was for confidants—he took that information to his paymasters. That was when the plot took on a definitive shape: they would find someone to go to Vilnius at the same time and assassinate Barbara, ensuring that suspicion would immediately fall on the queen's envoy. Pappacoda was therefore dismayed—as I had noticed without understanding the cause—when I arrived for the audience at which Bona entrusted me with the mission. He knew my reputation—most of the courtiers did—and worried that it might affect the success of the murder plot.

The Habsburgs pressed to continue regardless. Luck favored Pappacoda: around the same time he heard through his connections with the denizens of that shadowy world of spies and assorted assassins of a man looking for an Italian poison to kill the young king's mistress in Vilnius. His Habsburg handlers duly supplied him with St. Nicholas powder, which he then sold to Zaremba—at a profit to himself, no doubt—with the results described here.

One of the greatest ironies is that Jakub Zaremba, who thought himself so clever for using the Spanish wine to cast suspicion on the emperor, was in reality an unwitting tool in the Habsburgs' hands. You may wonder if Charles's ambassador took part in the plot. I, for one, do not think so. My years at court taught me a thing or two about diplomacy, and the rules and decorum with which it is conducted, even when matters of life and death are at stake. I suspect the ambassador had no idea his masters in Vienna sought to ensure that if my mission failed, Barbara would still be out of the way. If von Tilburg had been in on the scheme, I doubt he would have sent Zaremba that flagon of wine.

In the end, everyone failed in their quest. Zaremba most immediately and Bona most obviously, for Zygmunt married Barbara in 1547. The union lasted only four years, until Barbara died in 1551, but even that turn of events failed to bring about a reconciliation between the queen and her son—if anything, it pushed them farther apart. Two years later—driven by the need to father an heir, more than anything else—Zygmunt married again. His third wife was none other than Catherine Habsburg, his first wife's sister and Emperor Charles's niece. But even that seeming triumph is now in question, for it is well known that the marriage quickly foundered and the spouses live apart. The latest news from Chamberlain Opaliński, with whom I still occasionally correspond, is that Zygmunt is thinking of having it annulled. If that happens, the Habsburgs will lose their tentative foothold on the Polish throne.

Would Bona have avoided such a grim fate had she not returned to Bari? Despite my sympathy for her, I cannot help but think that throughout her life she laid the foundations for both her success and her downfall. Her reforms and the wise management of her possessions made her rich, but she was never content; her greed and ambition only grew as she aged.

When her son became the sole ruler of Poland-Lithuania on the death of his father, the room for Bona's aspirations shrank dramatically. Hating that lack of purpose, she eventually left Poland in 1556 in search of a new place in which to wield power. At first, she reestablished herself in Bari, where Sebastian and I had returned only a few months earlier when Giulio, a healthy young man of twenty, took over the management of Konary. Bona was still duchess here, and her subjects welcomed her back with great pomp. But she wanted more. Soon rumors began to circulate that she had set her sights on Naples, where she hoped to become viceroy. The exorbitant loan she made to Philip of Spain in the autumn of 1556 was meant to multiply her fortune and provide funds to buy that title. Instead, it led to her death.

Whatever her faults, Bona did not deserve to die that way. She had a forceful personality and she could be brash, qualities not welcomed in women anywhere but especially not in the land that destiny chose her to rule. She made mistakes, and enemies, but she also did a lot of good, not just in the agricultural realm but as a patroness of artists, supporter of monasteries' charitable work, and founder of schools and hospitals.

So I weep for her as I write these words and the inky sky begins to pale through the shutters. Sebastian is sleeping across the chamber from my desk, but I am often awake at night. It gives me plenty of time to reflect on the past and worry about the future of the country I consider my second homeland, where my son still lives. Queen Bona worked tirelessly for the kingdom and the monarchy, and now both are in danger: one from the continuing power struggle between the *szlachta* and the magnates and the ambitions of powerful neighbors lurking at its borders; the other from the ongoing lack of an heir.

Already some people call the days of Zygmunt Stary and Bona's rule the Golden Age. And they refer to it in the past tense.

Historical Note

As confusing as it may seem, both Zygmunts—father and son—held the title of King of Poland and Grand Duke of Lithuania concurrently from 1529 to the elder's death in 1548. Due to the maneuverings of Queen Bona, her son was declared grand duke in October 1529 and king in December of that year, when he was only nine. Her motivation was to secure the succession, because the monarchy was formally elective. However, in practice the ruling king's son was all but assured succession, so the move was largely symbolic. Worse, it made Bona more enemies—especially among the Polish nobility, which prided itself on its role in the election of kings, even if it was a rubber stamp. Moreover—and I allude to this frequently in the novel—Zygmunt August's formal assumption of the ducal role in 1544 was a political catastrophe for Bona, as he quickly moved to curb her power in Lithuania.

Elizabeth of Austria, the ill-fated wife of the young king, died in Vilnius and was buried there. I moved the location to Kraków to fit the narrative, but the other details are accurate. It was a short and unhappy marriage that ended when Elizabeth died of epilepsy on June 15, 1545, at the age of eighteen. Frail, shy, and deeply religious, she held no interest for Zygmunt, accustomed as he was (thanks in no small part to Bona's upbringing) to promiscuous and experienced women. During the two-year marriage, the couple spent much time apart, and it is likely that Zygmunt's affair with Barbara Radziwiłł (Lithuanian: Barbora Radvilaitė) started during Elizabeth's lifetime.

Mikołaj Rudy, although a real historical figure, is a composite character in this novel. In reality, there were two

Mikołajs in the Radziwiłł clan—Czarny (The Black) and Rudy (The Red), the nicknames deriving from the colors of their beards. Rudy was Barbara's brother, while Czarny was a cousin. Together they formed a powerful team of (relatively) young and ambitious noblemen who did everything in their power to see Barbara married to Zygmunt August in order to advance the family's standing. From the 1550s to the 1570s, both Radziwiłłs held some of the highest military and administrative offices in Lithuania, including those of the commander of the army, Grand Chancellor, and *wojewoda* of Vilnius. As their political interests, activities, and careers mirrored each other so closely, I chose to include only Rudy in this narrative to avoid confusion.

The relationship between Queen Bona and Captain Bernard Pretwicz is an interesting one. Pretwicz was a descendant of a German family from Silesia, which should have made it hard for him to enter the famously anti-Habsburg queen's trusted circle. But he was a successful army commander, particularly against Tatar invasions in Lithuania. For that, Bona respected him and supported his career, showing that she was as politically savvy as she was pragmatic.

The issue of Zygmunt's second marriage was of the utmost political importance. He was the heir to the throne with no living brothers, and the survival of the dynasty hinged on his fathering a son. Bona, in her typically energetic fashion, set out to look for a new daughter-in-law among the finest royal and princely houses of Europe. However, Zygmunt's affair with Barbara prevented any of these plans from materializing. Although Caterina's mission to the court in Vilnius is fictional, Bona did all she could to separate the lovers, even going so far as to dispatch the most beautiful courtesans to Vilnius. The women were sent back to Kraków without having rendered their service to the Crown, and Zygmunt married Barbara in 1547 in a clandestine, middle-of-the night ceremony straight out of the pages of a romance novel. The move marked the final break between mother and son. In 1548, when Barbara was on her triumphal way to Kraków, Bona left the capital to avoid meeting her daughter-in-law. Powerless, isolated, and resentful, Bona settled in Warsaw, in Mazovia, then left for Italy in 1556, a destination from which she was never to return.

The couple's happiness was short-lived. In the vein of a tragic fairytale, Barbara died in May 1551 at the age of thirty, just six months after being crowned queen at the Wawel Cathedral. Contemporary rumors abounded about poisoning by her mother-in-law, but modern scholars dismiss the theory. Based on medical reviews of the historical record, Barbara died of a disease of the reproductive system, possibly cancer. Zygmunt August was heartbroken. In the years that followed, he dramatically limited the entertainments at his court, spent more time hunting at Knyszyn, and focused on expanding the royal art and tapestry collection. The walls of his private apartments were lined with black cloth, and he abandoned the colorful Italian and Spanish outfits he had once favored for mourning black, which he wore until his death in 1572.

Though it was a love match, the marriage, as predicted, was politically disastrous. The kingdom's lower nobility (*szlachta*)—whose power was significant due to its representation in the parliament (which voted on taxes, conscription, and other important laws)—adamantly opposed it. They could not stomach a woman of inferior birth (and a mistress) being elevated to the ranks of royalty. Zygmunt August's relations with the *szlachta* were always tricky, as he was a proponent of a strong monarchy and central power. In the wake of the marriage to Barbara, those relations deteriorated further, preventing him from conducting several major, and much needed, judicial and administrative reforms. Some argue that this ongoing conflict laid the groundwork for the collapse of the Polish-Lithuanian state in the late eighteenth century.

There is some uncertainty regarding the birthdate of Bona's trusted courtier (and murderer) Gian Lorenzo Pappacoda, with some sources claiming it could have been as late as 1541. I do not think that is likely, but in 1545 he was almost certainly younger than my portrayal of him in *Midnight Fire*. However, I chose to include him as one of the characters because of the sinister role he was to play in Bona's life in 1557. After the queen's death, suspicion fell quickly on Pappacoda, and he promptly defected to Spain, proving once and for all that he was a Habsburg agent. Polish emissaries acting on behalf of Zygmunt August made an effort to apprehend him, but Philip II protected him, although later Pappacoda, too, was murdered.

The idea of a poisoned ruff was partly based on a rumor regarding the sudden death of Jeanne d'Albret in 1572. According to many contemporaries, the queen of Navarre, who supported Protestants, fell victim to the queen of France, Catherine de' Medici (who was Italian by birth and a staunch Catholic). Catherine was alleged to have sent Jeanne a pair of poisoned gloves as a gift. There is no solid evidence for this claim, but the rumor sufficed to blacken Catherine's reputation during her lifetime and for centuries afterward. Regardless of the true cause of Jeanne's death, I find the parallels between Catherine and Bona—both Italian, both powerful queens, and both largely rejected by their subjects—to be uncanny.

On a final note, there are no surviving records of the plan or the interior of the ducal palace in Vilnius. The reconstruction of the current palace (completed in 2018) is based on a modern design. The layout presented in this novel is therefore my own invention, although it is informed in part by historical drawings and paintings, all of which date from later periods than the setting of this story.

Thank you for reading *Midnight Fire.* I hope you enjoyed it. Would you kindly take a few minutes to support independent publishing by leaving a review on Amazon and/or Goodreads? I will greatly appreciate it!

If you want to stay up to date on my Jagiellon Mystery series or learn more about my other writing projects, feel free to get in touch via my website's Contact Me form at www.pkadams-author.com or my Facebook Author Page at www.facebook.com/PKAdamsAuthor..

You can also follow me on Twitter @pk_adams

Acknowledgments

I would like to thank my editor Carolyn Pouncy for helping me make this novel the best it can be. I am grateful to Jake Conner, Jena Henry, Gifford MacShane, and Wendy Stanley who read the full manuscript of *Midnight Fire*, as well as to Elaine Buckley, who read extensive excerpts, for their very insightful comments. This story would not be what it is without your honest and generous feedback.

I am also grateful to Jenny Quinlan for designing another excellent cover, and to Deborah Bluestein for making the map of Poland-Lithuania under the Jagiellon dynasty. I am in awe of your artistic skills!

About the Author

P.K. Adams is the pen name of Patrycja Podrazik. She has a bachelor's degree from Columbia University and a master's degree in European Studies from Yale University. She is a blogger and historical fiction reviewer at www.pkadams-author.com. Her debut novel, *The Greenest Branch, a Novel of Germany's First Female Physician*, was a semifinalist for the 2018 Chaucer Book Awards for Pre-1750 Historical Fiction. She is a member of the Historical Novel Society and lives in New England.

Printed in Great Britain
by Amazon

55602086R00162